THE PEN FRIEND

CIARAN CARSON

BLACKSTAFF
PRESS
BELFAST

First published in 2009 by
Blackstaff Press
4c Heron Wharf, Sydenham Business Park
Belfast BT3 9LE
with the assistance of
The Arts Council of Northern Ireland

arts
council
of Northern Ireland

The acknowledgements on pages 255–6
constitute an extension of this copyright page.

Typeset by CJWT Solutions, St Helens, England

Design by Dunbar Design
Printed in Italy by Rotolito Lombarda

A CIP catalogue record for this book is available
from the British Library

ISBN 978-0-85640-815-1

www.blackstaffpress.com

Against the cream blouse you
notice a little pendant cylindrical
jewel, some kind of etui or
lipstick-holder, I think. It's
done in a beautiful red and
black marble swirls that show
off the red highlights in your
Cleopatra-cut black hair and
it hangs from a lanyard that
is itself beautiful, interwoven
greens and reds and mauves
that have the sheen of silk.
You toy with it from time to
time, with one hand as the
other manages the business of
the tea and biscuits. Then you
reach for it with both hands
and you unclip it from the
lanyard, you rummage about
in your handbag and take out
a notebook, you unscrew the
little etui, and when I see the
gleam of a gold nib I realise
it is a YOUR fountain pen

THE PEN FRIEND

For Patricia Craig
and Jeffrey Morgan

IT'S BEEN
A LONG TIME

Wearever

Your postcard came like a bolt from the blue, and it was the spur that drove me to begin writing again. After my father died in 1998 – did you know he was dead? – I took early retirement from my position in the Municipal Gallery, partly to devote myself to writing a book about his involvement with Esperanto, the international auxiliary language devised by Ludwig Zamenhof. I had long been familiar with the salient details of Zamenhof's life. He was born in 1859 in Bialystok, in the Polish district of Podlasia, once part of the Duchy of Lithuania, and then of the Russian Empire. I began studying the history of the region, hoping to gain a better understanding of what made Zamenhof Zamenhof, without which it was impossible to imagine my father. I began to discover that Poland, and hence Polish Lithuania, had been partitioned and repartitioned by a series of treaties between Prussia and Russia, behind which lay such a series of insurrections, strikes, pogroms, feuds, plots, wars, commercial enterprises and business transactions, that I realised it would take me years to unravel the particular circumstances of the town which had brought Zamenhof into being, let alone how my father had come to learn Zamenhof's invented language.

I began to think of myself as an angler fishing a stretch of canal in the shadow of a dark semi-derelict factory leaking steam from a rusted exoskeleton of piping, who, after hours of inaction, feels his line bite, and, his excitement mounting, begins to reel in as his rod is bent by the gravity of what must be an enormous catch – a pike perhaps, glutted by its meal of barbel, perch, or one of the plump rats that scuttle through the soot-encrusted weeds of the canal banks – when to his consternation he finds he has snagged a smoothing-iron, which he discovers to be only the precursor of a series resembling an enormous charm bracelet dripping green-black beards and tendrils of slime, as the iron is followed by an iron kettle, pots and pans, a bicycle, a kitchen sink complete with taps, a pram, a harrow, a plough, forks and rakes, a gamut of broken looms, winding machines and spinning jennies, a string of dead horses, rotting straps and rusted buckles, tumbrils, wagons, engine tenders, locomotives, tanks, flat-bed trucks and howitzers, a crocodile of sunken barges, lighters, tugs, launches, cutters, gunships, battleships, amphibians and submarines sucked from the reluctant mud, the whole gargantuan juggernaut flying in midair for a second, as the angler's rod whips back, before collapsing all about him with an almighty thunderclap; and I would wake sweating and exhausted from my nocturnal Herculean labour. My book ground to a halt before it even properly began.

I realised that even my knowledge of my father was fragmentary and incomplete. I did not know, for instance, what he looked like as a child. Cameras were not readily available when he was growing up, at least not to his milieu; and whatever studio photographs might have been taken, for his First Communion, say, or Confirmation, have not survived. The earliest photograph of him is at the age of eighteen or nineteen, when his features had been fully formed. And yet, perhaps it is possible retrospectively to build an Identikit childhood portrait where none exists.

I was reminded of this when I got your card this morning, because it occurred to me that we read handwriting as we do faces, and yours – your handwriting, I mean – had changed little, even though it was over twenty years since we had last met, and parted. Not that I believed it was yours at first; for if seeing is believing, sometimes we look and do not see; and sometimes we only see what we want to see, or what we want to believe. And now, reading your brief message for the umpteenth time – It's been a *long time*, you wrote, that was all, and left it unsigned, knowing the gesture of your writing would be signature enough – I find it difficult, in retrospect, to understand my initial hesitation as to its provenance. Even when we purposely change the way we write, some ineradicable loop or slant, an identifiable arpeggio, betrays us. When we meet someone we have not seen for years, and it takes us a while to put a name to the face, we say, But you haven't changed at all. And even when we fail to know the person, when provided with the name, we see him then, we see her then, and say, Of course, how could I not have known you? For now the evidence is unmistakeable, and we read the face like invisible writing that blooms to the surface when exposed to heat. So, even in this brief flourish I recognised the character of your handwriting; I knew its physiognomy. As you would have anticipated. The words are written in fountain pen, and in blue ink, the colour of eternity. You knew I would remember that a fountain pen had first brought us together, all those years ago.

I picture myself sitting in the old XL Café, in Fountain Street as it happens, on a Saturday in May 1982. The day before I had bought a nice 1950s jacket in the Friday Market, lightweight grey Donegal salt-and-pepper tweed with heathery flecks, little hints of purple, blue and mauve that flicker in the sunlight. I'm wearing it with a pale blue soft-collared cotton shirt and white duck trousers, so when you appear through the door in a navy check box jacket over a high-necked cream broderie anglaise blouse and a flax-coloured maxi-skirt, like Bonnie of Bonnie & Clyde, I find myself indulging in a little scenario where we go well together, such a nice-looking couple, people would say. You sit down a table away from me and order some tea and biscuits, and when they come I watch you out of the corner of my eye as you dunk a biscuit into the tea, a gesture I think at first doesn't quite suit your style, but then I tell myself it reveals some character, it shows you're not afraid of what people think. Against the cream blouse I notice a little pendant cylindrical jewel, some kind of étui or lipstick-holder, I think. It's done in beautiful red and black marble swirls that show off the red highlights in your Cleopatra-cut black hair and it hangs from a lanyard that is itself beautiful, interwoven greens and reds and mauves that have the sheen of silk. You toy with it from time to time with one hand as the other manages the business of the tea and biscuits. Then you reach for it with both hands and you unclip it from the lanyard, you rummage in your handbag and take out a notebook, you unscrew the little étui, and when I see the gleam of a gold nib I realise it is a diminutive fountain pen.

You were poised to write when you caught me looking at you. You looked back. I must have blushed. Lovely pen, I said. You smiled. Yes, you said, it's what they call a Dinkie, Conway Stewart used to make them. A lot of people comment on it, you said, I suppose it's what you might call a conversation piece. Or lethal weapon, and you held it up briefly between thumb and four fingers like a dart. Its length was not much more than the breadth of your hand. Well, I said, I used to have a Conway Stewart, but I've never seen one like that. My father gave it to me, I said, I think it must have been the first fountain pen I ever had. It was a family joke of sorts, because our name is Conway, and my mother's maiden name was Stewart. So you might say I'm a Conway-Stewart myself. Gabriel Conway, I said, and I extended my hand awkwardly across the intervening table, and you moved to take it, and we ended up sharing the empty table. You did not offer me your name at first. Oh, you said, when eventually I asked, it's a very ordinary name, probably so ordinary you wouldn't guess. You paused, and smiled. So what do you think I might be called? you said. Oh, I said, looking you up and down, you look like an Iris to me. You laughed. Yes, you said, Iris, of course, how did you know? I was slightly taken aback; I'd been joking, and you didn't look at all like what I imagined an Iris to be. But I was flattered, too, that I had guessed right, and thought myself like the girl who discovers the name of Rumpelstiltskin. Iris what? I said. Iris Bowyer, you said.

It's been a long time. Such a lot has happened. My father, as I've said, died seven years ago. Some eighteen months ago, I was forcibly reminded of his aura – and of yours – when I was browsing in an annex of the Empire Auction Rooms. Amongst a job lot of odds and ends – a box of Veritas gas mantles, a dozen mismatched bone-handled knives, two battered brass candlesticks, a chess set missing the Black Queen – I saw a Conway Stewart. It was almost identical to my first fountain pen, an 84 model, my father's pen, iridescent green marble laced with gold veins, though somewhat muted by a layer of grime, but when I rubbed its barrel with the wetted ball of my thumb I could feel the raised imprint of the logo even before it became visible. It was indeed an 84. I unscrewed the cap and posted it on to the barrel end. It felt good in my hand as I wrote on the air, the gold nib shining in the gloom of the annex. I won the lot for a few pounds.

I bought ink on the way home. Miraculously, the pen still wrote, though the nib was a little scratchy. Again I thought of my father. At the beginning his pen, too, had snagged a little when I put it to paper. Everyone holds a pen differently, and the nib had taken on the quirks of his hand, but not irremediably so: the more I wrote with it, the more its path was smoothed as I wore away his influence and imposed my hand on his. Now, writing with its sibling, feeling the drag of the nib on the fibres of the paper, breathing the antique smell of bottled ink, I felt a powerful nostalgia steal over me, which led me, in the months that followed, to become a collector of vintage fountain pens. I haunted auction rooms, antique shops, the bric-a-brac stalls of Smithfield Market and the Friday Market. Before, I had been familiar with names that are still current: Parker, Waterman, Sheaffer, Mont Blanc. I had no idea of how many makes there were I'd never heard of: Mentmore, Swan, Condor, Miracle, Esterbrook, Packard, Fineline, Royal, Venus, Eagle, Stratford, Senator, Conklin, Avon, Merlin, Wing-Flow: pens as varied as their names, their companies defunct, their premises abandoned to other trades, or long since demolished. When I pick one up from a stall I touch the past.

I experienced a special frisson when I acquired a Dinkie, a 540 model like yours, though in a violet and ivory swirl instead of your red and black. *Le Rouge et le Noir.* I thought for a moment I might write this letter with it; but, looking at your card again, I decided on the Wearever de Luxe, made in North Bergen, New Jersey, in 1939. Not a luxury pen, despite its name; at the time, it was advertised as the Dollar Pen. Nevertheless, the Wearever has a beautiful casing of jazzy intermittent lanes of shimmering green on black, like strips of emerald laid into ebony, and when I first uncapped it I was struck by the Art Deco double-take of its nib, a gold open point overlaid by a stainless steel brace with a diamond-shaped aperture. It put me in mind of the Chrysler Building, and I visualised the steel ziggurat of its superstructure radiating a wintry light, and us together in New York. And here is your postcard of New York, a reproduction of a black-and-white photograph by Acme Photo Service, *Lightning striking the tip of the Empire State Building, July 9th 1945*, in which the lightning-bolt appears a luminous scribble on the dark lowering sky; one can almost picture the traffic moving like corpuscles through the bloodstream of New York, beeping longingly through the murk. And, as I write with the Wearever, the words borne forward in this flow of ink, I picture us in a thunderstorm in New York, laughing and running for shelter as the heavens open and pour down on us, and wonder what ulterior message lies behind your few words.

I turn the card over: I hadn't noticed the British stamp until now, nor that it was postmarked York, not New York, and your faint Yorkshire accent came back to me, how charmingly it had struck my ear when first I heard it, in the XL Café in Belfast in 1982. And then I remembered what I have often tried to forget, that your farewell letter came on 9th July 1984, the day that York Minster was struck by lightning, and its South Transept destroyed by the subsequent fire. I kept the letter for some weeks, reading and rereading it disbelievingly until at last, believing it, I burned it, together with all your other letters.

When inked paper is burned, the metallic components of the ink endure longer than the paper, and for a few brief moments I saw whole sentences stand out bold and clear on their silvery white leaves, before I poked at the ashes and watched them snow upwards into the grey July sky, and I breathed those ashes as your thousands of smouldering and dying words entered my bloodstream. It has been computed that with every breath we take we breathe some molecule of Caesar's last breath, and I wonder if I now breathe some minute fragment of those ashes, if sufficient time has passed for their particulate matter so to be diffused into the atmosphere that it too is breathed by everyone who breathes. Perhaps I am breathing what was your breath yesterday as I look at your words today and inhale them as I write my words. I put my face to the card and I smell the ink that was wet as you breathed on your words and perhaps whispered them or said them silently. At the very least you must have thought them. And when I trace the forms of the characters with my fingers I touch a substance that once flowed within centimetres of your pulse. The blue vein in your wrist. There's something else, a trace of perfume. What was it, *L'Air du Temps*? When I leaned over to you that day in the XL Café, I caught a faint bouquet, a hint of violet and musk-rose underlaid by sandalwood, a perfume that was nameless to me then.

Iris Bowyer. I didn't know then that in Greek mythology Iris was a sister of the Harpies. Iris personifies the rainbow, hence the iris of the eye. Iris is the messenger of the gods, for the rainbow unites heaven and earth. Iris conducts the souls of dead women to the underworld, just as Hermes does the souls of dead men. As for the flower known as the iris, the Ancient Egyptians considered it to be a symbol of eloquence, and placed an iris on the brow of the Sphinx. And Iris – only lately did I learn this – gives her name to iridium, the super-hard metal with which the gold nibs of fountain pens are tipped, because when dissolved in acid, iridium produces an array of colours like those in an oil slick, or the iridescent feathers of an exotic bird.

As I talked to you then, I noticed your left eye had a little amber fleck in the green iris. So what do you do? I said. Oh, let's say I'm in service, you said. I must have looked surprised. Well, I'm a Civil Servant, you said. I work for a Ministry. Which one? I said. Oh, that would be telling. And I wouldn't want to bore you. And you live in Belfast? I said. Well, sometimes, you said, I flit back and forth, you know, between Belfast and London. Where my Minister directs his Ministry. And you? I'm Assistant Keeper of Irish Art at the Municipal Gallery, I said, well, actually, Assistant to the Assistant Keeper. I suppose I'm in service myself, I said, and we both pretended to laugh. You must come up and see my paintings some time, I said, and you said, I will. Though I've already been to the Gallery a few times, you said. But it would be nice to get the inside picture, as it were. There's painting I liked a lot, it's a yellow room, sort of skewed dimensions, and a woman sitting with her arms folded, and a boy with a concertina or something on his lap, and there's a cat, I think curled in a yellow chair. It's a very bright painting, you know? you said. I know, I said, it's called *The Yellow Bungalow*, it's by Gerard Dillon. My father knew Gerard Dillon. It's a melodeon, by the way. Not a concertina. So what's the difference? you said. I said I'd written a catalogue text once for a show of Dillon's paintings, and it was important to name things by their proper names.

The Yellow Bungalow was and is a favourite painting of mine. I can see it in my mind's eye as I write. It's small, and almost square, some thirty by thirty-two inches, and shows the interior of the bungalow, whose walls are painted a bright yellow, its perspective tilted a little, as if in a fish-eye lens. A boy holding a melodeon and a piece of paper sits to our left, looking out at us; in the far corner a woman – she might be his mother, or a sister – sits with her arms folded, watching the boy. A cat lies curled in a yellow cane chair: it is either sleeping, or eyeing the three fishes arranged on a white plate on a yellow, patterned tablecloth. There is a black stove against the wall, with a pale blue kettle and teapot on it, and a hurricane lamp with a pale blue shade hangs from the ceiling. Through the window we see a fragment of a landscape: a path, some houses, a green field, a blue strip of sea and mountains of a darker blue beyond. I am reminded of the West of Ireland which I first saw at the age of five. I imagine my father and me opening an unseen door in the yellow bungalow and stepping out into the windswept landscape, where we would wander before returning to the animated murmur of stories being told around the fire at nights: stories of ancient Irish heroes which my father subsequently retold me over the years of my growing up. I remember, too, their opening scenario, where it is always nightfall, the hero has lost his way, and a few lights glimmer on a lonely mountainside. One of these represents a house which the hero will enter. Gorgeous food is arrayed on a table, and there are lit candles everywhere, yet the house seems empty. One can tell that mysterious actions are about to unfold.

I think *The Yellow Bungalow* is the first painting I ever really saw, I said. My father would bring me to the Gallery as a child. The Mummy in Antiquities was the big draw that had everyone peering over her glass case to see her blackened features and her flaxen hair. I can remember standing on tiptoe to look at her, and thinking she looked nothing like the picture on her coffin. Sarcophagus, my father would say, and proceed to tell me how the ancient embalmers drew the brain out through the nostrils with a hook, and would then discard it, believing it unnecessary to the reanimation of the body in the next life. The heart, the centre of intelligence, was left in place. After seeing the Mummy we would go to view *The Yellow Bungalow*, and I still remember the glow with which it hit me first. Though of course we don't know how many layers of remembering have been built on to that, I said to you. My father would point out how the three fishes were a reference to the Miracle of the Loaves and Fishes. The woman was a type of Madonna. As for the boy, who did I think the boy would be? Oh, the boy with the concertina, I said, as if there were another boy. Melodeon, said my father, it's a melodeon. And I should have known better than to call it a concertina, for my father played the melodeon himself, and I realised I had been trying to be clever.

So my father would lecture me on the importance of names, and when we emerged into the Botanic Gardens, he would point to the broad lawn surrounded by chestnut trees in blossom and ask me how many blades of grass I thought there might be on the lawn, and I said, I don't know, hundred of thousands, maybe, millions? We can be sure that it is a great many, said my father, but every one is different from its neighbour, because nothing in the world is the same as anything else. Because if any one thing was identical to another thing, then it would occupy the same space as that thing, and be that thing. And because God sees everything, we may be sure He has enumerated those blades of grass, and every blade of grass in the world. And in a like manner He knows all the names that Man has given to things, in every language, in order to distinguish one thing from another.

The trees swayed in the breeze like a line of galleons and I thought of the blue strip of sea in *The Yellow Bungalow* where ships of the Armada might well have foundered. Of course it was a melodeon, I said, and I could hear my father playing it on Sundays, 'Nearer My God to Thee', I said, with the slightly wonky treble notes shimmering above the dark bass, and my reverie was interrupted when my father said, Gabriel, are you listening to me?

So I'm writing this with the Wearever and I can feel the pen writing. The tip of the steel overlay of the nib is slightly upturned, allowing the gold point underneath some play, while keeping it in check when too much pressure is applied. If this were a car, you'd say it had a comfortable suspension. The writing has a spring to it, a bounce which I found difficult to control at first, accustomed as I was to the rigid point of a ballpoint pen or rollerball. But from the beginning I've enjoyed using the Wearever, writing whatever came into my head, practising my signature with it just for the feel of the nib and the measured flow of ink on paper. I'm writing this with the Wearever, I'd write, nice Wearever nib to use Wherever wears forever, before moving on to more elaborate nonsense – the quick brown fox jumped over the lazy dog, colourless green ideas sleep furiously. Or, driven by fountain-pen-induced nostalgia, I'd carefully delineate my name and address, as written in my school copy-books a good half-century ago, *Gabriel Conway, 41 Ophir Gardens, Belfast, County Antrim, Ireland, Europe, The Northern Hemisphere, The World, The Solar System, The Universe*, and wonder, as I did then, what came next in that hierarchy. Or did I write *Northern Ireland*? I can't remember. Wherever.

That's all very well, you said, but you can't expect everyone to know what you know when you're looking at a painting. And what do you know of what I knew when I looked at that painting? *The Yellow Bungalow*, whatever you want to call it. Don't you think *The Yellow Bungalow* is just a bit too easy, too descriptive? Why not *The Cat and Fishes*? What does it matter, if you're looking at it with your own eyes? you said. You bring yourself to a painting, you said.

So what brought you to write to me again? You remember our letters? We used to write to one another even if we were to meet that day, letters as addenda to whatever we'd discussed or fought about the night before, letters as agenda for the next day, adumbrations of the pros and cons, retractions or advancements of positions taken, communiqués that opened up the possibility of renegotiation or compromise; for we believed that written words were sometimes a more accurate record of our thoughts and feelings, because more pondered, whereas spoken words are often ill-advised or ill-considered, and once uttered cannot be retracted; but letters can be drafted and redrafted until they sit better with our thought than the words which first come to mind; moreover, as we write, trying to articulate ourselves, unexpected thoughts sometimes occur to us, that were not part of our original intention, and we change our minds as we write, arriving at conclusions wholly other than those we first envisaged, so that writing to each other, we discovered what we thought. We were the authors and protagonists of an epistolic novel. Meeting in the XL Café, we would read each other's letters in each other's presence, silently, as a long-established couple might read the morning papers. Then we would discuss our written statements, seeking clarification on this point or that, like negotiators of a ceasefire or a post-war treaty.

I used a Pentel rollerball then; I'd abandoned writing with a fountain pen some years before. I'd always disliked the slippery feel of a ballpoint, and the Pentel seemed to have more tooth when put to paper. I liked the firm black line laid down by its point, and its thick green plastic flat-topped casing, a classic design that remains unchanged to this day, for I saw one yesterday. And it seems to me now to have been inspired by the classic Parker Duofolds and flat-top Sheaffers of the 1920s, which leads me to put down the Wearever I've been writing with till now, and pick up a Gatsby era Sheaffer's ring-top pen in jade celluloid with little milky flecks in it – the ring would have been attached, as was your Dinkie, to a lanyard to hang from a lady's neck. As I write, I find myself touching my free hand to my neck for an invisible lanyard, and I think for a moment I could be you, toying with your Dinkie, red and black marble swirls and not this near-translucent green jade.

Made for and presumably used by a lady's hand, the Sheaffer sits tolerably well in mine, though I must hold myself somewhat differently, and there is only the ghost of a scratch to its nib as I write. The point is finer and more rigid than that of the Wearever, and it seems to discipline my writing to a different mode as the words come forth, and I wonder whose hand held this pen before me, what assignations it communicated, its jade cylinder resting on a dressing table between words, among scent bottles of pale amethyst and frosted lilac and delicate opal. It carries a perfume which is not ink alone, a residue of someone else, of chiffon scarves of coral and apple-green and lavender and faint orange billowing in the slipstream of a Duofold Mandarin Yellow open-topped tourer, colours dappling the faces of the laughing foursome as they drive through a leafy tunnel and faint jazz music ebbs and flows down through the trees from the white ocean-liner of a house built on the cliff edge.

I try to picture the face of the woman who held this pen before me, eighty years ago, and instead see your face, as you might imagine, for you knew I would be thus intrigued when you wrote that single phrase, that slender horizontal lightning-bolt, *It's been a long time.* I see you as you were then, but also as you might be now. You were two years younger than me, so you're fifty-five. I put lines in your brow, and guess what wrinkles might have accrued at the corners of eyes and mouth, and flesh out the neck a little, and add some pouches to the cheeks, streaks of grey to the black hair, and it is still you, what you have become. In any case I'd know you by the amber fleck in that left eye of yours, not so much flaw as beauty-spot. I'd know you anywhere.

When York Minster was struck by lightning in 1984, and its South Transept razed by the subsequent fire, it was discovered that the four-hundred-year-old stained glass of the great Rose Window, made to commemorate the defeat of the House of York in the Wars of the Roses, had been riven into some forty thousand fragments, though the panels had miraculously stayed intact within their embrasures, having been releaded some years previously. Restoration began. Adhesive plastic film was applied to the crazed mosaic of the glass panels, which were then removed one by one, disassembled, and reassembled, tessera by tessera, using a specially developed fixative which had the same refractive index as the old glass, whereupon the completed work was sandwiched between two layers of clear glass for added security, and mounted back in place: which intervention means we will never again see what was seen before the fire, the dims and glows of stained glass unmitigated by an added medium, however clear. We two saw the glass as it was, as it had been.

I write to try to see you as you were, or what you have become. You left no forwarding address: that was part of your intention. For when we wrote those letters to each other all those years ago, we wrote as much for ourselves as for each other; as much to ourselves as to each other. Promising to be in touch, you drifted out of the XL Café. Your perfume lingered. *Arpège*, that's what it was, not *L'Air du Temps*. Jasmine and rose borne by musk with a hint of sparkling green in its depths.

IT'S EASY
TO REMEMBER

Merlin 33

I had spent a week planning a new approach to my Esperanto book (it would be written in longhand with various fountain pens for one thing, each appropriate to a particular strand of the narrative) when your second card arrived, and threw me somewhat out of kilter. Lightning does strike twice. I remember hearing, in 1983, midway through our time together, of the death of the man – an American park-ranger – who had been struck by lightning seven times in his life. And statistics show that it is more likely for a person to be struck by lightning in the United Kingdom, than to be the victim of a terrorist attack; though whether that applied to Northern Ireland in the 1980s, and to Belfast in particular, might well require another computation. In any event I did not know whether to be more surprised by your second missive than by the first. On reflection, perhaps I had subconsciously expected it. Viewed by itself, that first postcard was unprecedented; or, retrospectively, it was a postscript, an addendum to our previous correspondence, however protracted the interval, the culmination of a long concatenation of mental processes which did not necessarily include me, of circumstances beyond your ken perhaps, of planetary influences for all I know, which led inexorably to your decision to communicate yourself to me again through those few words; and when I thought about it, I realised that when we say, It's been a long time, we usually intend it as the preamble to a mutual reminiscence, queries as to how the other party has been faring all those months or years. It opens up a conversation. And when we part we say, We must keep in touch.

This message was equally laconic: *It's easy to remember,* you wrote. Again, you left no signature. The stamp was post-marked London, one week after the first. I pondered the words for some time, thinking that there are many things which are not easy to remember, that there are things so forgotten as to be beyond recall, or that there are things whose implications will be fully realised only in the future, and even then perhaps not by the person whom they most concern. Be that as it may, I was more struck by the image on your postcard than by your words, as I presume you had intended. The caption on the back bottom left reads thus: *Two Dutchmen and Two Courtesans, Hanging Scroll, ink and colours on paper, Japan (Nagasaki), about 1800.* And on the bottom right, V & A *Encounters, the meeting of Asia and Europe 1500–1800, sponsored by Nomura.*

The image was familiar to me because I had seen its original in that very exhibition, held in the Victoria and Albert Museum in the autumn of 2004. On 9th October, to be precise, on which day I attained the age of fifty-six: it was my birthday gift to myself to spend a few days in London, a city I have always loved, a city that you loved. And it struck me that you might have been there that day in the V & A, that you might have seen and known me, however changed I was, whatever I'd become, you might have shared the same gallery space as me, and breathed the air that I breathed. We might have brushed against each other unwittingly, or unseeingly. I had visited the museum shop at the end of my visit. Perhaps you bought the postcard then, one of a batch as *aides-mémoire* of the exhibition, which had lain forgotten in a drawer until now. Or it was meant for someone else, and thinking twice you thought better of it. Perhaps it was intended for me all along, that even then you planned it. I could have bought that very card myself, but was distracted by a book on eighteenth-century costume; and perhaps as I browsed its colour plates of elaborate brocades you were paying for this card I keep flicking my eyes to as I write, and I was oblivious to the beep of the till that signalled the transaction.

Two Dutchmen and Two Courtesans: when we went out for our first meal together, you insisted it should be a Dutch treat, and when I demurred, you said it was only proper, since you were half-Dutch. I saw a glint in your amber-flecked eye. The name on your birth certificate was Bouwer, you said, and you had changed it to Bowyer by deed poll when your father died. Bouwer meant 'builder' in Dutch; you had always disliked it. Your father, Arie Bouwer, had been active in the resistance movement known as PAN – Partisan Action Netherlands – founded in 1943 in Eindhoven, where he was an electronics engineer in the Philips factory. As you told me something of his story, an image of the Philips Bakelite radio I used to listen to as a child flickered in and out of my mind's eye, and I saw myself spinning the needle past the lit linear blips of the stations, Athlone, Hilversum, Warsaw, Moscow, to a storm of gabbled languages and machine-gun bursts of Morse and static. The partisans, you said, had been organised into cells which communicated chiefly by telephone, and your father had been instrumental in further refining the system by linking it to the underground cabling of the Eindhoven factory. Everyone in PAN had a nom de guerre; when they did meet face to face they wore masks. No member knew the identities of the others, beyond their being agents of a common cause. And what was your father's nom de guerre? I asked. He was known as Harry, you said, and when I queried the efficacy of an alias that was so close to the original, you replied that the best place to hide a thing was in plain sight, and referred me to the Edgar Allan Poe story, 'The Purloined Letter', where the letter in question has been stuck by the thief in a letter rack, under the noses of the investigating constabulary, and only the private consultant Dupin – the precursor of Sherlock Holmes – has the eyes to see that the letter has been disguised as itself.

Given the Dutch connection, I thought it only proper to write this with a Merlin pen, made in the Netherlands in about 1948, the year of my birth and of your father's marriage to a Yorkshire woman, Eleanor Birtwhistle. You showed me a photograph once of her when she was your age, and you have her dark hair, her high cheekbones and slightly flattened, up-tilted nose, the same broad smile, the same assured stance. She is a Chief Executive Officer in the Imperial Civil Service, a rare achievement for a woman at that time. She is wearing a salt-and-pepper tweed suit with a box jacket; on a lanyard around her neck she wears your Dinkie pen, and its red and black candle-flame seems to glow against her white blouse, even though the photograph is in black and white. As for this pen I hold now, it is in mint condition, one of a number of new old stock recently discovered in a Delft stationer's. It had never been inked when I received it, and it is a paradoxically uncanny feeling, to be writing with a pen as old as I am when there are no ghosts of other hands behind it, as if I were writing when it was new, and I am born.

The body of the Merlin is patterned in shimmery layered feathery lines of tawny brown and cream, like the plumage of the bird it was named for; and I consider again how many fountain pens there are of avian nomenclature – for pen, after all, is from Latin *penna*, a feather, or a quill, an etymology I did not fully realise until I became, as it were, a fully-fledged collector of pens. There are pens called Swan, Jackdaw, Swallow, Blackbird, Eagle, Condor, and Wing-Flow. The companies that made them are all defunct. There is a pleasant story behind the German firm of Pelikan, still producing fine pens today. It was founded in 1878 by Gunther Wagner, whose family crest of a pelican was adopted as the logo of the company, to symbolise a familial allegiance to its employees, for the pelican is famously protective of its brood. The family pelican was depicted with three chicks; but another was added to the Pelikan logo at the last moment, when it was found that Wagner's wife was expecting their fourth child.

Some months ago I stumbled on a rare find in Smithfield Market, a Staffordshire ceramic quill-stand which more fully illustrates the pelican legend. In Christian art, the pelican is a symbol of charity; it is also an emblem of Christ the Redeemer. St Jerome gives the story of the pelican restoring its young destroyed by serpents, by feeding them with its own blood, and his salvation by the blood of Christ. The misconception as to the pelican's feeding habits apparently arose from the fact that the parent bird macerates small fish in the large bag attached to its under-bill, whereupon, pressing the bag against its breast, it transfers the macerated food to the mouths of the young. The quill-stand consists of just such a family group, with holes for two quills on either side, though apparently its makers have never seen a pelican, for the bird lacks its characteristic long beak; but it is clearly identified by the salient features of its legend. The pelican pecks angrily with its diminutive nib at a green snake coiled around its body; its breast is red with blood, and at its feet lie three pink featherless chicks, yet to be revived. Jerome, as the translator of the Bible into Latin, is the patron saint of translators and interpreters, and elsewhere he draws an explicit parallel between blood and ink: translation by transfusion, as it were. I am reminded that solemn covenants are often signed in blood, that thousands of Ulstermen did so in 1912, swearing allegiance to the King, and to oppose the plans to set up a Home Rule government in Dublin; and that four years later thousands of those Ulstermen would die in the blood-bath of the Somme.

I open my veins in a manner of speaking to write to you. I have been looking at your postcard on and off for some days, examining the poised, hieratic body language of the foursome, who are like partners in a stately minuet, the distances between them at once intimate and remote. The Dutchmen, who at the onset seemed to me both graceful and incongruous, like aliens in our depictions of them, have become more familiar now, and I can see a glimmer of meaning in the folds of the women's kimonos. But I cannot read the Japanese characters of what seem to be a good few sentences of writing in the top right corner – a bawdy song? A satirical verse, a description of Dutch costume? I decided to research the background to the image, and discovered the following.

The first contact between the West and Japan occurred in 1542 when a Portuguese ship, blown off its course to China, landed near Nagasaki. They brought with them something the Japanese had never seen: firearms. They also brought their religion, and in subsequent years converted a number of the feuding warlords of Japan, who were eager to trade with the bearers of guns and Christianity. In 1600 the first Dutch contact with Japan was made when a Dutch ship captained by an Englishman was also blown off course by a tempest, and landed near Nagasaki. Slowly the Dutch established themselves as rivals in trade to the Portuguese. They were careful not to proselytise; the standing of Christianity in Japan ebbed and flowed depending on political circumstances. In 1636

Christianity was banned, and the authorities ordered the construction of an artificial island, Deshima, in the harbour of Nagasaki, wherein the Portuguese were interned. Being man-made, it was not considered part of the sacred soil of Japan. A year later the Portuguese were expelled altogether, and the island was given over to the Dutch. It was tiny, with a perimeter of some five hundred metres, about half the size of Dam Square in Amsterdam. From 1641 until 1859 – the period of Japanese national seclusion – Deshima was the only place where trade between the West and Japan was permitted. The permanent staff of Deshima comprised a director of the Dutch East India Company and some ten employees, among whom were a physician, a cook, a blacksmith, a carpenter, a musician and a scribe. A short bridge connected the island to Nagasaki – to Japan – and for many years no Japanese, save prostitutes and interpreters, were allowed to cross over; nor were the Dutch allowed on to the mainland, except once a year, when they were escorted under armed guard to the shogun's court in Edo, where, as part of their ritual homage, they were required to perform Dutch songs and dances.

I had particular reason to be fascinated by this history of Dutch–Japanese relations, for my father had corresponded with representatives of both nations through the medium of Esperanto. I thought of how useful Esperanto would have been for that first contact in Nagasaki. As it was, the lingua franca at the beginning of East–West encounters had been Portuguese, and there were enough significant differences between Japanese Portuguese and Dutch Japanese as to make conversation occasionally hazardous. And I wondered what kind of linguistic relationships might have developed, what kind of creole might have evolved between the Dutchmen and the Japanese courtesans – did they have pet names for certain acts, or for each other? – though it also occurred to me that for certain physical engagements gesture alone would have been sufficient.

As time went by, the strict rules governing the Dutch factory, as it became known, were relaxed, and many samurai began to travel to Deshima for Dutch Studies, or *Rangaku*: medicine, chemistry, astronomy and weaponry. Deshima means 'fan-shaped island', and I learned that in Japan fans were not merely decorative, but were used as musical instruments, serving-trays, and umbrellas. Fans with steel ribs were employed as weapons by the samurai. The language of fans had an extensive lexicon of gesture, and virtually anything could be depicted on a fan: animals, flowers, peacocks, people, mountains, valleys, skies, and places such as Deshima itself, where the little maze of buildings is shown in all its micro-cosmic complexity: the reception area, the tobacco store, the vegetable garden, the kitchen, the pigsty, the music-room, the brewery, the bath-room, the still, the dining-room, the forge, the flag, the lookout post, the powder magazine, the guest-room, the gun-room, the chicken-coop, the workshop, and little vignettes of the entire population of Deshima in their offices, the company director being entertained by three courtesans, the physician by two, and the rest of the staff by one each, except for the scribe, who is holding a goose between his knees as he plucks it for quills, while through his window we see a ship about to set off for the Netherlands, laden with silks, jade, tea, porcelain, spices, ivory, and fans.

I open our past like a fan. Angel, you used to call me, for I had been named for the Angel Gabriel. Gabriel, the messenger of God, sent by Him to Mary to proclaim the mystery of the Incarnation, is patron saint of the postal services, and of stamp collectors: my father had been appointed Inspector in the Royal Mail, a rare achievement for a Northern Ireland Catholic, shortly before my birth. And you too were a messenger, not of one god but of many, so I called you Rainbow, Iris, that was what I called you then. Iris Bowyer. You remember? *It's easy to remember.* We'd been going out together for two or three weeks. You'd taken me up on my offer to take you to the Gallery on one of my days off. I'd met you in the XL Café first. You were wearing a lovely pre-war men's jacket, pale green linen, that you'd bought in Second Chance. I thought they only sold women's stuff there, I said, and you said, No, if you go upstairs there's a good few rails of men's, there's a very nice 1940s suit there, single-breasted, dark blue check tweed, about your size, it'd look great on you, though maybe you wouldn't wear it as a suit too often, too formal. But you could buy it for the jacket alone, not to mention the waistcoat. Wear them as separates. You put your hands to your lapels as if draping yourself in another, invisible jacket, and I envisaged myself wearing it, the soft fall of the tweed.

Under the linen jacket you'd one of those Indian silk tight bodices that were in at the time, a retro hippy look, bottle-green with red embroidery, and you were wearing loose white linen trousers with red wedge-heeled one-strap sandals. And what else? Yes, you were wearing a new perfume, it was like amber smoke over green leaves after a shower of rain. What's it called? I said. Ee, you said, and I thought this to be one of your Yorkshire turns of speech, and you laughed and said, Ee, maybe I should have said Why, you said, it's the letter Y. Ee as in Yves St Laurent. Ee, French for there. So here we are, I said, and you're wearing a perfume called There. You remember. A scent for every occasion, I said, you're like Andy Warhol's calendar of perfumes, I said, and you said, What? Not quite a calendar, more like a memory-bank, I said. He bought a different perfume every day or so and stored them in a writing-desk. Then he'd open a bottle every so often, maybe one from a couple of months ago, or last year, and sniff the perfume, get that powerful olfactory hit, just to remind him of that time, that period which was already history, or maybe he just wanted to remember when he'd bought them, there and then, the bright aura of that particular transaction. Warhol loved buying things. And selling things, of course. I do business, not art, he used to say, I said. You could say he sold souvenirs, you said, that's why they place the perfume department, the illuminated signs for Coty and Givenchy, Guerlain, Lancôme, Elizabeth Arden, at the entrance to the big stores, because the perfumes and the names remind you of the last time you were there, and all the other times, all those layers of pleasurable smells. And you want to buy that again and again, you said. Even though you pay mostly for the name, and not the thing itself. You remember?

And we talked a little more about Warhol. I'd been working on a rather fanciful essay linking Gerard Dillon and Warhol. Of course their methods were radically different. But it seemed to me that neither could be fully understood without reference to their Catholic backgrounds. Warhol, born in Pittsburgh, where he was raised as Andrew Warhola, was of intricately European ancestry. His parents had emigrated from Ruthenia, then in Czechoslovakia; they were neither Czech nor Slovak, and spoke a Carpatho-Rusyn dialect. They were devout Byzantine Catholics. From his childhood Warhol was continually in the presence of icons, and in a manner of speaking all his paintings are icons. As for Dillon, he came from the Catholic Falls Road district of Belfast, and he too was deeply influenced by Catholic iconography. My father and he were born in 1916, within a few days of each other, I said, within a few days of the Easter Rising in fact, and they went to school together. Slate Street School. You wouldn't believe it, I said, but my father learned to write on a slate, they still used them then. You shivered. Oh, I could never bear that squeak. Like chalk on blackboard. I imagined you writing on a blackboard as a child, standing on tiptoe, your careful embryonic handwriting. Yes, I said, and Gerard Dillon used to paint on slate. He'd paint on anything, old bits of cardboard or discarded timber. When he left school he was apprenticed to a house-painter. Learned to burn off old paint with a paraffin blow-lamp, scrape off wallpaper with a shave-hook, mix the paints, that kind of thing. He'd paint on the bare walls before they were re-papered. I'm sure there's still a few houses standing in the Falls Road that have early works by Gerard Dillon on their walls, and nobody knows it. And at home he begged his mother to teach him how to use a needle and thread. He did a few tapestries in the early fifties.

Both Warhol and Dillon, I said, were devoted to their mothers, and both were homosexual, Warhol more ostentatiously so, not that my father ever mentioned Dillon's sexuality. For him, Gerard Dillon was the painter of the Falls Road, and of the West of Ireland, and of icons. A good Catholic. There's a lot of death both in Dillon and in Warhol, I said, death and resurrection. The image as a way of circumventing death. Warhol's repeated takes on Marilyn Monroe and Jackie Kennedy, for instance. Their very repetition makes us remember them. And Warhol's obsessive repetitions are a refusal to let go of the image, an insistence that we look again and again, that we do not forget. It doesn't matter whether the image is of a soup can, or a Coca-Cola bottle, or a shoe, or a Chanel No. 5 bottle. Warhol also made repeated images of electric chairs, car crashes, race riots, the atomic bomb, he did portraits of murderers and movie stars, and they are all about death and memory, they glorify the image of the thing or the person. The memorable icon that outlasts its subject, or that represents eternal subjects.

And we can't imagine Warhol without his use of silkscreen printing. Silkscreen is actually a very fine nylon mesh, a gauze almost. You apply the ink with a squeegee and the ink is squeezed through the tiny holes in the screen to make the image. A surface of endless silkscreen dots which the viewer sees as a can of beans, a Coca-Cola bottle, a Marilyn, whatever. Imagine your skin's a silkscreen, and we wrap you in a winding-sheet, and you sweat blood or whatever on to the fabric. A kind of Turin Shroud effect. Not that you'd get too many prints out of it. A very limited edition. But you can print any number of copies off a silkscreen without the image deteriorating too much. But for all that, every print is unique, because the ink is applied a little differently each time, you get an uneven inking of the roller, or the screen slips a little. Warhol liked that degree of routine error, the porosity and seep and bleed of silkscreen. All my images are the same, he said, but very different at the same time. Isn't life a series of images that change as they repeat themselves? he said. And Warhol liked to quote Edvard Munch, who said, We see with different eyes at different times. We see one thing in the morning, and another in the evening, and the way one views things depends on the mood we're in. That's why one subject can be seen in so many ways, and that is what makes painting so interesting. I believe he said something like that, I said.

We were walking past the City Hall by now, and the Royal Ulster Constabulary band was playing in the grounds, their silver instruments shimmering and blaring in the heat. We were hand in hand, swinging along to the beat of the music. They were playing the First World War marching song, 'It's a Long Way to Tipperary'. As we threaded in and out of the crowds a man jostled accidentally against me, apologised, then took a little formal back-step of astonishment and exclaimed, Gabriel! Gabriel Conway! How long has it been! How are you? and then, as he registered your presence, another back-step, side-step rather, he cried, Miranda! and we disengaged our hands and moved apart a little, the whole sequence like a figure in a minuet, an intricate toing and froing, Miranda Bowyer! Well, well, fancy meeting you together! Small world, or what!

I stared at him, then at you, dumbfounded. I'd been trying to place him – the face was familiar, but the name eluded me – and now all that ran through my mind was Miranda, Miranda, Iris, Rainbow, and I stood not hearing your conversation, as the police band music dimmed and swelled around it through the buzz of the crowd. I felt weak. Miranda. In a kind of trance I noted his clothes, the charcoal chalk-stripe suit, a little heavy for the weather, but nicely cut, the blue silk tie with a muted silvery grey diamond pattern, the faint blue herringbone shirt, a legal kind of look. He had cupped his hand to his chin and was smiling at whatever you were saying, I caught a glimpse of a cuff and cuff-link, a black stone set in silver, and then, turning to me, he said, And you, Gabriel, still in the Gallery? I nodded. You? Oh, communications, that kind of thing, we should get together some time, I'll tell you all about it, but for now, must dash, do let's keep in touch. Gabriel. Miranda. And he vanished into the crowd.

Well, I said to you, so what's all this? Miranda, I said with heavy irony. Or Iris. Or whatever you might be. Oh, Angel, you said, don't be silly, you're not upset, are you? And I put my hands in my pockets and lowered my head and pouted my lip in a classic huff, and said nothing. But Angel, you said, what should it matter what I'm called? And am I not Rainbow, anyway? No, I brought myself to say, how can you be Rainbow, when you're Miranda? If Miranda you are. Or did you lie to him? And then it came back to me who he was; he was Tony Lambe – Baa, we called him, he'd been in my year at university, but he'd dropped out and gone to London, what, eleven, twelve years ago, he certainly seemed to have gone up in the world. Miranda's the name on my birth certificate, you said, but so what? Well, you didn't tell me the truth, that's what, I said. You didn't tell me your name. No, you said, it was you who told me, remember? And weren't you pleased that you were able to tell me my name? I was pleased that you were pleased, so I let it go. I quite liked being Iris. And then, with vehemence, you said, Why should we be bound by our names? Can't we be anyone we please to be?

I'm still writing this with the Merlin pen. Merlin the bird of prey, the little falcon, merlin that is related to the French or Scots word merle, a blackbird, Merlin the wizard and the architect of Camelot. To be precise, it's a Merlin 33 – I have another Merlin, in marbled grey and black swirls, called Merlin Elegant – and when I first got the 33 I wondered if this number were chosen for some esoteric or cabalistic significance. Pythagoras says that the world is built on the power of numbers: I discovered that in classic numerology the numbers 11, 22 and 33 are master numbers, not to be reduced to a single digit if they correspond to an individual's name, and that the number 33 is that of avatar. More interestingly, I learned that the Merlin was the last of a series of aircraft engines designed by Rolls-Royce, which included the Kestrel and the Buzzard; that versions of the Merlin engine had powered the Hurricane and Spitfire aircraft that were instrumental in winning the Battle of Britain; and that the Merlin 33, specifically, had been used in the De Havilland Mosquito night-fighter and reconnaissance aircraft which made forays into Dutch and German territory during the latter course of the war. It had also been used as a transport aircraft for the Dutch Resistance. So it was entirely possible that the Merlin 33 fountain pen, designed in the Netherlands in 1948, the year of my birth and of Arie Bouwer's marriage to Nell Birtwhistle, was a tribute to those missions, and to the engine which made them possible. The pen as bird of prey, the pen as aerial observer and communicator. And I wondered what connection your father – Harry the spy, as he was known to some – might have had with all this.

I discovered after some hours searching the Internet that on 11th April 1944 a group of six De Havilland Mosquitoes of 2 Group, 2nd Tactical Air Force, armed with five-hundred-pound incendiary/high explosive bombs, flew to The Hague. Their target was the Gestapo-controlled Dutch Central Population Agency, which PAN had ordered to be destroyed to prevent identification of the false IDs that were so crucial to their clandestine operations. The Agency was located beside the Peace Palace, which, as home to the Court of International Justice created by the League of Nations in 1922, enjoyed extra-territorial status, and was not considered to be part of the Netherlands. Great precision was required on the part of the bombers. In the event, the pilot of the second Mosquito reported that he clearly saw the bombs dropped by the first skip in through the doors of the target. The Peace Palace was unscathed, and the Mosquitoes, powered by their Merlin 33 engines, escaped with only minor damage to one aircraft. The Agency was totally destroyed, and with it the official identities of the entire Dutch population. In a footnote to the article which detailed this information, the name of the PAN agent who passed on the order was given as 'Harry'.

So what's in a name? you said. A rose by any other name, is that it? I said. It was true, I had felt rather pleased with myself when I named you; and now I realised the emptiness of that gesture. I'm sorry, I said. Rainbow. Miranda. The police band was playing 'Pack Up Your Troubles', and, as the chorus came round, we both burst into song together, Pack up your troubles in your old kit bag, and smile, smile, smile. And smile we did, if a little wryly. But I felt that both of us had betrayed ourselves, that we had participated a mutual confidence trick. And I didn't know whether to call you Rainbow or Miranda. Both seemed somehow false now.

Some days later I called into Isaac Beringer's antique shop in Winetavern Street. I've known Beringer for almost as long as I can remember, and he doesn't look much older than he did when I was a child, when I was introduced to him by my father. Beringer has a photographic memory, and knows not only the present contents of his shop, but can relate the history of every piece, clocks, watches, pendants, snuff-boxes, rings, spoons, anything that has passed through his hands over the years, its provenance, its defining characteristics, its current market value. I once asked him how he did it. Oh, it's very simple, Mr Gabriel, he said. I've been born into this shop – and it was true, his father, Isaac the Elder, had kept the shop before him – and I know it as well as myself. Better, maybe. Every display case, every shelf, every drawer, every cubbyhole – and he gestured around him – I can see them with my eyes shut. And I know where everything is. Where everything was. I've got them all filed away. You might say they're like people, and I remember their faces, and I have little stories for them, so one reminds me of another, the way you say so-and-so is like so-and-so. Take this piece, for example – and here he picked up a silver snuff-box – nice box, made by David Pettifer in Birmingham, 1854. Year of the Crimean War, Charge of the Light Brigade, got it last week for a song in the Friday Market. And I see this snuff-box in the pocket of an English officer, a tall man with big moustaches, you'd know him anywhere. In another pocket he's got his father's watch, nice movement by Barwise, 1790s, I sold it six months ago. You see how it works? I just make up stories about them.

But the watch wouldn't have been in the officer's pocket before you had the snuff-box, I said. No, said Beringer, I had another story for the watch then, involved an antique pistol, the case had a little dent in it when I got it, so I thought maybe there's been a duel, the watch belongs to this brash youth, you know the sort, all piss and vinegar, and the other chap's bullet hits the watch, youth escapes unscathed, you know the kind of thing that happens in stories. Or sometimes in real life, I said. True, said Beringer. That's why the stories change. Because things in real life change all the time, even when they stay the same. Depends on the way you look at them.

And what happened to the other chap? I said. Oh, said Beringer, brash youth, he's shitting himself, pistol all over the place, but he manages to get your man in the leg. Wound went septic, had to amputate. Chap's a cripple for the rest of his life. Most unfortunate, really, brash youth was in the wrong, chap hadn't been looking at his woman at all. But then there's never really much justice in these things, is there?

So there I was in Beringer's shop and I said I was looking for something special. For a lady. Lady friend? said Beringer. Well, acquaintance, I said, and Beringer gave me the ghost of a wink. Well, he said, maybe you wouldn't want to get too close then. A pendant wouldn't do. Certainly not a ring. Nor earrings. Now here's something – and he pulled open a drawer and took out a scent bottle – Lalique glass, he said, lovely thing, *L'Air du Temps* by Nina Ricci, 1948. He handed me the bottle. It was indeed lovely, with a swirled bowl of pale yellow, the stopper in the form of two intertwined doves in opalescent frosted glass. Yes, said Beringer, *L'Air du Temps*, Spirit of the Times, just after the war, you know. Love and peace, that kind of thing. Of course it's empty, but you can still smell the perfume. I unstoppered the bottle and put my nose to its mouth. Sandalwood, rose and jasmine breathed out at me. I thought of the paintings of Botticelli, of Venus emerging from the waters on her scalloped shell. So I bought the bottle, and I gave it to you. Of course you knew what it was at once, and you were delighted. *L'Air du Temps* by Nina Ricci, 1948, the year my parents married. The Lalique bottle came later, 1950. Thank you so much, Angel, do you know I used to call myself Nina when I was a child, because Miranda was such a mouthful, and my father called me Nina, though my mother would insist on Miranda. So you became Nina then, and you are Nina still to me. And I wonder if you still have the *L'Air du Temps* bottle, and if its perfume still lingers.

BUT SO HARD
TO FORGET

Onoto

When two similar and unlikely, or at least unexpected, events happen in relatively quick succession they achieve a certain equilibrium, a reciprocity: they are the two sides of an equation, and complement each other, like Yin and Yang. So it was with your first two messages: *It's been a long time, It's easy to remember.* But three? Three is a perfect number, the triangle of the Trinity, but triangles are notoriously tricky in human relationships, and I think again of the little accidental minuet we danced with Tony Lambe when I heard him call you Miranda. Nina. I write your name again this time in order to address you. Your third postcard was postmarked Stroud, Gloucs., a name which meant little to me. I looked it up in the atlas and found it to be a small town on the Welsh border, not far from Bristol, and I wondered what you were doing there. But then I used to wonder what you were doing wherever you were when you were not with me, when you were not in Belfast, away on one of your trips.

Stroud meant nothing to me, but the image on the postcard brought tears of recognition to my eyes. *Belfast 1954*, the caption on the back reads, *John Chillingworth,* © BBC *Hulton Picture*

Library. It shows a back street in Belfast. It could be Sevastopol Street, where I spent the first six years of my life before we moved to Ophir Gardens, but it is not. Nevertheless this grey pavement is familiar to me, the corner shop, the lamp-post, the water running down the pavement from a broken gutter. 1954. I would have been five or six. I could be one of these five boys in the foreground, wearing wellington boots, or I could turn a corner and appear in the picture any time soon. A game is in progress, Cops and Robbers or Cowboys and Indians, for the smallest two of the boys are wielding toy guns, drawing in on a third who is hidden from their view by a street corner; a fourth, evidently a passer-by and not part of the game, looks at the fugitive with amusement, and, from the eager expression on the face of the leading gunman, seems to have given the game away; the fifth boy, who might or might not be involved, is looking elsewhere. And I wonder what this little drama, so accidental, so inevitable in outcome because seen in retrospect, might have to say about our relationship.

I turn the card over. It took me a few readings of your brief message before I realised the link between it and your preceding one. *But so hard to forget*, those were your words, and suddenly I heard Billie Holiday singing, as you must have intended. It was you who introduced me to Billie Holiday.

> Your sweet expression, the smile you gave me,
> The way you looked when we met
> It's easy to remember, but so hard to forget
> I hear you whisper, I'll always love you,
> I know it's over and yet
> It's easy to remember, but so hard to forget.

And more than that, I heard her singing my favourite Billie Holiday song, as you must have intended, 'Gloomy Sunday'. It's playing on the CD player as I write, and I am hearing it, not now in my study at 41 Ophir Gardens, but in your flat at 70 Eglantine Avenue as I heard it over twenty years ago; for music, like perfume, has the power to abolish intervening time. The flat is more of a maisonette, the two top floors of a big three-storey Victorian house. We're sitting in what would have been the drawing-room. It's summer dusk, the curtains of the great bay window have not yet been drawn, and a tree bows and scrapes against the glass in the breeze which rises at dusk when the air grows chill; there's a bright fire burning in the grate. The only other light is the deepening amethyst of the sky beyond the trees and a dim lamp which shines on the hi-fi system. There's a gleam on the black undulating disc like silvery moonlight on a black ocean, and Billie's voice emerges from the speakers the ghost of a beat ahead of the backing, but slowly, skimming above the melancholy horns, dipping and soaring then slowing as she pauses on the last word of a line before letting it go into a temporary silence, and the band comes to the foreground for a second or two, echoing the phrase before last, then fades back behind her.

> Sunday is gloomy, my hours are slumberless
> Dearest, the shadows I live with are numberless
> Little white flowers will never awaken you
> Not where the black coach of sorrow has taken you
> Angels have no thoughts of ever returning you
> Would they be angry if I thought of joining you?
> Gloomy Sunday.

And I see the drawing room in its entirety, the big Kazak rug, faded reds and yellowed greens on the black-painted floorboards, the shelves of books, the framed Japanese fans, the Art Deco dressing table. You had another in the bedroom; this one was more of a display unit for your collection of scent bottles. I hadn't known, when I bought you the *L'Air du*

Temps bottle, that you were a collector, and it pleases me to see its pair of intertwining doves here now, even if perhaps you only brought it out because you knew I was coming. Either way, you had me in mind. On the dressing table you've arrayed bottles of cut glass and blown glass and marble-swirl glass and opalescent milk glass and Limoges porcelain and rose quartz and green opaline, square-shouldered bottles and round bottles and cylindrical bottles, bottles with stoppers of ruby glass and silver and guilloche enamel and diamond-faceted glass, stoppers in the shape of lilies and roses and pineapples, bottles shaped like pineapples and translucent pears and apples. Here is an especially beautiful one, with a reverse-painted Japanese scene showing two boys playing hide-and-seek. There are bottles shaped like domes and spires and cupolas, ranged like the buildings of a city reflected in the triptych mirror of the dressing table, glowing and winking in the firelight. Then there are the accessories, the atomizers with beaded bulbs and the hairbrushes with tortoiseshell backs, the enamelled powder compacts. I asked you what drove you to collect these things, and you said, Because they're beautiful, and as I write these words I think of my own collection.

I open the pen cabinet in my mind's eye to see the pens like jewels, no two of them alike, the Conway Stewarts in casings of Teal Blue with Green Veins, Blue Cracked Ice, Autumn Leaves, Peacock, Grey Jazz, Candy-stripe Relief, Red Jazz, Blue Jazz, Blue Rock Face, Moss Agate, Pink Moiré, and Salmon Pink with Grey-green Flecks, to name but some.

I have a tray of Pelikans, like German burghers in their uniforms of black tops and trouser-barrels of striped green, brown and blue and grey, and the long Pelikan beak-shaped clip sitting against the black top like a gold tie with an upturned tip. I have a block of Parker Vacumatics in silver blues and greys, and if you stand them on end they look like skyscrapers at night with patterned strips of lit windows. I have a sheaf of Sheaffers and a quiverful of Swans and Blackbirds.

I'm writing this with an Onoto, which I chose because its Tiger's Eye pattern of iridescent tawny browns and ambers matches the back of a hairbrush on your dressing-table. I got it from Beringer when I was starting off collecting, one of the first pens I bought. Lovely thing, Mr Gabriel, attractive name too, said Beringer, Japanese, wouldn't you think? But no, English as Brighton rock. Made by Thomas De La Rue and Company, London, best printers in the world, Queen Victoria grants them a licence to print the stamps of the Empire. Immensely wealthy. Literally printed money. Banknotes, run your fingers over them, you can feel the engraving. Made diaries, too, stationery, playing cards, that kind of thing. It's 1905, they decide to make pens. Fountain pens a new-fangled thing, expanding market. Logical step. So they look around for a new angle, most fountain pens were what they call eyedroppers, you had to unscrew them and fill them with an eyedropper. Messy business. So they get hold of this inventor chap, George Sweetser, comes up with a patent for a plunger mechanism, piston if you like, steam engine technology – here, I'll show you – and Beringer showed me how to unscrew the blind cap on the end of the barrel and pull out the plunger. Funny thing is, said Beringer, you push it in, it fills on the downstroke, not what you'd expect. Vacuum system, ingenious. Opposite of a syringe. And of course you use ink instead of blood. You won't be going signing your name in blood, Mr Gabriel? Funny thing about Sweetser, too, he was a roller-skating champion, did a music-hall act dressed up as a woman. If you made it up people wouldn't believe you. Anyway, 1905, they buy Sweetser's plunger pen. The same year, Battle of Tsushima, Admiral Togo blows the Russian fleet out of the water. End of Russo-Japanese War. So De La

Rue thinks, fair play, better keep in with the Land of the Rising Sun, British interests in the Pacific, don't you know. So they call the pen Onoto, Japanese ring to it. They have a sun logo on some of their pens, not this one. Here's a thing – he rummaged under the counter – novel by Onoto Watanna, real name Winnifred Eaton, English father, Chinese mother, born in Canada. Dresses herself up in kimonos, does the whole Japanese thing, Americans think she is Japanese. He proffered me the book. *The Heart of Hyacinth*, he said,1903, not that rare mind you, they printed a couple of hundred thousand, and not great literature, to tell you the truth, but a big hit in its day, and a nice genre piece. Lovely illustrations, I'll tell you what, I'll throw it in with the pen. Two Onotos for the price of one. Oh yes, said Beringer, the pen's a 1948 model. Year that you were born, if my memory serves me right. It does, I said.

So here I am in Eglantine Avenue in 1982, the 1950 Lalique bottle with the intertwining doves is on your drawing-room dressing table, and the hi-fi is playing 'Gloomy Sunday'. They called it 'The Hungarian Suicide Song', you said. Two Hungarians wrote the original, Rezso Seress the music, Laszlo Javor the lyrics, in, oh, 1933. The story goes that after it came out there was a spate of suicides among young lovers in Hungary. They'd find them dead in their apartment or whatever, empty syringe beside them, 'Gloomy Sunday' on the record player. Or the neighbours hear gunshots and when they burst in the record is still playing. Or the lovers leave a suicide note with 'Gloomy Sunday' written on it, nothing else. Well, it's the Depression after all, and Hungary's got the highest rate of suicide in the world, the song is in the air, so maybe there's some truth in the story. Then an English version came out in the States, about 1936, and the same thing began to happen, so they say, lovers killing themselves all over the place. They say they banned it from the airwaves, the BBC banned it, but no one seems to have been able to come up with any hard evidence. They say this, they say that. Maybe the whole thing's an urban myth. All we can be sure of, Seress jumped to his death from his apartment block in 1968. That's, what, thirty-five years later, very delayed reaction, I would have said. As you spoke, I thought of Andy Warhol's images of suicides, one in particular where the victim looks asleep amid the sculpted marble drapery of a baroque tomb; but when we look closer, we find her bed is the crumpled metal sheet of the car roof she has landed on. Yet she seems to have found some repose and grace, as if Divine mercy has been shown.

> Soon there'll be candles and prayers that are sad, I know
> Let them not weep, let them know that I'm glad to go ...

Funny thing is, you went on, the English lyrics are nothing like the Hungarian. Not that my Hungarian is up to much, but I came across a translation once, oh, something like, it is autumn and the leaves are falling, all love has died on earth, people are heartless and wicked, there are dead people on the streets everywhere, that kind of thing. Billie's version came out in 1942, not long after Pearl Harbor. Not the happiest of times, in any event. And they say that Billie's third verse was an afterthought, a kind of palliative to lighten the gloom of the first two.

> Dreaming, I was only dreaming
> I wake and I find you asleep in the deep of my heart,
>   dear
> Darling, I hope that my dream never haunted you
> My heart is telling you how much I wanted you
> Gloomy Sunday

It's dark by now and I'm in Ophir Gardens casting my mind

back to Eglantine Avenue over the dark gulf of intervening time, and it's dark by now there too. The record comes to an end and I think how there seemed to be more hiss and crackle on your vinyl copy, more of the atmospherics of lost time, forty years since Billie laid the track down and I imagine the dust of 1942 sifting down into the grooves of the recording back then, getting into the voice and the instruments, and making that slight lisp in her enunciation all the more poignant.

You got up and drew the curtains and the noise of the wind in the trees outside died to a whisper. I can see her with that white gardenia in her hair, you said, isn't it strange how the song makes you see the singer, she's standing in a spotlight in a bar in New York, you said, and it's dark but there's those little tea-lights in faceted glass holders on the tables and you can see hands holding cigarettes and cocktail glasses, a face or two maybe, the smoke curling up and drifting into the spotlight, and I think how strange it is that your few words, *But so hard to forget*, should make me see you as you were then, or what you have become to me since then. I see the blue vein in the back of your hand as you write and you go over to lift the needle from where it's bumping at the end of the last track. You know, she took her name from Billie Dove, you said, her favourite movie star, her real name was Eleanora Fagan Gough. Her father was Holiday but she hardly ever saw him, I think she took his name as a kind of accusation, or revenge. Not that you'd ever know from her autobiography, they say she made half of it up, you said. Billie Dove.

You went over and touched the two intertwining doves of the *L'Air du Temps* stopper. Nineteen forty-eight, you said, March 16th, Billie plays Carnegie Hall, she was released from the reformatory just eleven days before. So you see, your Lalique bottle will always remind me of that, of Billie's greatest concert. Do all your bottles have memories like that? I asked. Well, they're all souvenirs of one kind or another, you said. Some of this, some of that. Inconsequential things, sometimes. Business trips even, the little bits of pleasure that happen when you're somewhere on business, and you manage to escape the business for a while. Well, I don't know that much about your business, I said, and then you began to tell me.

I work for MO2, you said. You won't have heard of it. Technically – but unofficially, as it were – we're supposed to report both to Home Affairs and the Northern Ireland Office, but they leave us pretty much alone. MO stands for Mass Observation, you know the group that was set up in the Thirties? Only vaguely, I said. Didn't the film-maker Humphrey Jennings work with them? You know, *Night Mail*? My father loved the Auden poem that was written for it, and I recited

> This is the Night Mail crossing the border,
> Bringing the cheque and the postal order,
> Letters for the rich, letters for the poor,
> The shop at the corner and the girl next door …

And behind my own voice I could hear Auden's clipped English accent as the steam train trailed its long plume of smoke like writing across the English landscape. My father used to recite the fourth line in a broad Belfast accent, I said, it's a proper rhyme when you do it that way. Well, it's near a proper rhyme in Yorkshire too, you said. Anyway, you said, Jennings was one of the founders, it all started off quite by accident. By coincidence. It's 1936, the anthropologist Tom Harrisson, erstwhile poet, that's Harrisson with two esses, has a poem in the *New Statesman*, same issue as a poem by Charles Madge, and a piece by Jennings. Bunch of left-wing intellectuals, some might call them. They begin to collaborate.

The ordinary British people have never been looked at properly before, so they begin to observe them. They want to know how things are, so they can make things better. They get other writers and artists on board. William Empson, for one, you know, the *Seven Types of Ambiguity* bloke. They hire a team of investigators, young middle-class clerks mostly, set them up in a terrace house in Bolton, mix with the working class. The investigators go to the pub, mix in, watch the drinking habits of the men, how often they use the spittoon, that kind of thing. They keep a record of everything, down to the number of pints they drink themselves. The portions of chips they bought at the end of the night, they even used to count the chips in the bag and put that into the record.

Then Harrisson recruits the poet David Gascoyne, Marxist, surrealist, you said, and in a way this is really a surrealist enterprise. And Gascoyne gets them to take on Humphrey Spender, the photographer, brother of the poet Stephen. You know Spender, those classic shots of Bolton, all smog and grit and washing on the line. The famous one, the two little boys peeing with their trousers half-down, and the factory chimneys belching out smoke in the background. Spender felt a little guilty about it all, thought of himself as a snooper, an eavesdropper, which of course he was in a way. Which they all were, for all that they were doing it for the greater good. But no one had done this kind of thing before, and Spender loved the detail, the way the light shone on the cobbles. He's got a lovely picture, the chromium-plated parts of a Hoover someone had displayed on the mantel of their front parlour.

Mass Observation aimed to focus not only on the people, you said, but the things surrounding the people. Hence the mantelpiece ornaments, men's penknives, their pipes, their collar-studs, kitchen implements, women's hatpins, sewing-kits, anything they thought might represent the people.

Getting down to the nitty-gritty of dialectical materialism. There's a file somewhere of button-boxes and their contents, you know the sort of thing your mother might have had, biscuit-tins or tea-caddies filled with odd buttons – and here I remembered sifting through my mother's Quality Street tin of buttons, buttons of Bakelite and Celluloid, mock tortoiseshell and amber, buttons for blouses and shirts and jackets and overcoats – quite incredible, really, you said, the level of detail they went into.

Anyway, you said, that's where MO2 got its inspiration from, to begin with. Sometime in the early Seventies, some bright spark in Westminster decides Westminster doesn't really understand Northern Ireland. This is about the time when the Brits – listen to me talking, and I'm half a Brit myself – decide for once and for all to get shot of Northern Ireland. So the bright spark gets them to set up an MO-type organisation. Of course it's all done with a nod and a wink. They spend a couple of years putting wheels in motion, recruiting staff, before some other bright spark comes to the conclusion that the original MO methods wouldn't be entirely appropriate for Northern Ireland. Just think of it, the Bolton people sometimes thought the MO people were spies. Spender nearly got his camera smashed on a couple of occasions. So it's back to the drawing board, and they come up with MO2. And that's a misnomer, really, for what they decide to do is not Mass Observation, it's more like Focused Observation – FO, if you like – because they go for selected groups of people, not the ordinary folk, whoever they might be – and there's nowt as queer as folk, you said in a stage Yorkshire accent – and not so much the people at the top, but the people they think might rise to the top. The up-and-coming cream, the incipient meritocracy. For this is a long-term project. After so many centuries, what's another decade or two?

As I wrote these words the Onoto ran out of ink. I'd never got the proper hang of the plunger system; and to tell the truth, though it's a beautiful pen, it doesn't quite suit my hand, the nib has just that too much flex for me, and I find it difficult to control, sometimes there's a wobble to my characters, it would suit you better, you always liked a supple nib, and when I look at your card the writing betrays the weight you give to your downstrokes. So I look into my pen cabinet and select a Conway Stewart instead, a No. 17 in Blue and Black Candle-Flame, and I fill it with blue Pelikan ink that comes in a nice little dumpy round-shouldered Pelikan bottle. The Conway, like practically all of its kind, is a lever-filler, and the gold lever ends in a little round gold shield, just four millimetres in diameter, and when you look at it through a jeweller's loupe screwed into your eye socket you can clearly see the letters C and S emblazoned on it like a pair of intertwining snakes. The shield is set into a nice little groove in the barrel, which makes it easy to lift the lever with your thumbnail, it's a very thoughtful ergonomic design. They call it a lollipop lever. Sometimes when the ink is a little low in the bottle you get a sucking noise as the pen fills up, and lollipop sounds right. So now I'm writing with the Conway Stewart, but the Onoto is still at the back of my mind as it lies on the mahogany veneer top of my desk, its colours glowing with an almost hallucinatory intensity in the light of the desk-lamp, russets and ambers like those of a New England fall, and they could easily have called this pattern Turning Leaves, not Tiger's Eye. But I like the Raj implications of Tiger's Eye, for the Onoto, after all, was a very Empire pen, its demise as a writing instrument in the Fifties coinciding with the loss of British possessions overseas. I learned just the other day that Onoto have started making pens again, not the original De La Rue Onoto, but a new company that got the rights to the name.

They're making expensive pens for the top end of the market. It's 2005, they're bringing out a pen to commemorate Admiral Togo's victory at Tsushima in 1905, they're calling it the Admiral Togo pen. And to commemorate Admiral Nelson's victory at Trafalgar in 1805 – and Togo modelled himself on Nelson, he thought of himself as the Japanese Nelson, he'd studied his tactics at Trafalgar – they're bringing out a pair of pens, the Horatio Nelson and the Emma Lady Hamilton. So I can never write now with an Onoto without thinking of Tsushima, and the Russian fleet going down in a cataclysm of steam, and of shot and shell, and of the blood running down the decks of the French and British ships, and of HMS *Victory*, and of Nelson with his one arm and his blind eye, and of Nelson freshly brain-damaged from the Battle of the Nile, meeting Lady Hamilton in Naples under the glow of a restless Vesuvius, of the sultry night, and of their subsequent long correspondence, and of quill pens and penknives and inkwells and pounces and portable writing-slopes, and the hundreds of thousands of words that passed between them. I write this to you, Nina, with the Conway Stewart Blue and Black Candle-Flame as I watch the blue ink of my words flow on to the page.

You stared into the fire as you talked, and there was a soft crash as a coal collapsed. If ever you read these words I wonder if you will see them as a true account of what you said to me that night twenty-three years ago, for I know that there is no memory that is not permeated with subsequent memories. And I realise I might have interpolated your story with some details not known to me then.

For instance, Tom Harrisson had conducted an anthropological study of the cannibal tribe known as the Big Nambas, of Malekula in the New Hebrides, now known as Vanautu. In Vanautu the principal objects of wealth and of religious veneration were pigs. In this system only male pigs were valued, their tusks being especially valued; most valued of all were male hermaphroditic pigs, whose incidence in the swine population had been raised to an extraordinary fifteen per cent by generations of inbreeding. This phenomenon had previously been described in 1928 by the Oxford zoologist John Baker, in an article published in the *British Journal of Experimental Zoology*. Somehow, this obscure piece of research came to the attention of a group of Hollywood moguls who thought it a wonderful premise for a motion picture involving cannibals and pigs.

One day in the year 1935 Harrisson, by his own account, was wandering the shoreline of Vanautu in an emaciated and delirious condition after spending months in the highlands with the Big Nambas, when an immense yacht glided into harbour. On board was Douglas Fairbanks Sr., erstwhile star of *The Mark of Zorro*, who appeared to Harrisson 'like a vision' wearing orange-flame pyjamas. Fairbanks and Harrisson then spent the next few days drinking 'perfect gin slings' and discussing the logistics of the proposed motion picture. Harrisson was given firm indications that he would be hired as a consultant on the project, but it never materialised, perhaps cannibal movies had gone out of vogue, and he found himself back in England jobless.

It then occurred to him that he could easily transpose his anthropological methods to the English population, and so Mass Observation was born. The town of Bolton was not chosen by accident. It was the birthplace of Lord Lever, founder of Lever Brothers, the largest soap company in the world, producers of Sunlight, Lifebuoy, Lux and Vim, among other brands. In 1930 Lever merged with the Dutch company Margarine Unie to form Unilever, which had links with the electronics firm of Philips, where your father worked.

Unilever was one of the chief sponsors of Mass Observation. I note that today Unilever are the manufacturers of Dove deodorant, which makes me think of the intertwining doves of the *L'Air du Temps* bottle that sits on your dressing table; which is possibly neither here nor there, though it could be argued that any one thing in the universe implies the existence of every other thing.

So I was tempted to have you tell me things you had not told me: you might have said, for example, that the poet Kathleen Raine, the partner of Charles Madge and author of such poems as 'The Invisible Spectrum', 'Lenten Flowers' and 'The End of Love', conducted a survey on the incidence of handkerchief use among Bolton women, from which we learn that on a particular day in 1937 a woman in a plum-coloured coat stopped outside the Regal Gown shop in Bolton and paused for two minutes and ten seconds before taking a handkerchief from her handbag and blowing her nose. You might have said that the poet and eminent literary critic William Empson was assigned to detail the contents of sweetshop windows in Bolton, and that the journalist Woodrow Wyatt was given the job of playing George Formby records on the gramophone in Harrisson's rented house in Bolton, in order to give it an authentic Lancashire atmosphere. You might have told me that Harrisson's first discipline had been that of ornithology, and that his experience of watching birds and then of listening to a people whose language he did not speak had convinced him that speech often hindered understanding. We cannot afford, said Harrisson – you might have said – to devote ourselves exclusively to people's verbal reactions to questions asked them of a stranger in the street, without running a grave risk of reaching misleading conclusions. What people say is only one part – not a very important part – of the whole pattern of human thought and behaviour, said Harrisson.

There was a soft crash as an archway of coal collapsed in the fire and for a second I got the smell of coal-smoke, and then it died and your perfume came back to me as it does now. I remember wondering if Mass Observation had surveyed the fragrance departments of the big stores in Bolton, and I thought of what it must have been like to come from the Bolton smog into their brightly lit foyers. Andy Warhol loved the names of those perfumes in the Thirties fashion magazines he liked to read, and used to say them over to himself, imagining what they smelled like, I go crazy because I want to smell them all so much, he said, Guerlain's *Sous le Vent*, Worth's *Imprudence*, Lenthéric's *Shanghai* and *Gardénia de Tahiti*, D'Orsay's *Belle de Jour* and *Trophée*, Kathleen Mary Quinlan's *Rhythm*, Saravel's *White Christmas*. What's that? I asked. What's what? you said, a bit piqued, I thought, that I had interrupted the flow of your story. Your perfume, I said, and then you offered me the blue vein in your wrist. *Je Reviens*, you said. It works on two levels. First you get a woody base with green ferns running through it, then a heady rush of flowers. Wild narcissus, jasmine, a dash of ylang-ylang.

Let's leave the job for now, you said.

IN HOC
SIGNO VINCES

1939 Esterbrook

I've never met a person I couldn't call a beauty. Andy Warhol said that. I found you beautiful, Nina, and sometimes I think it's got to do with that photograph of your mother, Nell Birtwhistle, taken at the age you were when you showed it to me, taken before you were born, for you were a late child, her only child, though not your father's. That affair came later. And, because she looks so like you that she could be you, I used to think of you as being as old as her, were she alive — for she had died before we met — with all her experience inherited by you, her life enfolded within yours.

I always thought of you as much older than me even though you are younger. There was something in you I could never reach, something that always lay beyond my ken. Before I met you I thought that to be mutually in love would be to have a perfect understanding of the other, and she a perfect understanding of me, so that we would melt indissolubly into each other, and I hungered for that love by which I would be so understood.

But now I know it is different; and it is difference which makes that difference. For no two bodies can occupy the same space, for if they did there would not be two bodies, but one, and the other would not exist. And it is ignorance of the other which moves us to love the other, for there is always more to know in him or her, and they surprise us every day with the things they come out with, some newly minted phrase or slant on things we'd never heard or seen before, that we'd perhaps thought them to be incapable of, and so they rise forever in our estimation because each day our ignorance of them is proven, and we grow more and more attached to them because they are always one step ahead of us, like the legendary deer that will always elude the hunter. *Il y a toujours l'un qui baisse et l'un qui tend la joue*, according to the French proverb, and so it was with us, for you would hold your cheek for me and I'd catch your perfume as I'd kiss or try to kiss you before you would me. There is always one who kisses, and one who offers a cheek. And I wonder if it was like that between Harry Bouwer – as he became in England – and Ellie Birtwhistle. I looked at the photograph again, noting her firm stance, her broad smile that was your smile, the red and black swirl of her Dinkie pen against her white blouse, her strong hands at ease by her side. You could be twins, I said.

Your fourth postcard was not wholly unexpected, for by now the element of surprise had been diminished. And the image you had chosen, of Gemini, was appropriate. You were one of those people who do not believe in astrology, but nevertheless take its prognostications half seriously, as a playful basis for the conduct of their daily lives. Perhaps you still consult your horoscope. At any rate, you are a Gemini, and I a Libra. Your message was at first difficult to interpret – *In hoc signo vinces*, you wrote, In this sign shall you conquer, the words purportedly heard by Constantine when, on the eve of his victory over the pagan Emperor Maxentius in 312, an angel appeared to him in a vision, holding a Cross, which is a sign of victory over death. You had long lapsed from your mother's nominal Anglicanism, and I did not seriously believe that you would write these words in any literal sense. So I decided that the sign in question was not the Cross, but Gemini, and I decided to refresh my memory as to its attributes.

A Gemini is lively, skilful, versatile, intellectual, more interested in political theory than direct action. But she can also be unscrupulous, cunning, and evasive, and often contrives to escape blame by imputing it to others. She can be fickle and flirtatious; she is a butterfly, a chameleon. Famous Geminis include Bob Dylan, Paul Gauguin, Marilyn Monroe, Queen Victoria, Sir Arthur Conan Doyle, and Judy Garland. The colour associated with Gemini is not any one colour, but the rainbow, and I think of how you were once Rainbow to me, and of Judy Garland singing 'Somewhere Over the Rainbow'. Cities ruled by Gemini include London, Versailles, and New York. And it so happened that your card, postmarked London, had been originated in New York, for the image was from a Book of Hours in the Pierpoint Morgan Library in that city, which we visited in the summer of 1983. The Twin Towers of the World Trade Center were still standing then, of course, and I remember making a playful comparison to your status as a Gemini. Yes, you said, didn't you know that Geminis are very good at trade? We're ruled by Mercury, after all, the god of commerce. And of thieves, I said. I looked at the card again. Mercury, or Hermes, was the god of the corn-trade, specifically, and of music, so one twin holds a sickle, the other a lyre, emblems of these dual attributes. And Hermes is also the psychopomp, who conducts the souls of the dead to the underworld.

It was July in New York, and I had never experienced such heat, such humidity. But it was my first time in America and everything was beautiful to me, and as you conducted me through the sweltering, claustrophobic underground that smelled of metal, electricity and sweat, I was fascinated by the trains as they drew groaning and trembling into the stations emitting blue sparks from their undercarriages, their cars emblazoned with elaborate graffiti tags of letters amplified and puzzled nearly to deliberate illegibility, yet still names, their forms grappling with themselves in lime greens, glowing yellows and acid blues moving as if animated across the walls of the cars, blossoming from two dimensions into a thought-bubble cycloidal realm, or break-dancing as human figures sculpt the space around themselves, sometimes resembling the flight of birds above the city, or the intertwining pythons of the subterranean world, jagged as a city skyline sometimes, or nebulous as cloudscapes, flickering like neon in a baroque spectacle that belied the curt syllables they had been evolved from – ZINK, SHARP, TAKI 183, SKEME, STITCH, KASS, DAZE, DEAL, DURO, BAN 2, KIST, KEL, SLAVE, CRIME 79, MIN, KASE 2, SEEN. On one car I saw a Campbell's soup tin the size of a door, but the writing read ZIP.

In the numbered grid of the streets above, everything was sign, from the cupolas of the water-towers stilted on the flat roofs to the fire escapes that ran zigzag down the walls of tenement buildings and the subway trains glimpsed momentarily between buildings on elevated sections of the track. Underfoot there was writing in the shape of the manhole covers embedded in the sidewalk, massive cast-iron shields embossed with their makers' identities, Abbott Hardware Company Ironworks, Marcy Foundry, Etna Iron Works, Madison Ironworks, Cornell's Iron Works, long-gone companies that that made their names felt under our bootsoles as we walked over them.

I wandered the time-warp of the Garment District with you, engrossed by the window displays of haberdashery shops, with their cards of loom elastic, buttons, needles, pins and hair-clips, and the reels of cotton threads arrayed like colour charts, past run-down diners, delis, anonymous shops with windows of opaque glass, and high gables bearing the names of defunct businesses in letters of peeling paint, Mutual Storage Company, Kozma Bakery, Moyel Bros Fine Menswear, Arcadian Soup Company, Dubal Loans, Kitzler Cheap Novelties and Fancy Goods.

In Greenwich Village you brought me to a dark little ink emporium, a cornucopia of inks in hues of violet and pale green and bright orange and sepia, red inks and black inks, gold and silver inks, and you told me that every colour smelled differently. Try this, you said, and unscrewed a bottle, and another, and held them to my nose like perfumes. From the red there came an almost vinous odour, and the violet seemed imbued with tar. Like perfumes? I said, and you said, Yes, and I said, holding a bottle of black, If this was a perfume, what would you call it? and you said, Oh, I don't know, why don't we call it *Styx*? Then we went off the beaten track and in Alphabet City in a street between Avenues B and C we saw an elaborate *BELFAST* in graffito of green and gold on a gable wall, the cross-stroke of the *T* elongated into an arrow that doubled back on itself to emerge from the belly of the *B*, and I knew it must signify something different to the name of the city I came from.

New York was beautiful to me because of its difference, and in memory of that difference I am writing this with an American Esterbrook pen, American as Chevrolet, a 1939 model in iridescent red feathered lines with steel trim. It gleams as brightly as it must have done back then, like a red car parked on the lit forecourt of a filling (gas) station. The Esterbrook, like the Wearever I began with, was advertised as the Dollar Pen, but its selling point was a system of interchangeable nibs which could be unscrewed and screwed in at will, not gold but hard steel, sometimes tipped with iridium but more generally with just the steel rolled into an equally durable ball, and by the 1950s there were more than thirty different points, Firm Medium, Flexible Stub, *The Right Point For the Way You Write*, Extra Fine, Bold Signatures, *For Easier More Comfortable Writing*, Falcon Stub For Backhand Writing, Manifold For Carbon Copies, *The World's Most Personal Fountain Pen*, Bookkeeping, Firm Fine Clerical, *Affordable Writing Pleasure*, slogans I gleaned from a run of *National Geographic* magazines from 1955 that I got from Beringer many years ago and unearthed for this purpose, because when I began writing with the Esterbrook I remembered the name from the pages of the *National Geographic*, interleaved with ads for Mosler Safe and Western Union, Zenith Radio, Kodak, Zeiss, Hartford Insurance, not to mention the sleek low-slung chrome-trimmed automobiles, Pontiac and Buick and Thunderbird and Cadillac and Chrysler, *Put New Fun Under Your Foot*, *Spectacular from Takeoff to Top Performance*, *Long Sweeping Lines with Purposeful Meaning*, in vivid reds and bright yellows and pastel blues and greens, occupied by proud smiling new owners who signed the 'check' with an Esterbrook, *Every Inch Your Personal Pen – All Ways and Always*. The nibs were numbered. I'm writing this with a Firm Medium, 2668, and the Esterbrook glides across the page as smoothly as a pen costing many times as much, epitomising *Affordable Writing Pleasure*. And before I flew to meet you in New York I perused the *National Geographics* for their bright promise of an America in which everything could be bought.

I bought the Esterbrook on eBay. You might have wondered where I get all my pens. There are not that many outlets in Belfast for my passion. Beringer usually has a nice piece or two that he picks up at estate auctions, dead men's pens, he calls them, and I still browse the antique stalls of

Smithfield and Donegall Pass, though with diminishing frequency. Most of my stylophiliac transactions are now conducted on eBay. Before I ventured into that virtual market-place, my computer literacy had been confined mainly to the word-processing I used for my Esperanto book. I supposed the Internet to be a realm of dubious informational value, full of snares and pitfalls for the unwary, and I was nervous at first of entering a realm where the usual physical delineators of a transaction – speech, body language, facial expression – are absent, and where one cannot handle or examine in detail the item one is bidding on. But then I considered that those qualities of verbal and non-verbal language were precisely those used by any con man in the course of his profession, and that people can lie as readily as they tell the truth.

So I entered eBay cautiously, and over the next few weeks I bought a 1930s Conway Stewart Scribe in Green and Black Candle-Flame, a 1920s Gold Medal ladies' ring-top in Lapis Lazuli, and a 1940s Burnham in beautifully patterned Celluloid with lighter and darker shades of rose pink pearl outlined with black veins; as my confidence with these transactions increased, I became more and more drawn into the invisible international web.

Now that I have bought some two hundred pens on eBay my opinion of humanity has been revised upwardly: some people might lie as readily as they tell the truth; but the vast majority of them are honest, and are anxious to be seen as such. The pens come packaged with loving care, taped up in layers of kitchen roll inserted into plastic tubing which is then enclosed in a Jiffy bag, or enclosed in a pen-sized box surrounded by a cushion of polystyrene beans within a much larger box secured by layers of parcel tape that make access sometimes endearingly difficult, accompanied by handwritten notes, *Hi, Gabriel, hope you enjoy the pen, have left you good feedback, hope you do the same for me, warm regards,* and here the seller would sign themselves by their given name, Paul, Mary, George, whatever, to show that there was a human being behind their adopted eBay user IDs, semi-humorous tags like wadatz9, pentopl, bjaune, livia4, leftyy, mcgrrkk, xklepper, mrknipl, dizmusch, from which one could form some mental picture of the person – bjaune I saw as a yellow-haired Frenchman, or Francophile, maybe he was called Bernard, livia4 had to be a buxom Irishwoman, Anna Livia, and mrknipl was a New York Jewish marriage broker, Mr Knipl – while others called themselves by impenetrable strings of letters and numerals, 56mxot99f, xh17mq555, pp97304, and from these I deduced either that they were nervous individuals, overly security-conscious, or were so secure in themselves that they did not feel the need to present an almost recognisable face to the virtual world.

At any rate, the whole eBay system is based on mutual trust. You bid, you buy, you sell, and every one of these transactions receives Feedback, so that a cumulative profile of your honesty is built up which can be consulted by any other eBay member at any time. In this manner I have bought pens from people all over the world, from Kansas, Minnesota, Taiwan, Paris, Augsburg, York, Swanage, Brighton, Hamburg, Greece, New Zealand, Hong Kong, the Balearic Islands. You could say that eBay is a kind of Esperanto, or free-market communism, except its members are invisible.

My own eBay ID is goligher. In the course of my Esperanto researches I had been following a tenuous link between Esperanto and spiritualism, and I'd taken the name from a spiritualist group known as the Goligher Circle, of Belfast, who between 1915 and 1920 were the subject of investigation by W.J. Crawford, a lecturer in Engineering at Queen's University. The Circle was essentially a family affair. Mr

Morrison, in the attic of whose home the Circle met, was a hard-working committee member of the Spiritualist Society. Mrs Morrison was a sister of the principal medium, Kathleen Goligher. The other participants were Mr Goligher, Kathleen's father; Kathleen's older sisters, Lily and Anna; and her younger brother Samuel, who was thought to have some mediumistic gifts. There is no mention of a Mrs Goligher. I first came across the case when I picked up Crawford's book, *The Reality of Psychic Phenomena* (1916), in the Excelsior Book Store in Skipper Street. Over the next few months I managed to get my hands on the rest of Crawford's oeuvre: *Hints and Observations for Those Investigating the Phenomena of Spiritualism* (1918), *Experiments in Psychical Science* (1919) and *The Psychic Structures at the Goligher Circle*, published posthumously in 1920. Crawford, after many painstaking experiments, concluded that Kathleen in particular was a medium of extraordinary power, and that the phenomena were genuine.

As described by him, the séances which produced the phenomena differed little from those conducted all over Europe and America at the time, when spiritualism was re-energised by the grief of those who lost their loved ones in the Great War. The participants would enter an attic room, and form a circle around the séance table. The room would be illuminated by a dim red light, in this instance a gas jet ensconced in a lantern having a red glass sliding front, for normal light was thought to be injurious to the phenomena. The sitters, said Crawford, clasp each other's hands in chain order, and the séance begins. One of the members of the circle begins the proceedings with a prayer, and then a hymn is sung. Within a few minutes, sounds – *tap, tap, tap* – are heard on the floor close to the medium. They soon become louder and stronger, and occur right out in the circle space, on the table, and on the chairs of the sitters. Their magnitude varies in intensity from barely audible ticks to blows which might well be produced by a sledgehammer, the latter being really awe-inspiring and easily heard two storeys below, and even outside the house. The loud blows perceptibly shake the floor and chairs. Sometimes the raps keep time to hymns sung by the members of the circle; sometimes they tap out of themselves complicated tunes and popular dances on the top of the table or on the floor.

Other extraordinary effects include imitations of a bouncing ball – one would really think there was a ball in the room – the sawing of the table leg, the striking of a match, the walking of a man, and the trotting of a horse. Sometimes the raps sound perfect fusillades, for all the world like gunshots. After a quarter of an hour or so the rapping stops, and another type of phenomenon takes place. Remember, said Crawford, that the members of the Circle are simply sitting in their chairs holding each other's hands in chain order. The little table is standing on the floor within the circle, and is not in contact with any of them, or any portion of their clothing. Suddenly the table gives a lurch, or it moves along the floor. It lifts two of its legs into the air. Then all four. The table rises completely into the air of itself, where it remains suspended for several minutes without support, said Crawford.

According to Crawford, the phenomena were produced by 'psychic rods', which emerged from the orifices of Kathleen Goligher's body, and, anxious to verify their physical existence, he made several attempts to photograph them. On 23rd October 1915, as described by him in *The Reality of Psychic Phenomena*, he succeeded in obtaining an image which seemed to corroborate his theory. On the developed plate, plainly visible within the Goligher Circle, was a vertical column of whitish translucent material, about four inches in diameter and rising to a height of about five feet. The pattern of the wallpaper was quite easily seen through it, said Crawford. At its summit, however, it appeared quite opaque, as if the psychic stuff, issuing from its source, had exhausted its velocity at the top, and had doubled over on itself. The column, moreover, had several arms or branches, one of which appeared to terminate in or emanate from the chest of the medium. Others were joined to Miss Anna Goligher and Master S. Goligher. The whole photograph suggested to Crawford that the medium was in reality a psychic pump, with a complete pressure system. Perhaps, during levitation, the vertical column was under the table, in which case the pressure range would appear much greater. As it was, the psychic fluid appeared to be losing its energy much in the same way as a vertical jet of water, projected upwards against its own weight only, inevitably loses impetus and falls back.

Interestingly, Crawford failed to reproduce the photograph to support his verbal account, though it appeared in his posthumous book, *The Psychic Structures at the Goligher Circle*. In like manner, wanting to show that the sounds produced by the Circle were not the result of a collective hallucination, he hired a phonograph – an Edison Standard model – from a local dealer and, on 14th April 1916, ten days before the Easter Rising in Dublin, he successfully recorded the phenomena, which according to Crawford were produced by spiritual 'operators' who manipulated the psychic rods that emanated from Kathleen Goligher's body.

I was struck not so much by this alleged proof as by the fact that the recording session took place on the same day that my father was born, and I was struck by a powerful nostalgia for a time I had never known. The Golighers were textile workers, and I imagined Belfast as it would have been then, its air trembling with noise from the linen mills which were then producing fabric for British aeroplanes in the Great War, and

I indulged myself in a fancy that, since everything affects everything else, so Crawford's phonograph had recorded not only the sound of the psychic raps but a trace, however subliminal, of the whole aural hinterland of Belfast, including the voices of its people, and that the wax cylinder contained in one of its grooves a series of infinitesimal pits and tics, a wavering scratch a fraction of a micron deep, caused by the first cry of my father as he came into the world.

I told you, Nina, how Billie Holiday's singing affected me when I first heard it on your hi-fi system, little altered from the original recordings; and I think the hiss and crackle of old wax cylinders or shellac discs is even more atmospheric, for the dust which surrounds the music, as it drifts into the grooves, provides a more faithful molecular record of the sound in the air than is possible in a modern, hermetically sealed studio. So, when I hear Caruso's singing – his 'Ave Maria' of 1914, for example, a favourite recording of my father's – it is like dust-motes drifting through a shaft of sunlight in an empty room. The door has closed. The person has gone but the voice remains. I dreamed about my father that night, singing 'Ave Maria', as he used to do on Sunday evenings, sitting in the gloom of the parlour at Ophir Gardens.

A few pages later I came across a detail that once again fleetingly reminded me of my father, who happened to be born precisely one year after the death of Ludwig Zamenhof, the inventor of Esperanto. In October 1916 Crawford asked the 'operators' if any languages besides English were spoken in the other world they inhabited. By now it had been established that the operators were indeed entities who had once lived on this planet, but had passed on to a higher plane, this information being relayed by a system of coded raps, somewhat like Morse. After some hesitation the operators rapped out, $E \dots S \dots P$. Crawford could make no sense of this, beyond the speculation that the letters might stand for English, Spanish and Portuguese; the term ESP, meaning extrasensory perception, had not yet been coined. I was disappointed that Crawford had not entertained the possibility that it might be the beginning of the word *Espagnol*, or *Esperanto*; but I thought no more about it, until, several months later, I came across an article, in the journal *Esperanto Studies*, that made an explicit connection between Esperanto and the Brazilian version of spiritualism known as Spiritism, or Kardecism. Allan Kardec is the pseudonym of Hippolyte Léon Denizard Rivail (1804–1869), who was born a Catholic in Lyon, but was educated in Protestant Switzerland under the famous pedagogue Pestalozzi. After completing training as a teacher, Rivail returned to France, where he taught French, mathematics and sciences at various schools. Around the years 1854–55 the 'talking-table' fad had swept through the salons of Europe, and Kardec, initially sceptical, began to examine the extraordinary claims made by its practitioners. He found to his satisfaction that many of the phenomena were genuine, and summarised his findings in *Le Livre des Esprits* (1857). He concluded that the spirit world was made of souls in various stages of enlightenment, as the living on earth are in various stages of ignorance.

Kardec's philosophy was enthusiastically embraced in Brazil, where it was assimilated by the less educated classes into the various 'umbanda' sects, which recognise not only the saints of the Catholic Church, but the old Amerindian spirits, and the trickster Yoruba spirits. 'Pure' Kardecism seems to be mostly a middle-class phenomenon, and its followers, aware of the marginalised status of Portuguese among European languages, actively promote Esperanto as an excellent vehicle for promoting their beliefs. A key text for the Spiritists is John 10:16: 'And other sheep I have, which are not of this fold:

them also must I bring, and they shall hear my voice; and there shall be one fold, and one shepherd', meaning, to the Spiritists, that there will be not only religious but linguistic unity when the word of God is fulfilled. For, as we read in the first verse of John, 'In the beginning was the Word, and the word was with God, and the Word was God'; and Esperanto is a means of salvation from the curse of Babel.

In 1958 the Brazilian medium Yvonne Pereira published a novel, *Memórias de um Suicida* (Memoirs of a Suicide), which she claimed was dictated to her by the spirit of Camilo Castelo Branco, one of the greatest Portuguese prose writers of the nineteenth century. It is not a literary work, said Branco, but rather fulfils a sacred duty of warning against suicide by revealing the truth about the abyss that the suicide will find himself in after death; and Branco did indeed commit suicide in 1890. However, this abyss, unlike the conventional Christian hell, is not forever: one can escape it through enlightenment in the other world, and eventual reincarnation; and one of the chief instruments of enlightenment is Esperanto, which Branco learns by graduating through successive levels before enrolling in the celestial Embaixada Esperantista, the Esperanto Embassy.

Castelo Branco was only one of many spirits who made themselves known to Yvonne Pereira. In her work *Devassando o Invisível* (Penetrating the Invisible) she recalls that one of the 'better dressed' and most beautiful spirits she observed as a medium was that of Zamenhof, who appeared to her clad in his characteristic wool suit. He bore a halo of concentric waves, highlighted by a jet of brilliant green light. As I write to you, Nina, I recall the green star of my father's Esperanto lapel badge, and I cast my eyes towards the portrait of Zamenhof which still hangs in my study where my father hung it when I was a child, opposite the crucifix. *In Hoc Signo Vinces*.

And you, Nina, will see the pattern in all of this. You are a Gemini. Your dual nature enables you to be a skilful gatherer and disseminator of information. You are a good communicator. You were in New York at the behest – the invitation – of the Irish Embassy, which was entertaining a group of American-Irish businessmen, some of whom were known to be financially implicated with the IRA. It was July, the marching season in Northern Ireland, when sectarian tensions rise to a predictable annual pitch, and when you suggested that I join you in New York, I was glad to get out of Belfast. By then I had as good an idea as I ever had as to what it was you did for a living. I'm a communicator, you said that first night in Eglantine Avenue, don't you know that's what Geminis are good at? You might call me a diplomatic aide, but I'm not. But what's your job title? I asked. Oh, technically I'm called a Field Officer, but there are quite a few of us, and we all have different areas of expertise, you said. When I first got the job I duly reported in at nine o'clock sharp in the morning. The only person in the building was the receptionist, who was doing her nails and reading a Mills & Boon novel. The title stuck in my mind: *Ask Me No Questions*, it was called. Eventually some of the other staff straggled in, and by maybe eleven o'clock there were seven of us there, all of us in separate rooms. I was given a room with a desk, a chair, and a filing cabinet in it, you said, and when I was asked what I was supposed to do they looked at me with some surprise, and they said, Well, how on earth should we know? You're the expert. That's what we hired you for.

So what did you do? I said. Oh, first of all I got myself a phone, you said. Or rather, I spent four weeks getting a phone. They weren't too stuck on phones. Face to face is what we want, they said. You're a Field Officer, after all. So I went into the field. I met people. Got myself invited to exhibition openings, that kind of thing. Privately I call myself a style consultant, you said.

So there you were in New York, Nina, in your role as style consultant, and we were at this reception with the Irish mafia when the news came in that four Ulster Defence Regiment soldiers had been killed in Tyrone by an IRA landmine. It was the 13th of July 1983. You remember. We'd drunk a lot of champagne. You were wearing a pale green linen suit and a jade pendant, I remember, with green amber earrings. We talked about the Troubles and we drank some more champagne and it was then that I told you that my mother had been killed in 1975 as she was driving to her school on the Antrim Road. She had stopped at traffic lights when a white laundry van drew up beside her and the bomb it was carrying, intended for God knows what target, exploded prematurely.

You were silent for a while, and then you said, I know what it's like to lose a mother for no good reason. My mother took her own life in 1965. She was forty-eight. I was fifteen. I won't go into the reasons now as to why I think she did it. But for months afterwards I used to dream that she wrote to me. Letters from beyond the grave. They came in pale blue envelopes addressed to Miranda. I would open the envelope excitedly, thinking she must be still alive, but then the letter would say something like, I am happy where I am now, and I am still watching over you, that kind of thing, you said. And I remember again, Nina, how I burned your letters in 1984, hoping that by so doing I would expunge all memory of you from my system, and as I watched their ashes snow upwards into the grey July sky I wanted you to be dead for me, I wanted that part of me that loved you to be dead.

But there was something else in the dream that made me feel that she was indeed watching over me from somewhere, you said, for the letters bore something else beyond the clichéd words, something more immediate and tangible, her perfume. The perfume that she wore the morning she kissed me for the last time, as she went her way and I mine. In the dream I'd bury my face in the pages of her letter and I would wake with my eyes full of tears. And every year on her anniversary I open a bottle of that perfume. You were silent again. What was it? I said. What was what? you said. Her perfume, I said. *Après l'Ondée*, you said, After the Rain-shower. A warm musky base, almond top-note. Then you get the scent of hawthorn and violets doused in rain, cold and shivery.

Berlin. Bahnhof Friedrichstraße

EINE KLEINE
NACHTMUSIK

Conway Stewart 58 Green Hatch

I wonder what you wonder, when you wonder how your postcards might affect me. After your last card I was tempted to buy a flacon of *Après l'Ondée*, to experience your mother's perfume, but that would have been trespass, and I am content to make do with your remembered words, for I think you must intend me to find a narrative in your semi-disconnected messages, and so arrive at an understanding of our time together that has long been hidden deep in my memory. And your fifth card made me remember something I had forgotten. For when I read the words, *Eine Kleine Nachtmusik*, I heard them playing the acoustic perfume of Mozart that night in New York, and I could hear the top-note clarity of newly rinsed hawthorns and violets shimmering over the bass cellos of the musk-roses that crowded the great bay window. And when you told me of your mother's suicide, I imagined I could smell her perfume, emanating from you as you spoke those words, as if you had enfolded her aura within you, and had taken on her spirit as it left her.

The classical ensemble had been hired by you, as style consultant for the evening. You had stipulated that there was to be no Irish music. We want to throw them off balance a little, you said, skew the received ideas a little. It'll be warm, but we won't have the air-conditioning all the way up as they come in, we want it just a little sultry, and then when it starts to feel a little stuffy, we'll turn it up, and introduce a little apple-blossom scent into the air, it'll be like an Irish spring evening. We want muted Irish, no Paddywhackery. I'll have a little pale shamrock motif in the table-linen, more apple-green than shamrock, you said. You chose the flowers, the silverware, the menu. It was to be a stand-up buffet affair, you wanted good circulation, when people have to juggle drink and food and talk they're put off their dignity a little, you said, and if a little champagne is spilled so much the better. Helps them unwind.

I'd been sceptical of your plans. These are not only hard-nosed businessmen, I said, but sentimental bigots, they don't want their preconceptions upset. Yes, you said, so we won't give them any. But we'll give them something else, an aesthetic experience. No one is immune to beauty. You had the whole place lit with candles, candelabras with real candles that formed cataracts of wax as the evening progressed, and the scent of candle-wax and apple-blossom wafted through the pools of light and shade in the room and flickered on the silverware and linen with an almost ecclesiastical aura, and it occurred to me that some of these hard-nosed businessmen would have been altar-boys once and that you had taken that into consideration. Yes, you said, I want to remind them of the numinous, the things that are important beyond all this fiddle. Let them think they are cardinals, you said, not gombeen men, as I watched them form little dark-suited groups and eddies of conspiracy, well-fed faces nodding and smiling in the shadows and oases of light thrown by the candles amid the cut-glass vases full of white gardenias.

And, thinking of your mother's otherworldly perfume, I was reminded of the nineteeth-century mediums who specialised in olfactory effects. The Rev. Moses Stainton, for one, who in the course of his séances would produce liquid scents, sometimes of familiar perfumes, such as jasmine, heliotrope, verbena, sandalwood, new-mown hay, sometimes of perfumes unrecognised. Sometimes it appeared sprayed from the air, sometimes poured as if from a vial into the cupped palms of the sitters; often it would be found oozing from the medium's head and running down into his beard. Stainton was also capable of introducing objects into the room, seemingly from mid-air – pearls, rubies, sapphires, and emeralds, as well as more common objects such as books, opera-glasses, gloves, pin-cushions, shells, thimbles, snuff-boxes, kitchen knives, and candlesticks. The celebrated medium Mrs Guppy once asked each of the nineteen people present at a séance to wish for a fruit. First a banana appeared, then two oranges, a bunch of white grapes, a bunch of black grapes, a cluster of filberts, three walnuts, thirteen damsons, a slice of candied apple peel, three figs, two apples, an onion, a peach, five almonds, four very large grapes, three dried dates, a potato, two Conference pears, a pomegranate, two crystallised greengages, a pile of dried currants, a lemon, and a bunch of raisins, all in the order in which they had been wished for.

There were various theories to account for these phenomena: some thought them to be ectoplasmic emanations, or that they had been transported from another corner of the universe, or from another plane, or that they had been produced from Platonic forms. Whatever the case, the raps and levitating tables of the Goligher Circle paled beside these baroque manifestations. Yet the Goligher phenomena were perhaps all the more mysterious for their banal austerity. After examining them closely for some six years, W.J. Crawford claimed to have found no evidence of imposture. However, on 30th July 1920 he committed suicide, and the suspicion that his action had something to do with a discovery about the Golighers is unavoidable. A few days before his death he wrote to a friend:

> My psychic work was done when my brain was working perfectly. I derived great happiness from it, and it could not be responsible for what has occurred. Possibly some anatomical change has suddenly taken place in the brain substance which would have occurred in any case. We are such complicated bits of mechanism that it does not require much to put us out of action. I wish to reaffirm my belief that the grave does not finish all. I trust that I will find myself with a renewed energy, and able still to further the work in which we are both interested. With regard to my present condition, I feel there is absolutely no hope. The breakdown is making further way and I am getting worse daily. I feel that in a short time I might become a danger to those I love. You may think it strange that all this could take place inside a couple of weeks, but so it is. But what I wish to affirm now with all my strength is that the whole thing is due to natural causes and that the psychic work is in no way responsible.

Crawford had been found lying dead on the rocks of the foreshore of Belfast Lough, a blue poison bottle beside him, and I remember the little silver-mounted blue glass salt cruets you had placed on the table like sacramental receptacles that evening in New York.

I cannot remember what scent you wore that night, so firm is my recall of those imaginary musk-roses, violets and hawthorns. But I can see your jade pendant with the amber fleck in it that matched your eye, and the faint sheen of your pale green linen suit, and I was proud of you as you flitted in your Gemini mode from group to group, directing the waiters with discreet attention, chatting to the musicians when they took a break. And though, as a Libra, I am one who always seeks another for balance, I knew from experience when to leave you alone, and when to wait for you to come to me, for a Libra, according to the books, is also harmonious, diplomatic, and peacemaking – ambassadorial qualities, though I doubt if I ever could have made an ambassador. I was, however, tempted to write this letter with an Ambassador pen, made in the USA in the late 1930s or early 40s, to judge from its looks. Not that any ambassador would be seen dead with such a pen: like the Wearever De Luxe, this Ambassador's name belies its low cost. It might be a Dollar Pen, maybe a dollar fifty. It's modelled on the much more expensive Conklin pens of the same era, with a streamlined cap reminiscent of the nose of an airplane or a locomotive; but the clip is a little flimsy, brushed with a gold wash rather than gold-plated, and the nib, too, is gold-washed steel, rather than solid gold.

Nevertheless, like the Wearever, it has a lovely bright jazzy feel to it, the body patterned in black 'railroad tracks' laid on to an iridescent red ground. But I chose instead a Conway Stewart 58, top of their range in the late 1950s, as being more appropriate to your 'muted Irish' theme: the pattern is called Green Hatch in the catalogues, and it's a patchwork of subtle Connemara marble greens overlaid with wavy black cross-hatched lines. It's chunkier and heavier than most Conways, and the three gold bands on the cap give it a magisterial air: I can see this pen clipped into the breast pocket of a 1950s Irish senator or ambassador, and I wonder what pen, if any, the Irish Ambassador sported that night of the reception in New York. If I could go back in time, with what I now know, I would know, but I would not have known then. I was not a collector then, and, beyond your Dinkie, I was oblivious to pens, and what they might signify about their owners.

I am pleased to write with the Conway Stewart 58 Green Hatch because when it first came to me, it would not write properly. The ink flow was reluctant, the writing had a dry, parsimonious feel to it. So I read up on it and discovered what had to be done. First I unscrewed the section – the bit that holds the nib – from the barrel with a pair of rubber-covered section pliers. I took the ink-sac, that's the closed rubber tube that holds the ink, off the end of the section, they call it the section nipple, where it fits into the barrel. Then I got what they call a knock-out jig, that's a metal cylinder closed at one end, with holes of various diameters drilled in it to accommodate the various section sizes, and I matched the section up with the correct hole, and with a tack hammer and a brass rod I knocked out the nib and the feed, that's the black plastic bit at the back of the nib, that has a capillary groove to carry ink from the sac to the nib. So now the pen is broken down into its component parts: barrel, sac, section, feed, nib. I hold the gold nib between my finger and my thumb – how delicate and light it is, divorced from its body, like a child's fingernail! – and I wash it under a tap, for there's ink encrusted on it where it fitted into the section, until it glitters. I look at it through a loupe and I see that it is as the book said, the slit between the tines of the nib is too tight, it needs opened up, so I take a scalpel and ease it between the tines, gently, for I don't want to break off the iridium on the tip, and I work the scalpel backwards and forwards a little to widen the slit sufficiently to ease the flow of ink.

I put the nib to one side for a while. There's a residue of hard shellac on the section nipple, where the sac was attached, so I scrape that off with the scalpel, and smooth it off with a nail-file, and wipe it with a damp cloth till it looks clean and shiny, then I dry it, and paint a little fresh shellac on to it, it comes in a bottle like nail-varnish, with a tiny integral brush that is also its cap. That done, I screw the brush back into the bottle. I've already prepared a new ink-sac which I've cut to the proper length, making sure it doesn't press against the end of the barrel when I try it for size. I take the section in my left hand as I ease the end of the sac on to the nipple with my right thumb and forefinger – a tricky operation this, I have to use the left thumb as well, but I manage it. I straighten it up, give it a quarter turn to spread the sealant, and I put it aside for ten minutes or so to dry.

Then I push the section with sac attached back into the barrel, and twist it with the pliers to a tight fit. Now it's time for the nib. I fit the feed to its back and put the ensemble into a nib-fitting vice, and tighten the vice on it, and push the open section end on to it, making sure the nib is not set too deep nor too high into the section, and it's done. I open a bottle of Conway Stewart ink – the name, like Onoto, is back in business again, making expensive status symbol pens – and I fill the pen. I take a clean sheet of paper and begin to write, *Gabriel Conway*, and lo and behold! it works perfectly, not too wet and not too dry, nice and smooth, *Gabriel Conway*, I write, *41 Ophir Gardens, Belfast* ... and I feel pleased with myself at having resolved this problem, as I am pleased to write now of our time together in New York twenty-two years ago, when I did not know what I know now.

I did not know then, for example, that Conway Stewart was founded in 1905 – the same year as Onoto – by Frank Garner and Tommy Jarvis, who, reluctant for whatever reason to give the firm their own names, purportedly called it after a music-hall double act, Conway and Stewart, who regularly performed in London at the time. You remember that George

Sweetser, the inventor of the Onoto plunger system, appeared on the stage as a roller-skating female impersonator, and you will wonder, with me, at this curious fellowship of music-hall performers and pen manufacturers.

Nor did I know, in 1983, that many fountain pens, and Conway Stewart pens in particular, were made not only from Celluloid, but from a plastic called casein, a by-product of the dairy industry. Casein is made from milk curd. A basic casein can be made in the home with milk and vinegar. Bring a cup of milk to a simmer and slowly dribble in twelve tablespoons of vinegar, stirring all the time as if you were making mayonnaise. When lumps begin to form and coagulate, drain off the excess liquid. When these curds have cooled, form them into whatever shape or shapes you please – milk buttons, perhaps – and leave overnight, by which time they will have set rock solid. Casein can be made into sheets, rods and tubes. It has been used for imitation jade, tortoiseshell, and lapis lazuli, and in the manufacture of various articles besides pens, such as buttons, buckles, knitting needles, combs, hair-slides, pocket mirrors, door handles, knife handles, walking-stick handles, cigarette cases, radio cabinets, and electrical plugs, sockets and jacks. And that, until some hours ago, was the extent of my knowledge of casein, so I decided to research it on the Internet. This is what I found.

Casein was first developed and patented by two Germans, Spitteler and Kirsch, in 1899. It was then taken up by firms in Germany and France and used for industrial purposes under the name Galalith. Subsequently other countries produced their own casein under a range of names: Aralac, Aladdanite, Ameroid and Pearlolith in the USA, Akalit in Germany, Ambloid and Ambroid in Japan, Beroleit and Casolith in the Netherlands, and Estolit in Estonia, to name a few. In Britain, casein was produced under the name Syrolit by Syrolit

Limited, in their factory at Enfield, North London, the home of the Lee-Enfield rifle. In 1911, the firm moved to Lightpill in the town of Stroud, Gloucestershire, where it set up in a derelict cloth mill once used for making 'scarlet' for British Army uniforms. In 1913 the firm renamed itself Erinoid because the raw milk solids used in the process were imported from Ireland through the nearby port of Bristol, and I thought of boats crossing the heaving green Irish Sea with their holds full of a pale green cheese that would end up as buttons, fountain pens, and electrical plugs. With the onset of the Great War, supplies of Galalith from Europe ceased, and Erinoid found a ready home market. Soldiers' uniform buttons were made from Erinoid.

And then I remembered your third card had been posted in Stroud, and wondered how I could have forgotten the Stroud connection. But then we were more than a little drunk by then, that night in New York when you told me of your mother's suicide, and the next morning I had forgotten some of the salient details. After the war, you said, your father emigrated from the Netherlands to take up a position in the London branch of Philips, and it was in London that he met your mother. In 1958 or so – you were seven or eight – your father was assigned to the Lightpill factory in Stroud to oversee the production of a new design of light-switch; he worked there for two years, sometimes staying all week, sometimes commuting home in the evenings, for London was only two and half hours from Bristol on the Great Western Railway, and as I try to piece together your story from my fragmentary recollection, more lines from Auden's 'Night Mail' come into my head:

> Letters of thanks, letters from banks,
> Letters of joy from the girl and the boy,

Receipted bills and invitations
To inspect new stock or visit relations,
And applications for situations
And timid lovers' declarations ...

and I think of the train bearing its long plume of smoke through the darkness.

Where's Daddy? you used to ask, when you woke from one of your nightmares. You slept badly for those two years. Daddy's in Lightpill, your mother would reply, and you would envisage him standing in a pool of light, near yet far away, bent over a workbench, and he would turn his head as if he heard something, and look into the distance with a puzzled look, and then he would smile as if he had seen you, and he would wave his hand. And sometimes you thought Lightpill was a holiday resort, like Blackpool, and you were angry with him because he'd gone on holiday without you. Daddy's in Lightpill, your mother would say, he's just telephoned to say he's working late. That was in the days when you said 'telephoned', you said. Sometimes the phone would ring when you were still up, and you would answer it, and he would say, I'm sorry I can't be at home, Nina, darling, but I'll be home soon, and he would tell you stories about Stroud. Did you know that the man who wrote the *Thomas the Tank Engine* stories came from Stroud? you said. The Reverend Wilbert Awdry. My father would tell me how the Reverend Awdry used to live beside the railway depot at Stroud as a child, and he would lie awake at night listening to the groans and clanks of the goods trains, their whistles sounding in the dark like cries of happiness or sadness, and how he imagined personalities for them, and made up stories for them, you said. It was funny, because as a child I never thought of the stories as having an author, you said. And when I remember these details I find it difficult to understand how I could have forgotten Stroud. Then your mother would come in and say, Miranda, is that your father? And she would talk to him then, but sometimes not for long.

Sometimes she would appear upset, but maybe that's only in retrospect, you said, after I got the postcard. The postcard? I said. It was long after my mother's death, you said, about 1975, eight, nine years ago, I got a card from Stroud. I hadn't thought about Stroud for about fifteen years, you know? A typical postcard image, it showed the vicarage and church in Stroud, very idyllic, and on the back it read, *Dear Nina, maybe see you some day*. And that was all, it was creepy, no signature, but it was a woman's writing. No one else called me Nina, only my father, and by then he was dead too. And then I began to think that maybe he hadn't always been working late in Lightpill, you said.

I look at your own postcard again, trying to glean what I can from the image. *Berlin. Bahnhof Friedrichstrasse. Berlin/ Historisches Stadbilt, 1930*, it says on the back. The station is thus in Berlin, not East Berlin as it would become. The stamp hadn't been postmarked, it was one of those that sometimes slips through the franking machine, so I had no idea where you were when you sent it. We'd gone together to West Berlin in November 1982, I was curating a show by a young Belfast painter, Gerry Byrne, at an obscure gallery called Kunstwerkstatt, run by a group of West Berliners who had contacts with the East, and they managed to get us into East Berlin for a day. You remember. It is a summer's day in 1930 in the photograph. On the viaduct above Friedrichstrasse a massive steam locomotive is about to pull a train out of Bahnhof Friedrichstrasse. Because I come from a city in which there are no elevated tracks, such a sight always seems magically incongruous to me, it adds another dimension to the cityscape. The train has a massive, spectacular presence, and I study it for some time before my eye is drawn to the details of the street. There is a *Parfumerie* in the left foreground, and I wonder what fragrances were in vogue in Berlin in 1930, and further on in, in the shade of the viaduct, is a Foto sign, and a row of boutique windows, and a stream of passers-by, and when I examine their clothes and their faces through the loupe, the closer I get the more abstract they become, because everything – shops, people, signs, traffic, clouds – is composed of the same matrix of black and white dots, yet I am still convinced of the solidity of that world as it registers the light that fell on it then, that summery moment in 1930 when the number 10 bus is passing under the viaduct, with the word *JUNO* inscribed on its brow. I take it to be a brand name rather than a destination. Soap, perhaps. But Juno is also the moon-goddess, wife of Jupiter. She is the goddess of war, but also of married women and of children born in wedlock. And in East Berlin we'd been taken to the Pergamon Museum. You'd been impressed by a sculpture of the Babylonian fertility goddess Astarte, with whom Juno is associated, and you bought a postcard of it, you remember. Wedlock, you said, what a strange word. I take it you were born in wedlock, Gabriel. Oh, my father and mother wouldn't have had it any other way, I said. My father especially was a devout Catholic. Tell me about him, you said, I wonder if he was anything like my father. Remember?

As I write this with the Conway Stewart pen I am reminded that casein has one weakness as a material: it becomes unstable when it comes into prolonged contact with moisture. In the manufacturing process, the casein is laid down in very thin slabs like sedimentary rock, at the rate of one millimetre per week, so it takes sixteen weeks to build up the sufficient thickness required for a pen casing. The material is then hardened by placing it in a solution of dilute formaldehyde, the chemical used for embalming; this can take up to five months, so that the whole process, like human gestation, takes nine months. If a casein pen is placed in water for any length of time, it will soften and warp, as it tries to return to its original slab shape, to the womb of the vat in which it was formed. Casein has a memory. I write through the layers of intervening time, and find it difficult to separate what I might have told you about my father then, or what I might have already told you, or what you might have known without my telling you, from what I know now. So much has been laid down in the meantime.

My father, like others of his social class, left school at fourteen and joined the Post Office. It was there that he first heard Irish spoken by two fellow workers. By eighteen he was fluent in Irish and began teaching the language. He met my mother, Mary Ellen Hanrahan, in 1942 when she began attending his classes, and they married in 1944, just before the end of the Second World War. They brought up their children in Irish, so Irish was my first language, though I hesitate to say that it is my first language now, so deeply am I imbued with English. In the meantime my father had learned Esperanto. A certain Willie Tomelty, an Esperantist, came to my father's Irish class. He kept badgering my father to learn Esperanto but my father had no initial interest. However: Tomelty had lots of pen-friends throughout Europe, one of whom was a Dutchman, Johann Wouters, who lived in your father's native town of Delft. As you know, Delft is a small place, and I wonder if Wouters and your father knew each other.

After a while the Dutchman began to express an interest in Irish affairs, and he asked Tomelty to teach him Irish through the medium of Esperanto. Tomelty was ashamed to admit he was only a beginner at Irish himself, so one day he asked my father if he would teach Irish to the Dutchman. My father agreed; Tomelty gave his address to the Dutchman, and the next week my father got a letter, in English, from the Dutchman, saying he hoped my father had English, and if my father would teach him Irish, the Dutchman would teach him Esperanto as a recompense. So they began to write to each other. In a couple of months my father had learned Esperanto, he sported the Esperantist green star on the lapel of his postman's uniform, and Johann Wouters was making good progress in Irish. English was soon dispensed with. They corresponded for some fifty years.

As I write this account I wonder, as I have always done, what sort of single-minded young man my father was. To learn Irish was regarded as eccentric then, even among the Nationalist population; Esperanto even more so. And Esperanto brought my father into contact with some strange people, notably Harry Foster, a spiritualist whom my father would engage in endless theological wrangles in the study of Ophir Gardens, where I am writing now. My father, as a fervent Catholic, subscribed to the Church's orthodoxy that the supposedly paranormal phenomena produced by spiritualism were cheap conjuring tricks devised for the gullible, and that in the few instances where the phenomena were inexplicable by science, they were likely to be the work of the devil. Yet my father, as a Catholic, believed in the communion of saints, and looked forward to the resurrection of the dead, and the life of the world to come, a position, it seemed to me even then, to be not so far removed from that of the spiritualists. The relationship between Foster and my father was complicated by Foster's claim that Esperanto was making great progress in the afterlife, and that the spirits of the dead had spoken in Esperanto to him and to others through Foster's wife, a medium of some repute in spiritualist circles. And I wondered if the green star was in heaven as it is on earth, an emblem of the communion that is still possible after the fall of Babel.

And now I remember what perfume you wore that night in New York, chosen to go with the muted Irish theme. It begins as a powerful evocation of newly cut grass, a flower-strewn field of oakmoss, bergamot and orange blossom, sandalwood and fern, and there's a whisper of a breeze carrying it elsewhere, a spicy note of cinnamon that clings as the bright green image fades: *Vent Vert* by Pierre Balmain. Green Wind. Though Green Breeze would sound better.

ALL MANNER OF
SERVICE IN THE FIELD

Swan self-filler

Of course you knew I'd recognise the image immediately – Jan Vermeer's *Lady Writing a Letter with Her Maid*, which hangs in the National Gallery in Dublin. And you knew I would think immediately of the bizarre set of circumstances which preceded its being placed there. In April 1974 Bridget Rose Dugdale, daughter of Lieutenant Colonel James Dugdale, a wealthy landowner and former chairman of Lloyd's, led a gang of three armed IRA men to Russborough House, the home of Sir Alfred Beit, whose family had made its fortune in partnership with Cecil Rhodes in the De Beers Consolidated Mines of South Africa. Beit and his wife, Clementine, were dragged by them to the library, where they were bound and gagged. The gang then proceeded to cut nineteen paintings from Beit's priceless collection from their frames. Among them were works by Goya, Rubens, and Gainsborough, and the most valuable of all, Vermeer's *Lady Writing a Letter with Her Maid*. Dugdale had already achieved some notoriety: a year previously she had received a suspended sentence for her part in an art theft from her family's country house near Axminster; and she was wanted by the police in

Northern Ireland for her suspected involvement in the hijacking of a helicopter which had bombed an RUC station in Strabane, in January 1974.

Following the raid on Russborough House, the thieves demanded the release of the Price sisters, imprisoned in England for their part in a London car-bombing, and a ransom of £500,000 in exchange for the paintings. Eleven days later the paintings were found in the boot of a car at a rented cottage in Glandore, County Cork. Dugdale was arrested, charged and sentenced to nine years' imprisonment. The paintings were returned to Russborough, and two years later Beit established a trust to retain the house and its collection for the Irish state, and the National Gallery thus became the custodian of the Vermeer, though it was still *in situ* in Russborough. Twelve years later, in May 1986, twelve masked and armed men, led by the notorious Dublin criminal Martin Cahill, aka The General, broke into Russborough and stole fifteen paintings, including the Vermeer. In September 1993 a cache of stolen paintings was discovered in the boot of a car at Antwerp airport. The Vermeer, somewhat scratched and dented, was among them. It was given to Andrew O'Connor, the chief restorer at the National Gallery of Ireland, to repair the damage.

I look at your postcard again. A long dark green curtain seemingly has been withdrawn as if to invite us to gaze into the room, where a woman sits writing intently at a table covered with an oriental rug. The bodice of her dress is pale green, her sleeves and cap snowy white; she is wearing pearl earrings. Behind her, and to her right, more plainly dressed, stands a woman whom we take to be her maid. She gazes as if her mind has wandered out the tall leaded window, her mouth showing the glimmer of a smile. On the tiled floor in the right foreground is a little still life which includes a letter with a crumpled wrapper, a stick of sealing-wax, and a red wax seal. The seal, which was only discovered during O'Connor's restoration of the painting, is a typical Vermeer conundrum, for it invites us to consider if a seal could remain unbroken if the letter we imagine it belongs to has been ripped open and discarded with such apparent haste – and recently, for we imagine the efficient-looking maid would have dealt with the mess on the floor. Perhaps the seal betokens a miraculously intact virginity. And why the empty chair in the foreground, which has not been tidied away against a wall, as it should in a Dutch household of that period? It looks as if a person unknown to us has been here not that long ago, a guest or messenger whose annunciation the writing woman is about to answer.

I turn the card over. It's postmarked Berlin, which leads me to suspect that your previous card contained implications I failed to grasp. And it took me a while to arrive at the source of this message, which read, *All manner of service in the field*. The expression had an archaic, familiar ring to it. I looked at the Vermeer again for clues. The painting of a painting on the rear wall of the room is a message within a message, a depiction of The Finding of Moses. I turned to the Bible, to Chapter 2 of the Book of Exodus, which contains the story of how the Pharaoh commanded every Israelite male child to be killed at birth; but one mother consigned her boy to a vessel made of rushes and pitch, and laid him in the weeds by the river's brink, where he was discovered by the daughter of Pharaoh, and she called him Moses, because Moses means 'saved'. Moses is like a message in a bottle, delivered from his mother's womb into the bosom of the Pharaoh's daughter, who is a surrogate Madonna; and he will later become a messenger, as he delivers the Commandments to the people of Israel, all of which is appropriate to Vermeer's painting. We take it that the maid will be asked to deliver her mistress's letter: she is thus a messenger, a kind of Gabriel, for Gabriel is the messenger of God. And in the Dutch tradition, Moses represented God's ability to unite opposing factions, which had some relevance to my own divided city of Belfast.

As I pondered your card and its manifold implications, I began to think of myself as an angler fishing a stretch of canal in the shadow of a dark semi-derelict factory leaking steam from a rusted exoskeleton of piping, who, after hours of inaction, feels his line bite, and, his excitement mounting, begins to reel in as his rod is bent by the gravity of what must be an enormous catch − a whale of a pike perhaps, glutted by its meal of barbel, perch, or one of the plump rats that scuttle through the soot-encrusted weeds of the canal banks − when to his consternation he finds he has snagged a smoothing-iron, which he discovers to be only the precursor of a series resembling a gargantuan charm bracelet dripping green-black beards and tendrils of slime, as the iron is followed by a sewing-machine, an ironing-board, a shopping trolley, a tangle of barbed wire, bits of corrugated iron fencing, rusted automatic weapons, a wire mesh security shutter, and a string of police motor-cycles, like stuff spewed from the maw of some legendary behemoth, a galleon or two with their full complements of cannon, barrels of biscuit and nail and wine and shot and oil, cases of carpenters' tools and swords and needles and astrolabes and viols and pistols and flutes and crucifixes, and I still had not got to the bottom of your message.

Another detail besides the wax seal was discovered during the restoration of the Vermeer. Before its return to Ireland, the painting had been stored in Antwerp, where O'Connor was working on it when he was visited by Jorgen Wadum, conservator in the Mauritshuis in The Hague. Wadum had long been dissatisfied with the theory that Vermeer used a camera obscura to achieve his almost photographic perspectives. When he examined *Lady Writing a Letter with Her Maid* he found a pinhole at the centre of the writing woman's left eye. On an impulse he fished in his bag, found a piece of string, and, holding one end to the eye, ran the string along the various lines of perspective. The lines met at the pinhole. Vermeer, he immediately conjectured, had rubbed chalk on a string, snapped it onto the canvas, and used those lines as a guide. And when I fish out a Perspex ruler from my drawer and try the same experiment, I find that it is so. The woman's eye is concentrated on her writing, yet radiates invisible lines out into the room and beyond the window of the room, embracing the outside world to which her letter soon will be delivered, and, imagining the faint whisper of her quill upon the paper, I see you sitting in a Berlin café, perhaps, writing this card to me, *All manner of service in the field*, and I think of me fixed in your inner eye as you write my name and address on the card, *Gabriel Conway, 41 Ophir Gardens, Belfast* ...

I turned to Exodus again, and found the source in Chapter 1. Verses 13-14 read, 'And the Egyptians made the children of Israel to serve with rigour: And they made their lives bitter with hard bondage, in mortar, and in brick, and in all manner of service in the field'. I took this to be an ironic reference to what you did. You described yourself as a Field Officer, Nina, though the bondage, I assumed, was voluntary. And what exactly is your field? I'd asked you. Well, it's more like *the* field, you said. The field of information, you said, the field of enquiry, if you will, though of course we all have our own field. Like a spy ring, I said jokingly. Like a spy ring, you said, though we're perfectly open about what we do. The best place to hide a thing is in full sight, you said. The early Mass Observation surveys were criticised because of their seemingly covert methods. The lower classes felt they were being spied upon by the upper. In MO2 we gather information, yes, but it's no different from the kind of information anyone would gather in the course of their work, be they postmen or publicans or seamstresses or clerks or whatever. Every job implies a field of social and economic relationships.

As for my job, well, I spent a good few weeks looking out the window, you said. They'd given us the top floor of an old linen warehouse in Bedford Street, you know, at the back of the City Hall. My room overlooked the street, five storeys below, and I used to amuse myself by tracking the pedestrian traffic – people-watching, if you like. Monitoring the flow, the little knots and eddies, accidental encounters, people bumping into each other in the street, I'd see their backward steps of surprise, and imagine them saying, How are you, I haven't see you for years, what have you been doing? And I took a special interest in people window-shopping. You know Lazenblatt's antique shop, beside the Ulster Hall? you said. Yes, I said, those terrible Irish landscapes, *The Bridge at Cushendun, Fair Head on A Summer's Day*, that kind of thing. But he's got some nice stuff, too, though a bit outside my price range. I'd seen a snuff-box there the other week that Beringer was selling for half the price. Anyway, you said, I'd watch Lazenblatt's over the course of a day, see who would stop at the window, while others wouldn't give it a second look. There was one guy I remember, oh, dressed a bit like you, Gabriel, nice Donegal tweed jacket, green and grey fleck, good brogues, he stopped one morning and looked in the window for about five minutes, then he was back later in the afternoon, looked in the window again for quite a while. And the next day, the same thing, and the next. It took him four days to go into the shop, and then he came out empty-handed. Unless, of course, he'd bought something small, some kind of trinket, maybe a watch for himself, maybe a brooch for his girlfriend, who knows? and it was in his pocket.

Then again I'd sometimes look across the way, there was a building with an office floor just below my eye-level. There was one office, man at a desk, grey suit, every morning about eleven he'd take a chair and place it opposite his on the other side of the desk, then a secretary would come in, she's in a grey suit too, except with a skirt, knee-length, hair in a bun, he'd gesture to her to sit down, she's got a notebook ready, and he'd dictate to her. When you said this, I thought of the rapid whisper of her shorthand pen, and visualised an Edward Hopper scene, sunlight falling into an almost empty room. *Office in a Small City*, 1953, perhaps.

I could see his lips moving, you said, and we must have then discussed the various surveillance devices which were known to be in use throughout the city. The laser voice interceptor, specifically, which I'd learned about from McWhirter, you met him once, the computer buff at the Gallery, they'd brought him in to develop a cataloguing system, very advanced stuff for 1982. It's really very simple, said McWhirter, like everything else we think is new, the Victorians had a version of it, they called it the photophone. It's really a telephone, except you use light instead of electricity to project the information. Alexander Graham Bell, he hooked up a mouthpiece to a diaphragm that's a mirror, so it vibrates to the sound of a voice, and that modulates a beam of sunlight aimed at the diaphragm by another mirror. Then you get a photovoltaic cell and an earpiece, that's your remote receiver, you position it in the beam, and away you go. The sound comes over the light-beam.

And as McWhirter told me this I remembered manipulating a piece of mirror glass as a boy to dazzle the eyes of neighbours, aiming the blip of light through the windows of rooms to dance mysteriously across the walls and ceilings.

Of course, said McWhirter, it was very weather-dependent. No sunlight, no communication, and I imagined rain-spattered voices flickering and fading as a scud of April cloud passed overhead, and thought that dust-motes falling through the beam might produce a background drizzle like that on old cylinder recordings. Then, in the Sixties, said McWhirter, Bell Laboratories – quantum electronics chap, Charles Towne – developed the laser. Acronym. Light amplification by stimulated emission of radiation. Ordinary light's like white noise, the photons are all over the place. But your laser releases all the photons in one direction, at one frequency. It's a sine wave, pure, coherent tone. Beam of tightly packed light, razor-sharp, nearly incorruptible. Like a magic wand. Point it at a window. The window is your diaphragm, you see. And the room's an acoustic chamber. The sound waves generated by conversation will cause the glass in the window to vibrate ever so slightly. If you bounce your laser beam off the window, the reflection gets modulated by the vibrations. Then all you need to hear what's being said is some kind of demodulating thingamajig to extract the audio from the reflected laser beam. And there you have it. Your laser voice interceptor. Mind you, it's not one hundred per cent perfect. Proximity of fluorescent lights, neon, sodium, might cause a buzz, that kind of thing. Air currents, strong winds, you get an effect like blowing into a mike. And direct sunlight can swamp the beam. But you'd be surprised at what you can hear from a couple of hundred feet away. And beyond that, well, you can hook it up to a telescopic gunsight, mount it directly on to the laser housing. Pretty accurate for a mile or two, said McWhirter. And you really think they're using this device in Belfast? I said. McWhirter looked at me over his glasses and gave me a pitying smile. What do you think? he said.

So there I was staring out the window one day, you said, I'd been there about a month, and Callaghan comes in, he's the boss of the outfit, if you could say there was a boss, because everyone seemed to be doing their own thing. At least, he was the person who recruited me. Recruited? I said. Well, of course we all had to go through the motions of an interview process, the jobs were advertised, and all that, though not very well. Anyway, I was recruited, if that's what you call falling into conversation with a man in a hotel bar who ends up telling you you're perfectly cut out for a job in his firm, you said, and you think nothing more of it till a few days later he gives you the call, like he said, that you thought he wouldn't. So Callaghan comes in and says, We feel it's about time you made your differentiation. Differentiation? you said. Yes, says Callaghan, we let people find their feet for about a month or so, and then they do their differentiation. Ask Tony Lambe how it's done, he'll put you right. Tony Lambe? I said, the guy we met at the City Hall that day? When I found out you were called Miranda? Yes, you said, and you had the grace to blush a little. Baa Lambe's one of you? And how many are you, exactly? Oh, there's quite a few of us, you said, I'll get round to that in a while.

So anyway, what's this differentiation business all about? I said to Tony Lambe. Oh, it's just another name for project management, forward work plan, whatever you want to call it, says Tony. You differentiate between what you want to do, and what you don't want to do. And what do you do? I asked Tony. Oh, basically, I'm in menswear, I sell ties, he says. Ties? I said. Yes, you know, neckwear, says Tony, ties, cravats, you know I'm a bit of neckwear freak, Miranda. And this has been a great opportunity for me, developing my own brand of ties. Lavelle & Smyth? Well, maybe you haven't heard of us, we're very discreet, says Tony, but I can assure you a lot of the top people are wearing Lavelle & Smyth ties. Our Irish poplin line is doing very well. Poplin, the Pope's linen, though we don't advertise the etymology, says Tony, but really, a lovely material for ties, nice ecclesiastical feel to it, pure silk on the outside, woollen worsted yarn on the inside, you get the best of both worlds, the sheen of the silk and the elasticity of the wool, a poplin tie keeps its shape wonderfully. Then we've got a lovely line in Japanese handwoven silk, said Tony.

As you know, I wasn't much into expensive ties then, Nina, not on my salary, I tended to buy the few I wore in charity shops, or in the Friday Market, ties from the Forties and Fifties, but I did know Lavelle & Smyth's shop in Crown Entry, and had sometimes paused before its window to admire its many-coloured display, ties in coral and apple-green and lavender and faint orange, ties in needle stripes and pinstripes and wide stripes, and ties with diamonds and gleaming lozenges, and delicate pink flowers on a deep blue ground, and peacock's eyes set amid glowing russet silk, they were really beautiful if unaffordable ties, and I marvelled that Tony Lambe should be their commissioner, Baa Lambe who when I knew him had hardly an eye in his head for such things, but then I suppose people change, or are changed, or can be made to change.

Anyway, you said, Tony explained this differentiation thing. Essentially you just draw up what you want to do, a business plan, cost it all out, give them a budget, he said. I've never known them to turn one down. Once you're recruited, you stay recruited, says Tony, they'll give you what you ask for, and more, they'll disburse a little of their largesse. Compared to the millions they spend on Northern Ireland, it's pin money. And what do they get out of it? you asked. Well, you have to file a report once every so often, customer profiles, that kind of thing, nothing that you wouldn't be doing anyway, says Tony. They're not too demanding, they're happy if you're happy. The main thing is to get to know your clients, find your niche. And what's your niche, Nina? I asked. Interior design, corporate events styling, that kind of thing, you said. And have I heard of you? I said. Oh, probably not, you said, I'm Fawcett & Jones, they like us to have those kind of joint-venture names, gives an impression of class. Or music-hall double-acts, I said, like Conway & Stewart? Yes, you said, like Smith & Wesson. And you toyed with the Conway Stewart Dinkie that hung from the mauve silk lanyard about your neck.

I didn't have to think twice about which pen to write this with, for it arrived in the post together with your card. It was an eBay item I'd been expecting for some days, and to tell you the truth I barely glanced at your card before attacking the package. I took a box-cutter to the layers of parcel tape, slicing through them with some difficulty before I could open the cardboard box which spilled a good few of its white polystyrene packing beans among whose remnants I discovered a section of plastic piping, taped at both ends, which contained, swaddled in kitchen roll, the pen. I wish you were here now to see it, for the red and black marbled wood-grain effect of its body would remind you of your Dinkie. This is a Swan, made in England in the 1920s by Mabie Todd and Co., and it's got a stylised swan engraved on the barrel and a white swan in intaglio on the top of the cap. At five and a half inches capped, and seven inches with the cap posted, it's a longer pen than most, slender, elegant, dignified. It was made without a pocket clip, perhaps to sit impressively on the desk of a person of discernment. I took it out to the better light of the back garden and I was holding it up to let the sun play on it, turning it this way and that to admire the patterning, when two swans – a pen and a cob – flew overhead honking mournfully to each other, and I knew then that I was obliged to write this letter with the Swan.

I watched the swans till they were out of sight, thinking of the story of the Children of Lir, who were turned into four swans by their jealous stepmother. My father had often told it to me as a child, and I can hear the slow-quick-slow narrative pulse of his voice, and I see in my mind's eye again the snow softly falling on the grey waters of the Sea of Moyle as the Children of Lir flew between Rathlin and Erin, uttering their mournful songs, for they still retained their human voices. And I wondered why a female swan should be called a pen, when it was from the wings of geese that one commonly obtained feathers for quills. My father, indeed, had shown me how to make a quill pen when I was in my teens, and how to make the oak-gall ink used by the medieval Irish scribes.

The oak-gall, or the oak-apple, is an excrescence formed on some species of oak by the larvae of gall-wasps, the females of which lay their eggs in punctures made into the bark. As the larvae grow, the gall develops and forms a home for them, until they finally eat their way out. To make ink, you grind the tannin-rich oak-galls, and add water, ferrous sulphate and gum arabic; and the whole process, from wasp to ink, as my father explained, was a symbol of the transformation of the soul through writing. A wasp is an inverted bee, he said, and as the bee represents the Virgin Mary, and goodness, so the wasp means evil. The wasp, unlike the bee which spreads good by pollinating, merely scavenges and lays its eggs. But the oak tree where it lays its eggs is the sacred tree of the Druids, a repository of deep and aged wisdom, said my father. So when the wasp lays its eggs in the tree, the tree winds its fibres of wisdom around them to protect itself, and thus evil is transformed into good.

He showed me how to grind the oak-galls. Slowly, slowly, he said, use your whole arm, not just the wrist, and relax, take your time, imagine you're saying a rosary, breathe steadily, for you're putting your whole body into it. Now add the water. Remember that water is life, the life of the spirit. Now add the ferrous sulphate, he said, and as I did so, I watched the thick brown mud of the ground oak-galls turn magically black. Ferrous sulphate, that's iron and sulphur mixed. The alchemists used sulphur in their quest for making gold, said my father, but they did not realise that the real gold is God's word, which is spread by this ink we're making now. Now the gum arabic, that's a binder, it binds the body of the ink to its soul, and it binds it to the parchment. Well, of course we must make do with paper. And he would get me to transcribe a few verses of the Bible with the quill pen and the oak-gall ink.

My father was one of the few Catholics I knew who habitually read the Bible, not only in English, but in Irish, Scottish Gaelic, and in Esperanto, and when two Mormons would call at our door, he liked nothing better than to invite them into this study to engage in a bout of theological wrangling; and when they spoke of God's word as represented in the Bible, he would say, which Bible? I used to hear him sometimes trying to convert them to the cause of Esperanto, citing Zamenhof as if he were a Christian prophet, or a Catholic saint, and not the agnostic son of an atheistic Jewish father. And I, with my quill and oak-gall ink would transcribe from the King James Bible, *Therefore is the name of it called Babel, because the Lord did there confound the language of all the earth: and from thence did the Lord scatter them abroad upon the face of all the earth.*

Not that I am writing now in oak-gall ink. The gum arabic in the recipe would irremediably clog the feed of a fountain pen, and the ferrous sulphate – also known as copperas or green vitriol – would corrode the rubber ink-sac and the metal nib. There is no green vitriol in this modern chemical ink. Nevertheless, as I pour these words on to the page, you must believe that they are imbued with the urge of the medieval scribe to realise the unity of all things. And yet, how hard it is to write the truth sometimes, to make everything connect, to give an accurate account of what was said or done. I realise, for example – since my father never spoke anything but Irish to me – that when I here report his words I must be translating them, and thus interpreting them. Not that I do so consciously, for my memory is not so much of the words themselves, but of the flow of the words, the thoughts communicated by the words, and the images aroused by them.

For I see the Children of Lir in their lonely flight from one abode to the next, and the snow falling softly on the dark, mutinous waves of the Sea of Moyle, without considering what language they are couched in. They are swans in any language. So I think. I wonder if it were so for my father. In many respects, he had a better command of Irish than of English, having come to it with the zeal of a convert who takes nothing for granted. He learned his stories from master storytellers, and learned them properly, complete with the ornate, alliterative leitmotifs that ran as mnemonic and rhythmical devices throughout the narrative, which could not but affect his everyday speech, so that when I transcribe or translate his instructions to me, they appear overly stilted or formal in English; but it was not so in Irish, because those mechanisms are part of the inherited grain of Irish speech. Irish was not his first language, but he spoke it better than I, whose first language it was, and who took it for granted.

As I write with the Swan it makes a little whispery music as it traverses the page. Every pen, every nib is different, and sometimes I fancy I can identify each pen in my collection from its sound alone, the different faint scratches and squeaks they make. And I think of the room depicted in the twice-stolen Vermeer, silent but for the faint music of the quill.

Vermeer never sold this painting in his lifetime: after he died penniless on St Lucy's Day, 1675 – the darkest day of the year – it was one of several given by his widow to the local baker in exchange for a long-overdue bread bill. It then passed through a series of ownerships, some unknown. During its restoration in 1993, it was discovered that not only the wax seal but the stick of sealing-wax had been overpainted, perhaps at the request of a previous owner who considered these to be untidy details. And, thinking of these thefts and veilings and revelations, I now remembered that Gerry Byrne, the artist whose show I curated in Berlin, had made his reputation by reinterpreting iconic works of Irish art: to a mountain landscape by Paul Henry, for example, he would add British army watchtowers, and helicopters in the sky – helicopters, in particular, became a kind of signature of his, an emblem of surveillance.

Byrne was particularly fascinated by the work of Sir John Lavery, who had donated some thirty paintings to my employers, the Belfast Municipal Gallery, in 1929. Among these was the work entitled *The Daylight Raid from My Studio Window, 7th July 1917*. It commemorates the occasion when twenty-one German Gotha biplanes carried out the second aerial bombing of London, and were engaged by aircraft of the Royal Naval Service and the Royal Flying Corps. It is a big painting, some six feet by three. Lavery depicts his wife, Hazel, at a window, which, given the scale of things, would be about fifteen feet by eight in real life. When I was first shown this painting by my father I thought the window looked like a real window in the wall of the gallery, giving out on to another world. Hazel Lavery is kneeling at the windowsill, apparently watching the aircraft swirled like insects in the sky beyond.

I seem to remember that the scene prompted my father to embark on a reminiscence of the Belfast Blitz of 1941, but I might be wrong on that point. What I do know is that neither of us were then aware of the painting's most curious feature, which was pointed out to me by Gerry Byrne some time in about 1979 or 80. See here, said Byrne, and he grasped me by the elbow, you can't see it unless you're low down, you have to get the light hitting it at the right angle. See here? and he pointed to an area of the painting which I had always taken for a rolled-down blackout curtain, just above the windowsill. And, as I squinted at it, I could see a darker patch on the putative curtain, shaped a bit like a keyhole. Do you know what he did? said Byrne, there used to be a statue of the Virgin Mary there, he painted it out before he gave the picture to the Gallery, back in the Twenties, and to hide that, he made up a blackout curtain, first curtain I ever saw that rolls from the bottom up. Stroke of genius, or what? and he laughed ironically. And, as he spoke, the keyhole blotch assumed a ghostly figural presence, and there flashed into my mind a vision of just such a statue – Our Lady of Perpetual Succour, to be precise – which had adorned my childhood bedroom. I could see her blue robes, her hands extended in that archetypal gesture of maternal comfort. Old bugger, I suppose he couldn't have the good Unionist trustees of the Belfast Gallery thinking he really was a Catholic, and his lovely wife a Catholic too, kneeling before an idol of the Madonna, said Byrne.

For I knew that Sir John Lavery had been born in Belfast of impoverished Catholic parents in 1856 or so. The exact date of his birth is unknown. Orphaned at an early age, he was taken into care by relatives in Scotland. He began his working life in a Glasgow studio, retouching photographs, but when the studio burned down he began painting. His reputation was made when he was commissioned by Queen Victoria in 1888 to paint her state visit to Glasgow. Thereafter he moved in the highest echelons of British society. I had thought myself something of an expert on Lavery's work, and I was a bit piqued when Byrne told me of this sleight of hand. But how did you spot it? I asked him. Oh, I always thought there was something fishy about the blackout curtain, you know, it's very sloppy painting, unlike the rest of it. So I asked Burrows about it. Burrows? I said. This was Freddy Burrows, the Keeper of Irish Art, my boss; we'd never got on, and he made a point of telling me as little as possible. After all, Conway, he'd say, we're not here to educate you, I think you're well able to educate yourself, so just get on with it. Yes, Burrows, I got him over a couple of drinks, and he spilled the beans, said Byrne. I'd always thought of Burrows as an archetypal Presbyterian, certainly not one given to casual drinking. Oh, said Byrne, you'd be surprised, everyone's got a guilty secret, and he tittered meaningfully. So we'll have to put things to rights, said Byrne, and over the next few months he worked on a version of *The Daylight Raid*, painting a garish Madonna on the windowsill, and replacing the German bombers with British helicopters. He called it *The Daylight Raid by Sir John Lavery, 1929.*

But of course, Nina, much of this was known to you, for when I mentioned it before our trip to Berlin in the winter of 1982, you said, Burrows? Yes, he's a client of mine. Charming man, if you get to know him. You were wearing an unfamiliar perfume that day. What's that? I asked. What's what? you said. Your perfume, I said. Oh, *Vol de Nuit*, you said, Night Flight, by Guerlain, 1933. You offered me your wrist and I caught a burst of orange, then cool wood and balsam notes followed by an enigmatic hint of spice.

WHEREVER
YOU ARE

Porte-plume réservoir

As I write to you, Nina, a surveillance helicopter is poised
motionless in the sky to the east of Ophir Gardens, and
the windows of my study tremble to its broadcast reverberant
din. There have been many changes in Belfast since you left in
1984, though of course you might well have returned at
intervals without my knowledge, and for all I know you might
be in Belfast now. Your card is postmarked Paris, but that was
last week. If you are here – the possibility disturbs me – you
might have noticed that your old MO2 offices have been turned
into penthouse apartments, and the ground floor of the
building is now the Linen Warehouse Restaurant and Bar. In
the side streets are cafes, gyms, aromatherapy boutiques and
retro clothing stores. Belfast is booming, and not with bombs.
Yet beyond the bright clatter of the lattes and Manhattans, the
gleaming dishes, silverware and linen, are dark recalcitrant
zones where July bonfires have been smouldering for days, and
the reek of burning tyres sometimes infiltrates the inner city.
Above the fragile periphery the helicopters maintain their
desultory watch, scanning the ruined terraces, the blasted
interfaces and the paint-bespattered Peace Walls. Every

summer the Loyalist housing estate on the other side of the Cavehill Road from Ophir Gardens blooms with paramilitary regalia, flags that become tatters over the winter.

It was not always so: the estate went up in the late Seventies, built on a former allotment site which I imagine had been established during the last war, given the shortage of fresh vegetables. By the time we moved to the district in 1955, it was already semi-derelict, a few little ordered plots surviving among the encroaching brambles, nettles and chickweed, gooseberry bushes and tall rhubarb plants gone to seed, tumbledown potting-sheds overgrown by convolvulus and ivy. It was a kind of paradise for us children, where we could get pleasurably lost in war games. Later, when I read *Portrait of the Artist as a Young Man*, and thought myself to be James Joyce, I posed before a derelict greenhouse wearing an outfit bought in the Friday Market – a Forties jacket and waistcoat and white duck trousers that emulated his turn-of-the-century gear – and had my photograph taken by Paul Nolan, who thought himself to be Cartier-Bresson. You met Nolan once or twice: a good fellow. Like me, he took early retirement, a victim of the creeping bureaucracy that finally overwhelmed our vision of what we thought we were doing.

I remember telling you how the allotments had been swept away, and you said yes, your grandfather in Delft had kept an allotment, and grew cucumbers, lettuces and cabbages. Dill, too, that your grandmother would use for pickling the cucumbers. As you spoke, I thought of cool tiled pantries, and could see the tidy Dutch allotments, occupying strips of ground by the sides of roads and canals, the sheds painted in bright greens and reds, like toy houses, the rows of flowers and vegetables. I had not been to Holland then, and much of my conception of it was based on Dutch painting, which I loved, and the postcards sent to my father by his pen friend in Delft.

I thought again how appropriate it was that my father should have learned Esperanto from a Dutchman, for the Netherlands seemed to me, as it did to him, a peaceable realm in which tolerance for one's neighbours was both desirable and necessary. These were Esperantist virtues, said my father. The people of the Netherlands, he said, not having been granted much land by God, made land for themselves; but realising they could never make enough, they made space for each other. I was somewhat disappointed that Johann Wouters, like my father, was a devout Catholic, not an Orange Protestant, and that they hence had much in common to begin with. The One, Holy, Catholic and Apostolic Roman Church was itself a kind of Esperanto, for you could hear the same Mass in exactly the same language anywhere in the world; and when the Latin Mass, under the New Liturgy of the 1960s, was abandoned for a multitude of vernaculars, my father regretted the change. But like a good Catholic, he submitted himself to it. I think it was about the time of the New Liturgy that he threw himself even more wholeheartedly into Esperanto, as a substitute for the universality of Latin. As for me, I never properly learned Esperanto. Much as I admired it, I was uncomfortable with its dream of universal brotherhood.

Only after my father's death did I begin to examine the history of Esperanto. I discovered that Ludwig Zamenhof had been given the Jewish name Lejzer, or Lazarus, at his circumcision, but had adopted the Christian name Ludovic, or Ludwig, in his teens, following the custom of the aspiring Jewish middle class of his milieu. Likewise, his father, a teacher of languages, had changed his name from Mordecai to Marcus. Ironically, Mordecai itself, then perceived as wholly Jewish, was once a disguise too, for in the Book of Esther it is the name of the Chief Minister of Ahasuerus, or Xerxes, the despotic king of Persia: it was the custom then of the exiled Jews to mask themselves in names familiar to their captors.

So what's in a name, Nina? If I am Gabriel, the angel of the Annunciation, you are Miranda by another name, the admirable maiden of *The Tempest*. But it would also seem that names can mean anything you want them to mean, for the rabbis say that concealed in the pagan name Mordecai are the syllables for 'pure myrrh', and so it bears a holy perfume, an incense I remember from the Latin Masses of my childhood. I daresay Marcus Zamenhof would have been aware of this nominal labyrinth, for his own father was a noted Talmudic scholar, well used to pondering the intricacies of the Word, and Marcus himself became a teacher of languages. He also became an atheist, and in 1857 married Rozalia Zefer, the pious daughter of a Bialystok Jewish tradesman. Lazarus – Ludwig, as he would become – was the first of their eight children. Bialystok, as I mentioned in my first letter, was then in Polish Lithuania, and part of the Russian Empire. The town was a Babel. The native upper classes spoke Polish, the lower Lithuanian; a population of Yiddish-speaking Jews had long been established; there was a substantial German mercantile class; the administration and the army were Russian, and the golden domes of a Russian Orthodox church shone in the main square. The language of the Zamenhof household was mainly Russian, because Marcus believed it an essential tool to their progress. But Yiddish was also spoken, and by his teens Ludwig had also a fair command of Polish, German, and Lithuanian, as well as the Hebrew and Greek taught to him by his father. From an early age, said Ludwig Zamenhof, I was anguished that men and women everywhere looked much the same, yet spoke differently, and thought themselves to be Poles, or Russians, Germans, Jews, and so on, instead of human beings. Thinking that grown-ups were omnipotent, I resolved that, when I was grown up, I would abolish this evil; for no one, he said, can feel the misery of barriers as strongly as a ghetto Jew, and no one can feel the need for a language free from a sense of nationality as strongly as the Jew who is obliged to pray to God in a language long since dead, receives his education and upbringing in the language of a people who reject him, and has fellow-sufferers around the world with whom he cannot communicate, said Zamenhof.

As you might imagine, Nina, I am not penning these words in a smooth consecutive flow. Zamenhof's words are not ingrained in my memory, the history of Esperanto is not at my fingertips, and I have to interrupt my writing every so often to rediscover passages scrawled in notebooks a good few years ago, when I began my Esperanto project, or to consult more fully drafted pieces, stored on the computer. And, as I transcribed Zamenhof's words from the screen before me, in pen and ink, I felt, as my hand moved across the page, that it was somehow guided by the spirit of Zamenhof, that I felt as he felt, knowing just a little of the linguistic despair that was his, that his words were both his and mine, though written in a different language, for he had written them in Esperanto, not English. And, rewriting those words by hand, I began to see nuances in them I had not hitherto suspected, for my view of them is different now that you have re-entered my life. So much has changed.

While still at school, I had written on the computer, Zamenhof began thinking of a universal language, and by 1878 he had invented one. Five years previously his father had moved with his family to Warsaw, where, in order to supplement his income as a teacher of German in the Veterinary Institute, he took on extra work as a state censor. In 1879, when Zamenhof went off to study medicine in Moscow, he left his extensive notes for the new language in his father's care. Immediately recognising the danger of possessing such documents, written in a secret language by a poor Jewish student, his father burned them. In Moscow, Zamenhof became involved with Zionism, but grew disillusioned with the movement, which he found too exclusivist. He returned to Warsaw, and to his dream of an international language. Finding it destroyed, he reconstructed it from memory.

In 1886, the year in which he matriculated in ophthalm-ology, he became engaged to Klara Zilbernik, the daughter of a prosperous businessman. For two years Zamenhof had unsuccessfully sought a publisher for a booklet in which he which described the new language. Klara's father, impressed by the idealism of his future son-in-law, offered to have the book printed at his expense. This was done; the proofs were held for two months in the censor's office, but fortunately the censor was a friend of Zamenhof's own father, who by now had withdrawn his objections to the project. On 14th July 1887 the censor authorised the booklet, and it was published in Russian; Zamenhof soon afterwards translated it into Polish and German. An early follower translated it into French under the title *La Langue Internationale*.

These editions all contained the same introduction and reading-matter in the international language: the Lord's Prayer, a passage from the Bible, a letter, poems, the complete grammar of sixteen rules, and a vocabulary of 900 roots. The work was signed with the pseudonym 'Doktoro Esperanto' – *esperanto* meaning 'one who hopes' – and the new language, by general usage, became known as Esperanto. Dr Esperanto and Klara Zilbernik were married on 9th August 1887, and the first few months of their life together were spent promoting Esperanto, putting the booklet describing the new language into envelopes and posting them to foreign newspapers and journals. It was known as the *Unua Libro*, the First Book.

There was no English translation for some time; Zamenhof considered his own English insufficiently adequate for the task. A German friend did produce one, which Zamenhof published, but English speakers found it incomprehensible.

In the autumn of 1887, a certain Richard Henry Geoghegan read an article about the new language. The Geoghegan family lived for many years at 41 Upper Rathmines Road, Dublin. Richard's father was a doctor who emigrated in 1863 from Dublin to Birkenhead in England, where Richard was born on 8th January 1866. At the age of three he suffered an accident which left him crippled for the rest of his life; but the good Lord, as my father might have said, by way of compensation, gave him extraordinary linguistic gifts: he had a perfect command of French, German, Italian, Spanish, and Latin, and became a noted expert in Chinese, Japanese, Hindi, and other oriental languages. He considered himself an Irishman: he spoke and wrote fluent Irish, and often visited the land of his fathers. In the autumn of 1887 he happened to read an article about the new international language and wrote in Latin to Zamenhof, who sent him the German edition of the *Unua Libro*. Geoghegan immediately learned the language from it. When Zamenhof sent him the English translation, Geoghegan pointed out its many shortcomings, and undertook to translate the book himself, publishing it in 1889. The German–English translation was withdrawn.

So began the Esperanto movement in Britain and Ireland. Geoghegan and Zamenhof became lifelong correspondents and friends. Geoghegan also had a hand in the adoption of the green star as the Esperanto emblem. Years later, Zamenhof wrote:

> About the origin of our green star I no longer
> remember very well. It seems to me that Mr

Geoghegan drew my attention to the colour green,
and from that time I began publishing my works with
a green cover. About one brochure, which I quite by
chance published with a green cover, he remarked to
me that this was the colour of his homeland, Ireland.
Then it came into my head that we could well regard
this colour as a symbol of Hope. As for the five-
pointed star, it had already been adopted as
representing the five continents; and so the green star
was born.

As I write to you, Nina, I have before me a postage stamp
bearing that very emblem. You know I was a stamp-collector
in my youth, and so, when researching the Esperanto story, I
was interested to see what Esperanto-themed stamps might
exist. I acquired a little collection of such stamps, issued by
countries sympathetic, or once sympathetic, to Esperanto:
Hungary, Bulgaria, Poland, Brazil, China, Croatia, Germany.
Many of them bear an image of Zamenhof. This particular one
is the Belgian commemorative of 1982, issued to coincide with
the 67th World Esperanto Congress, which was held in
Antwerp that year, the year that we first met. It features the
smaller of Pieter Bruegel the Elder's two versions of the Tower
of Babel. Above the Tower is a green shooting star bearing a
rainbow-coloured tail, whose trajectory suggests it has come
not from the heavens, but from Earth. And I am tempted to
address this letter simply to Miranda Bowyer, Earth, and use
this stamp for its delivery. But that would be wishful thinking.
Instead, I affix it to this page, in the less forlorn hope that we
might once more meet each other in the flesh.

As for your postcard of July 2005, it has been sent from Paris,
and bears a French stamp commemorating the French statesman Alexis de Tocqueville, author of *Democracy in America*,
who thought that association, the coming together of peoples

for a common purpose, would bind America to an idea of nation larger than selfish desires. It was he who said that it is easier for the world to accept a simple lie than a complex truth. It was he who said that all those who seek to destroy the liberties of a democratic nation ought to know that war is the surest and shortest means to accomplish it. And the image on your card was made not long after the war. The caption reads

Renée
The New Look of Dior
Place de la Concorde, Paris, August 1947

I wonder if Renée is the name of the model, or a reference to the New Look, since it means 'reborn' in English. Perhaps both? I look again at the New Look, Dior's response to the austerity of wartime, an extravagant look, the soft-shouldered, slim-waisted jacket and the voluminous, exuberantly swirled skirt of the model contrasting with the almost military deportment of the three young men, whose eyes have just swivelled right to take in the gorgeous apparition.

Place de la Concorde. We were there in Easter 1983. We might have walked in the very footsteps of the model, or those of the three young men. You had had your hair cut in a Leslie Caron fringe, and you wore an outfit that was a kind of homage to the New Look, a dark plum-coloured alpaca waisted jacket over a flared ivory cambric skirt, high heels very like the one visible beneath the hem of the model's skirt in the photograph.

Earlier that day, I was moved by a nostalgia for the Catholic ritual of my childhood, and we had gone to Easter Sunday Mass at Saint-Eustache, that strange architectural mix of the classical and Gothic which flanks one side of Les Halles. It was beautiful. From the inside the church seemed even taller, more vertically compressed, the Gothic columns soaring up to arch and meet each other in their slender trajectories, and the Easter light fell in shafts through the high windows of the clerestory. Here dozens of pigeons had roosted, and, as organ music announced the beginning of the ceremony, some of them flew from one alcove to the other, their wings beating against the dusty light. A choir sang. A chinking thurible dispensed a smoky perfume. The priest delivered a sermon in an elegantly modulated French that spoke of the mysteries that lie beyond language: *l'homme est comme un paysage dans le brouillard*, he said, Man is like a landscape lost in fog, which is pierced by the light of the heavens, by the redeeming light of the resurrection, and as he spoke, we could hear the pigeons chirping and cooing behind his words. *Je suis toujours avec vous jusqu'à la fin du monde*, I am with you always, even unto the end of the world. Then came triumphant organ music, the bright peal of the treble sailing above the reverberant thunder of the bass, and the pigeons scattering everywhere. We emerged stunned into the sunlight. Some time later we found ourselves in Place de la Concorde.

Until today I had little idea of the history that lay behind Place de la Concorde. When I looked it up on the Internet I discovered that it was called Place Louis XV when completed in 1763, for it was Louis XV who had commanded it to be built, and an equestrian statue of himself to be placed at its centre. In 1770, 133 spectators were trampled to death at a huge fireworks display on the occasion of Marie Antoinette's wedding to the Dauphin. In 1792, the equestrian statue was removed, and the Place became Place de la Révolution, home to the guillotine that beheaded, according to various accounts, some 1,200, 1,800, or 2,800 people, among them Marie Antoinette, Louis XVI, Danton, Charlotte Corday, and Robespierre. In 1797 it was renamed Place de la Concorde; in 1814 Place Louis XVI; in 1828 Place Louis XV; and in 1830 it was finally designated Place de la Concorde.

More importantly, perhaps, I found what you surely must have meant me to discover, that the architect of Place de la Concorde was called Jacques-Ange Gabriel. Angel, you'd said, Gabriel, I'm glad you took me to Mass. I could nearly become a Catholic myself, you said. But I'm not one, I said. Oh yes you are, you said, once a Catholic, always a Catholic. It's ingrained in you, you said. But can't we change ourselves? I said. The way we change our names? Why do we have to be what we were born into? Oh, let's not argue about what we might be, you said, *que sera sera*, let's enjoy ourselves as we are now, this moment, and you kissed me, and I remember the soft wool aroma of your jacket warmed by sunshine. I will always remember it, wherever you are.

Wherever you are, you had written on the New Look card. Besides the caption, there was an acknowledgement:

Printed by Rapoport Printing Corp.
© Fotofolio, Box 661 Canal Sta., NY, NY 10013

and I realised that the photograph was not so much of Paris, as by Richard Avedon who was of New York. Very possibly you had bought it there. Wherever you are. I thought of the jazzy green Wearever pen I used for my first letter, and thinking again of our time in New York, I remembered another detail I had put to the back of my mind since then. At the Embassy reception you'd been standing chatting to a blue-suited, red-faced man with pendulous blue jowls, or rather, he was chatting to you, maybe even chatting you up, he had that chatting-up stance, legs apart, wineglass in one hand, the other supporting the elbow. I made my way nonchalantly over and he made a neat little demi-pirouette as I came from behind him, and then, Gabriel Conway! he exclaimed, has it been years, or what? and it took me some interminable seconds to put a name to the face. Tommy Geoghegan! he cried, just as it was on the tip of my tongue. Of course! I cried back, how could I not know you?

In truth, he had changed somewhat, and the Tommy Geoghegan I once knew was buried like a ghost in the flesh of this other. His accent had changed, too, from broad Belfast to more than a touch of Dublin 4. A waiter was passing by, and with one fluid movement he knocked back the remains of his wine, placed the empty glass on the waiter's tray, and helped himself to a full one. There was something about this gesture, at once graceful and transgressive, that made me see him more clearly as he was. He had been an athlete once, a good footballer by all accounts, and a Celtic supporter, the only one in our A-level class. The only football supporter of any kind; sport was not in vogue in our literary set. The trouble was, Geoghegan also read books, voraciously, and could more than match any of us in his enthusiasms for Joyce, or Beckett, or Dylan Thomas, whose verse he loved especially for its sonorous obscurity. 'Do not go gentle into that good night,' he would intone in a passable imitation of Dylan's plummy voice, 'rage, rage against the dying of the light.' And, true to his old form, without further preamble, he put a hand on his heart, held his glass aloft, and declaimed, 'The force that through the green fuse drives the flower/ Drives my old age ...' Well, we're not getting any younger, are we? he said. I was just telling Miranda how much I liked her muted Irish theme – you know Miranda, I take it? Everyone knows Miranda. I nodded uncomfortably, and tried to catch your eye, but you refused to meet mine. Yes, the subtle wearing of the green, said Geoghegan, to which I've made my own little contribution, and he thrust forward his jacket lapel, in which was embedded a tiny green star. I didn't know you spoke Esperanto, I said. Well, to tell you the truth, I don't, said

Geoghegan, though I can read it a bit, the old school Latin does come in handy, but I feel obliged to wear it every so often in honour of the Geoghegan connection, let's say it's a conversation piece, and he proceeded to tell me something of what I now know, but didn't know then, about Richard Henry Geoghegan's contribution to Esperanto, and of Tommy Geoghegan's discovery that he was a distant relation of the great man.

It was back in '79, he said, I was sent to Alaska, such is the life of the diplomatic aide, don't you know, I had to attend the official opening of the new Fairbanks Public Library, quite a big deal in that neck of the woods. So I'm introduced to the Chief Librarian, and he says, Geoghegan, you wouldn't be anything to the famous Richard Henry? He was quite a figure here, you know. Harry Geoghegan, secretary to Judge James Wickersham back in the Noughties. Judge James 'The Terrible', they called him, ruled the territory with a rod of iron, says the Chief Librarian. We've got all Geoghegan's journals here, says he, written in Esperanto, we had an Esperanto chap here a couple of months ago to translate them.

And Tommy Geoghegan proceeded to give me an account of his distant relative's life – quite a tall story, it seemed to me at the time, but I have since found it to be more or less true. Father a doctor, lived in Rathmines, he said. Funny, I used to live there myself, then went to Liverpool, Harry was born there, fell down the stairs at the age of three, broke his leg, seems the doctor father set it wrong, cripple ever since. Then he goes to Oxford, studies Chinese, wants to join the Foreign Service, must run in the family, the diplomatic Geoghegans, don't you know, but then he finds out they won't take him on because of his bad leg, then his father dies, he's got his mother and six siblings to support, so they hear there's great opportunities in Canada, and they move there lock, stock and barrel, steamer across the Atlantic, train across to Vancouver, must have taken them months, then another steamer to Orcas Island, have you heard of it? I hadn't. They get themselves a homestead there, do some farming, but Harry Geoghegan's not cut out for that kind of thing, so he moves to Seattle, various clerical jobs, stenography mostly, they say he knew all the various shorthand systems, could transcribe two at a time, one with each hand, incredible, like he's got two brains. And all this time he's learning languages – Russian, Sanskrit, Tibetan, Korean, Swahili, Arabic, Khmer, Lepcha – Lepcha, for Christ's sake, I don't even know what Lepcha is – they say he knew two hundred languages, seems he had a photographic memory, had only to look at a word and he'd remember it, and of course all the time he's working away at the old Esperanto connection, corresponding with Zamenhof. Gives him the idea for the green star. 1904, he goes to Alaska, meets up with The Terrible Judge, the circuit takes them all over Alaska, husky dogs, sleds, real Jack London story, said Tommy Geoghegan. As for the journals in the Fairbanks Library, he went on, seems there were quite a lot of fairly graphic bits in there, Harry was quite a ladies' man, stuff about his relationships with the Fairbanks line girls, as they called them, gammy leg doesn't seem to have affected him much in that department, sort of Toulouse-Lautrec figure, you might say. Seems he taught them a little Esperanto, made up words for specialities of the house, that kind of thing. So I thought I'd have a bash at the old Esperanto myself, being a Geoghegan and all, said Geoghegan. Not that I got that far with it. But listen, must dash, chap over there I've been trying to talk to all night, great to see you, and he wandered off into the crowd.

Quite the diplomat, Tommy Geoghegan, I said drily to you, Nina. Oh, he's not so bad if you get to know him, you said, that clumsy manner of his, it's part of his charm, people tell him things because they think he's guileless. Whether what they tell him is true, that doesn't really matter. It's all information, people reveal as much about themselves by their lies as they do the truth. Anything we know, at any given time, it's as much disinformation, or misinformation, as it is information. More, sometimes. The edges are always fuzzy. Bluff and fuzz. Tommy Geoghegan fits very well into that picture. That's why he's one of us. One of you? I said. Yes, you said in a mock conspiratorial whisper, we have our people everywhere.

And then there's Declan Tierney, you said, the time you told me about Tony Lambe's tie emporium. He's one. Declan Tierney? I said, the art dealer? Well, he's the only Declan Tierney I know, you said. And, when I thought about it, I wasn't entirely surprised. Declan Tierney had arrived on the art scene in Belfast seemingly from nowhere. Began dealing in those terrible Markey Robinson rip-offs, stylised Connemara landscapes, whitewashed cottages, doe-eyed Madonnas in shawls, that sort of thing, not that Markey himself was that much better than his rip-offs, but then Tierney moved on, got in with Gerry Byrne, went to all the graduate shows, began putting together a stable of young artists, cutting-edge stuff. Though there was always something dodgy about him, he tried to sell me what he called a Gerard Dillon once, claimed he picked it up from one of the Friday Market dealers who'd just made a house clearance in West Belfast. Maybe he did. But the painting wasn't right. There's a *faux-naïf* thing about Dillon's brushwork, but this was just plain amateurish. Declan Tierney? I said, well, I suppose that figures.

And then there's Archie Chambers, you said. Archie Chambers the ventriloquist? I said. Archie's dummy was called Bernie Buttons, he was one of those Champagne Charlie dummies, with a rather predictable line in double entendres.

You know the routine, Bernie says to Archie, May I have a goodbye kiss? And Archie says, Well, I can't see any harm in that, and Bernie comes back with, Oh, I wish you would, a harmless kiss doesn't sound very thrilling. Yes, Archie and Bernie both, you said, you'd be surprised how many of us there are. For instance, for all you know, you might be one too. Without my knowing it? I said. Yes, you said, without your full knowledge. Or consent, for that matter, you said. You'd learned to twin those words from me, it's a Catholic concept, a mortal sin can only be committed with full knowledge and complete consent. Does anybody really know who they are? or what they are? you said. Billie Holiday was playing in the background, I can't remember what song, but it occurs to me now, as I write, that 'Wherever You Are' is the title of a Billie Holiday song, recorded in 1942. Not her best song: the lyrics are trite, the music slightly incongruous, but, given what I presume to be their purpose – to offer comfort to American troops in Europe – perhaps the song is redeemed by that very banality, that all-inclusive 'you' which is both singular and plural:

> Everywhere in every home
> Hope is burning bright
> While millions of hearts
> Are kneeling, saying, Tonight
> Wherever you are
> Our hearts are with you.
>
> Wherever you are
> Our prayers are with you too
> All through the darkness
> Our faith is your guiding star
> May God bless you all
> Wherever you are.

So, wherever you are, Nina, I know that this wartime song must have been in your mind when you wrote those words to me. And wartime must have been in your mind when you booked us into the Hôtel Scribe in Paris, for in 1944 it was the HQ of the Allied press corps, which included Lee Miller, erstwhile model, photographer, a war correspondent for *Vogue* magazine, and one of your great heroines. And with all that in mind, I've been writing this letter with two pens, alternating them according to whatever voice I have in mind. One is a French pen, which came in a box bearing the inscription *Porte-Plume Réservoir*, which I take to be an elaborate synonym for the more usual word for fountain pen, *stylo*. The pen itself has no name stamped on the barrel, as is customary with good pens, but the classy 18 carat gold nib has 'Paris' engraved on it, and, in a diagonal cartouche, the initials D & D. Whatever they might stand for, I like their doubleness. It is a very elegant pen, and again, like the Swan, it is done in a mottled red and black wood-grain pattern, le rouge et le noir, that bears a striking resemblance to the Dinkie you wore when first we met. The other is an English pen, a Conway Stewart Scribe in Green and Black Candle-flame. Both were made in wartime. That first night in the Hôtel Scribe, before we went out for dinner, you dabbed a little perfume on your breast and wrists. The casement windows of our room on the fourth floor were open and the voile curtains billowed gently in that breeze that comes on at dusk, you'd ordered a great bunch of Easter lilies to be placed on the windowsill, and their scent mingled with yours, a bittersweet tang of aniseed and musk followed by jasmine, rose and bergamot, and, as I write this in blue ink, the colour of eternity, the nib of my French pen whispers across the page till it falls silent after these words, *L'Heure Bleue*.

FEELING
BLUE

Waterman's Ideal

I'm writing this in blue ink with an American Waterman's Ideal fountain pen made in 1927, the year that Lee Miller, aged twenty, was about to step off a sidewalk in New York into the path of an oncoming car, when she was saved by a passer-by. When her panic had subsided, he introduced himself to her as Condé Nast, the owner of *Vogue* magazine. I'm writing this with the Waterman's Ideal because its swirled faded green and amber colours are like those of a dress you wore in Paris, made of a billowy moiré tulle, that shimmered as you walked. You'd bought it for a song in the Friday Market, a copy of a Dior number you'd seen in a 1947 *Vogue*. And the pen also goes well with your postcard, the rusts and metallic grey-greens of the Turbine Hall of Bankside Power Station before its conversion to the Tate Modern Gallery in 1997. Not to mention the tawny fleck in one of your green eyes.

At first I took your message, *Feeling blue*, to be a reference to a song, but when I thought of it in the context of the Tate Modern, I knew that you meant me to think of Yves Klein's IKB 79, which hangs at this moment in the Tate Modern, and which we both saw in the old Tate in October 1982. It consists of nothing more than blue paint applied to a canvas-covered plywood panel some five feet by four, one of almost two hundred such monochrome paintings made by him before he died from a hereditary heart condition in 1962, aged just thirty-four. Klein had left these works untitled, but his widow posthumously numbered them IKB 1 to IKB 194, a sequence which did not reflect their chronological order, possibly because even she could not determine when each had been composed. The letters stand for 'International Klein Blue', registered by Klein as a trademark in 1960. He had long been fascinated by the incandescent luminosity of pastel colours. In the early 1950s, noting how the glow of pigments in their powder forms invariably dimmed when mixed with oil to make a paint, Klein had begun a quest to find a means of preserving what he called the 'affective magic' of the colour. In 1955 he found the solution: a colourless fixative called Rhodopas M60A, manufactured by the Rhône-Poulenc chemicals company, consisting of a vinyl chloride resin, thinned with ethyl alcohol and ethyl acetate. When M60A was mixed with a pigment and applied to a surface, the highly volatile ethyl derivatives would evaporate, leaving behind the pure colour suspended in the transparent resin.

Klein's all-blue paintings were first seen in Milan in 1957, where he exhibited a series of eleven such works. To a casual observer they all looked the same, but Klein assigned different prices to them, claiming that each reflected not what the painting 'looked like, but the intensity of feeling that had gone into making it'. The blue was a feeling blue. In any case, the pieces were not identical, said Klein; and I am reminded of my father's observation regarding the blades of grass on the lawn of Botanic Gardens, that every one is different from its neighbour because, despite appearances, nothing in the world is the same as anything else. The blue world of each painting, said Klein, although the same blue and treated in the same way, presents a completely different essence and atmosphere. None resembles any other – no more than pictorial moments resemble each other – although all are of the same superior and subtle nature, marked by the immaterial, said Klein.

Your card is postmarked Nice, where Klein was born in 1928. Blue always evoked to him the Côte d'Azur. When he embarked on his Blue project, he searched for some time before finding a suitable canvas, a cotton sailcloth used for the canopies of Paris street-market traders. He liked its artisan quality, its association with both sky and sea. Every piece was a unique textural field of nubs and bracks and flaws. As he proceeded with the IKB series, the individual panels began to come out differently. Some were utterly flat and thinly painted; many were dry and grainy, or lush and velvety; the surfaces of others were undulating, swirled, grooved, rutted, or embossed. Though every moment in time had its unique quality, all could be absorbed by blue, said Klein.

I knew little about Klein's work, or the philosophy behind it, when I first saw IKB 79 with you, but I was immediately attracted by its intensity of colour. Only in subsequent, closer viewings did I realise that its surface was not entirely uniform, but had a dimpled, translucent shimmer like that of distemper paint, though I do not know how much this might be due to the passage of time. It reminded us both of the stained glass in York Cathedral, and I was not surprised to discover that Klein had been influenced by the ethereal blue of the stained glass in Chartres Cathedral. Klein espoused a peculiarly mystic brand of Catholicism, immersing himself in Rosicrucianism, and becoming a Knight of the exclusive Order of the Archers of St Sebastian. One of his most sumptuous works is the votive offering he made for the shrine of St Rita of Cascia, a Perspex box containing rose pigment, blue pigment, and gold leaf. Viewed in this light, IKB 79 is a religious icon. Through blue and beyond blue, said Klein, he felt himself grazed by the quivering of the absolute, a tangible representation of celestial space.

Klein had visited Hiroshima in 1953. As he was being shown around the city he remarked on the beautiful, cloudless blue sky, and was told that the atom bomb had dropped out of just such a sky on 6th August, 1945. In that immaculate summer light of 1953, the few relics of the city's most defining moment – that of its erasure – stood out clearly amidst the ongoing work of reconstruction. The ruined dome of the once beautiful Art Deco Hiroshima Prefecture Industrial Promotion Hall, still left partly standing when everything around it had been levelled to the ground, had been preserved as an admonitory feature, as were the white shadows imprinted on hard surfaces by things and people vaporised by the explosion. Etched into the wood of an electric pole were the bold, serrated leaves of a *Fatsia japonica*, which reminded Klein of reports he had heard of the patterns burned into the skin of some women, from the shapes of flowers on their kimonos. He learned that in the immediate aftermath of the explosion people supposed they had been the victims of a *Molotoffano hanakago* – a 'Molotov flower basket', the Japanese name for the self-scattering cluster-bomb known to the Americans as a 'bread-basket'. When the full extent of the devastation began to be realised, a rumour circulated that an aircraft had dusted all of Hiroshima with a special magnesium powder so fine as to be invisible, which exploded like a gigantic photographic flash when ignited by a spark from an overhead power cable. At the Red Cross Hospital, word went around among the staff that there must indeed have been something very peculiar about the bomb, because on the third day the second-in-command had descended to the basement, and, opening the vault where the X-ray plates were stored, found the whole stock exposed as they lay. Only gradually did the truth emerge, and then it was not believed by many.

Klein's visit to Hiroshima was by the way. He had gone to Japan principally to study judo. He became an expert practitioner of the art, being awarded the fourth dan black-belt on 14th December 1953. He had long been fascinated by how the body cuts a shape in space, leaving behind innumerable, invisible impressions of itself on the air. Although the principle of judo was not one of staccato aggression, but of a seamless flow, Klein recognised that its repertoire of actions could be broken down into a series of pivotal moments. In his book *Les Fondements du Judo*, published in 1954, he analysed the syntax of judo movements in meticulous detail, accompanying them with hundreds of still photographs derived from film footage taken in Japan: illustrations of the importance of timing, of recognising the split second when the opponent's equilibrium can be turned to disequilibrium, his apparent greater strength to weakness. Learning to fall, one learned to overthrow. Gradually, through practice and inner visualisation, the most effective attitudes were remembered by the body, so that its responses to attack became second nature.

Klein was deeply affected by Hiroshima. He paid homage to the ghostly presences of its atomic silhouettes in a piece he called *Hiroshima*. This was one of a series of 'anthropometries', made by spraying blue pigment around live models posed on a large sheet of white paper, who, when they removed themselves, left behind a shadowy, retrospective choreography of body-shaped spaces. At the back of Klein's mind were apparitions of the Virgin Mary; the miraculously preserved bodies of saints, particularly that of St Rita of Cascia; the 'mummies' of Pompeii; and the faint impressions left by a person on a judo mat.

As you know, Nina, blue is a favourite colour of mine. You remember that first day I showed you around the Municipal Gallery, when we looked at Gerard Dillon's *Yellow Bungalow*. Then, by way of contrast, I showed you, as my father had first shown me, the Gallery's most prized exhibit, J.M.W. Turner's *Dawn of Christianity*, subtitled *Flight into Egypt*. I had always loved the blue of the sky in this painting, which is inspired by the Gospel story according to St Matthew: 'And when they were departed, behold, an angel of the Lord appeared in sleep to Joseph, saying, Arise, and take the child and his mother, and fly into Egypt, and be there until I shall tell thee. For it will come to pass that Herod will seek the child to destroy him' – a text my father would habitually quote to me each time we saw the painting, as I did to you, for it was ingrained in my memory. And I told you that my father would explain to me that Herod was an agent of the Roman Empire, comparing its jurisdiction in the Holy Land to that of the British in Ireland. I saved you the gory details of my father's account of the Massacre of Innocents that followed, but when I mentioned that the Catholic Church considered the Innocents to be martyrs, you asked if one could be a martyr without full knowledge and complete consent. You'd make a good Jesuit, I said, you know they were trained to be devil's advocates, to see both sides of an argument. Yes, you said, I know, it's useful to imagine what it must be like to be somebody else, to see things from another's point of view. And we gazed into Turner's opalescent blue sky, below which the fugitive Holy Family were almost indecipherable details in a dream landscape. My father would say that blue signifies a detachment from the things of this world, I said, an inclination of the liberated soul towards God. In other words, it was the colour of flight.

Years afterwards, I discovered that these were precisely the attributes that Yves Klein ascribed to his trademark blue. He had always been fascinated by the concept of flight. Today, said Klein, the painter of space must actually go into space, but without aeroplane, parachute, or rocket. He must be capable of levitating. From his judo experience, Klein believed that levitation – he liked to think of it as a form of ascension, a victory over death – was indeed possible, through a regime of breathing exercises designed to free the body – physically, mentally, and spiritually – from the constraints of weight. In October 1960 the French journal *Dimanche* carried a photograph of Klein which became known as *The Leap into the Void*. It shows Klein, dressed in a business suit, soaring into space just off the ledge of a mansard roof, his torso and head turned towards the sky and his arms extended outwards in a convincing simulacrum of flight. The setting is a nondescript Parisian street, empty except for a man on a bicycle who has just passed by, his back to the viewer, oblivious to the marvellous event. When I first saw a reproduction of this photograph I was struck by the quotidian beauty of the scene, the crooked kerbstones, the empty bus-shelter, the tarred roadway patched and laddered with repair-work, light glinting off the leafy trees and the iron railings of a garden. How wonderfully the cyclist defies gravity, how intricate are the folds and puckers of his overcoat, caught in mid-flap behind him! Klein's *Leap into the Void* might have been a camera trick; but the street is miraculously real.

I write this in blue ink, the colour of liberation, the colour of France. You remember that week in Paris, Nina, you told me about Lee Miller. We were in Cimetière du Montparnasse, where Samuel Beckett is buried, except he was alive then, and we walked the avenues between the tombs and sepulchres and monuments as they glittered in the immaculate Paris light. We stood at the grave of Baudelaire as you recited his poem

'Parfum Exotique' – *l'odeur de ton sein chaleureux*, the odour of your warm breast – and we stood silently a while by the grave of Jean-Paul Sartre, who would be joined in four years' time by Simone de Beauvoir; and then we went to Man Ray's grave, Man Ray who was once a lover of Lee Miller. A string of coincidences, if you like, you said. Imagine, 1927, New York, Lee Miller's about to step in front of a car, and of all people, of all the millions of people in New York, she's saved by Condé Nast, who owns *Vogue* magazine. A few weeks later she appears on the front cover of *Vogue*, full face, with the lights of New York behind her, lovely Art Deco cover, she's wearing a blue cloche hat, and she's got this look, uninhibited yet relaxed, a look of worldly sophistication. Someone who knows who she is, yet the viewer can project her own fantasies on to her. Edward Steichen, the great photographer, takes a real shine to her, that's when she starts to get interested in photography, she watches how it's done, how an image is created. Then Condé Nast pulls some strings for her, gets her a research assignment in Paris with French *Vogue*, she's to go and look at Renaissance paintings, make detailed drawings of costume adornments, buckles, buttons and bows, haberdash-ery, as it were, and Steichen gives her an introduction to Man Ray. Man Ray, he was born Emmanuel Radnitzky, decides at the age of fifteen he's going to be Man Ray, anyway, Paris in the 1920s, he's at the forefront of the whole Surrealist enterprise, there's Paul Éluard and André Breton, there's Max Ernst, Yves Tanguy, Magritte, Picasso, and there's Man Ray – what must it have been like?

Lee Miller goes and looks at the buckles and bows, and decides that drawing them is a bit silly, why not photograph them instead? All she has is a folding Kodak, she has to take close-ups in bad light with low-speed film, but she learns how to do it. She knows now she wants to be a photographer. She goes to see Man Ray, calls at his apartment, but the concierge tells her he's just left for Biarritz. She goes to a nearby café, Le Bateau Ivre, she's sitting there all disappointed sipping a Pernod, when who walks in but Man Ray. She tells him she's his new student, he says he doesn't take students, and anyway he's leaving Paris to go on holiday, and she says, I know, I'm going with you, and she does, and they end up living together for three years. Ends up driving him near crazy. But at the beginning, she's going with Man Ray, she's the talk of Paris, there's images of her all over the place, a glass manufacturer designs a champagne glass modelled on her breast, as photographed by Man Ray. She gets her own apartment, look, over there, and you pointed to a high mansard roof in a street that overlooked the cemetery, 12 rue Victor Considérant, you said, she sets up a studio, gets to photograph high society, the Duchess of Alba, Duke Vallambrosa, the Maharanee of Cooch-Bihar, whoever, it's like something out of Proust. And one thing leads to another.

Skip to 1940, she's in London, she gets to know the Mass Observation people, you know, Jennings, Gascoyne, Spender, all these poets and photographers, she's at all their mad soirees, and they all idolise her because the Mass Observation thing was really a Surrealist enterprise, and here's Lee Miller who was at the heart of it all in Paris, worked with Man Ray, Jean Cocteau, Picasso, all the big names. Of course, by now Mass Observation's a propaganda tool, they're in league with the Ministry of Information, they assess the morale of the civilian population, see what might perk them up. So a few strings are pulled, she gets a photography job in British *Vogue*, they called it *Brogue*. And *Brogue*'s doing the British stiff upper lip thing, photographs of well-bred, elegantly dressed ladies, aloof from the terrors of the Blitz, even when their offices were bombed it didn't rate a mention in the magazine, the show must go on.

Lee gets a bit restless, starts to look around for something to do on the side, she meets up with the American broadcaster Ed Murrow, they collaborate on a book, he writes the text, she takes the pictures, they call it *Grim Glory, Pictures of Britain under Fire*. I got a second-hand copy a few years ago, cost me a small fortune, but it was worth it, I can see some of those photographs still, one of a bomb-damaged typewriter, she called it *Remington Silent*, the keyboard's all twisted, the ribbon's unspooled all over the place, it looks like some kind of Surrealist object, but really it's a very simple shot, there's no tricks with it. It just shows it as it is, a typewriter that's been in the war. Then there's one of a terrace of grand houses in Knightsbridge, it's got a house-sized gap blasted right through the middle of it, you can see the back of another terrace through it, but the top storey with the mansard windows is still intact, she called that one *Bridge of Sighs*. Or maybe Murrow made up the captions, I don't know. Personally I find the captions a bit sentimental, the pictures speak far more clearly.

Then she meets the photographer David Scherman, she teams up with him, in more ways than one, eventually. *Brogue* gives them assignments with a bit more grit to them, seems the Ministry of Information people, or the Mass Observation people, whatever, they want *Brogue* to change its slant. Lee comes up with some great photographs, the ATS searchlight operators, women, they've got this padded body armour on, they look like gladiators. Londoners sleeping in the Tube stations, she makes you aware of fabric and texture, the folds and furrows in the blankets, there's a sculptural quality to the rows of people wrapped up for the night, yet they're still people, you can see how the light falls on an old man's hand, a child's face. There's a great one of a barrage balloon that's settled in a field, terrible caption, they called it *Eggceptional*

Achievement, because there's a pair of geese standing in front of it, like they've just produced this wonderful giant silver egg, a Surrealist thing, except it's not. It's real. That's the beauty of the pictures, they show how things pressurised by exceptional circumstances, by war, take on interesting new shapes, you said.

Then in 1944 *Vogue*, *Brogue* that is, make her their official war correspondent, they send her to France to cover the period after D-Day. She photographs Saint-Malo being bombed, and the rubble of the aftermath, tall chimneys standing alone giving off smoke from the burning remnants of their buildings at their feet. She's the only woman war correspondent in Paris when it's liberated, what must it have been like? you said. I used to put myself in her shoes, the long graceful avenues crowded with flags, girls, bicycles, kisses and wine, and around the corner sniping, a bursting grenade and a burning tank, the bullet-holes in the windows like jewels, the barbed wire strung like decorations in the boulevards, urchins playing in the wrecked German war machines. And the smell has changed, it used to be a combination of patchouli, urinals and the castor oil burned by motorcycles. Now it's air and perfume wafting across a square or an avenue, and everywhere the dazzling girls, cycling, climbing up tank turrets − full floating skirts and tiny waistlines − the GIs gawping, they think their dreams of wild women in Paris have come true, the girls in high wedge-heeled platform shoes and pompadour hairstyles, blowing kisses everywhere. And whenever I'm in Paris I imagine I see it through Lee Miller's eyes, I see photographs on every street, I think my eye is a camera, and I have only to blink to capture it, you said. Which one? I said. Which one? you said. Which eye? I said. This one, you said. And you winked at me with your amber-flecked eye.

I was interrupted just now by the postman ringing the

doorbell. This was not the letter post, which brings your postcards, and sometimes pens, if they're in sufficiently small packages, but the parcel post, which comes later. The postman had a package for me to sign for, a substantial cardboard box typical of meticulously responsible eBay sellers, which contained, I knew from the sender's New York address, just one pen. I signed for the package and brought into the kitchen, where I slit it open with a chef's knife. Inside, cocooned in bubble-wrap surrounded by crumpled newspaper, was the pen, described by the eBay seller as a Conway Stewart Duro in Golden Pearl Basket Weave laminated plastic. The pattern is also known as Tiger's Eye, but it's very different to the Tiger's Eye of the Onoto I used in an earlier letter. To be finicky about it, I knew in advance that this was not a Duro pen: from its eBay photograph I knew it to be a Conway Stewart 58, made in the early 1950s, and not, like a Duro, in the early 1940s: the seller had been misled by the fact that 58s usually come, as this one does, with a Duro nib. But 58 is clearly marked on the barrel. No matter: it is a beautiful pen, in near mint condition. The laminated body twinkles and glows with deep ambers and golden browns, like spiral-twist, translucent toffee, when I revolve it in the light. I filled it from a bottle of Conway Stewart black ink, tried it out by writing my name and address on a piece of scrap paper, and found that it wrote beautifully, with a confident wet firm line. So I'm laying down these words on the page with it now, delighting in the feel of a new instrument.

I was about to throw the packaging in the bin when a headline word in the crumpled newspaper caught my eye: GUNMAN, it said. I smoothed it out on the kitchen table. CHURCH GUNMAN, it read in total, there must be more, I thought, and then I realised that this must be one half of a double-page spread; the other half was missing. The newspaper was the *New York Post* of 18th July 2005, last Monday. 'Many cops rely on St Michael the Archangel, the patron saint of police officers, for protection, but Dominick Romano and his NYPD colleagues have also a back-up – their bullet-resistant vests. Romano was shot nine times in the back by a crazed gunman – and eight of the buckshot pellets were stopped by his bulletproof vest', one paragraph read. And the story, which I pieced together from the newspaper account and a little research on the Internet, went more or less as follows.

At 2 a.m. on the morning of Sunday, 17th July, a man wielding a spear and a tyre iron – or a sword, or a machete, according to other accounts – was seen attacking the statue of St Anne and the Virgin Mary outside the Roman Catholic church of Saints Joachim and Anne in Queens, New York. The police were called, by which time the man had hacked off the left arms of St Anne and the Virgin Mary, and was now firing at the head of St Anne with a shotgun. The statue was decapitated. As the two police officers, Dominick Romano and David Harris, attempted to apprehend him, he turned the shotgun on them. Romano was grazed on the head and eight pellets were embedded in the back of his bulletproof vest; Harris received five shots in the leg, and suffered a broken femur. A passer-by, Tyrone Murphy, who happened to be a registered nurse, struggled from his car – he was on crutches, following an automobile accident some weeks previously – and applied a tourniquet made from his own T-shirt to Harris's leg, possibly saving his life. It transpired that the attacker was one Kevin Davey, otherwise known as 'Gambit', a 25-year-old New Yorker with a history of psychiatric problems. According to some, he held strong anti-immigration views and had got particularly worked up in the wake of the London under-ground terrorist bombings the week before. Davey was shot four times by the police officers, in the right arm, shoulder, ankle, and side, and was brought to the nearby Hospital of Mary Immaculate.

His mother told reporters that he was just sick, a good kid with some mental problems. His brother Keith, however, said he understood 'the logic involved' in the attack on the police, whom he branded as 'devilish' and he spoke with contempt of the 'white' statue, which suggested that the Daveys were black, though at first I had presumed it to be an Irish name. It transpired that their father was a subway preacher who had issued a homemade DVD which included rants against the Bush administration, the police, and white people in general. The parishioners were particularly upset because the attack occurred on the first day of a Novena – nine days' solemn prayer – to St Anne, who is specially revered as the mother of the Virgin Mary; St Joachim, the other dedicatee of the Queens church, is her father, and together they are a holy family, precursors of the Holy Family of Joseph and Mary and Jesus. A poignant photograph in the *New York Post* showed the parish priest, Monsignor Joseph Malagreca, cradling the decapitated head of St Anne, whose lips and jaw had been shot off. I have this head in my room, he said, I picked it up out of the bushes, and what am I supposed to do with it?

As I read this bizarre account of modern iconoclasm I was reminded of the icon of the Holy Family – a Nativity scene – which I bought when I was with you in Paris, Nina. You remember? We had wandered into the Marais, which at that time was not the fashionable quarter it has recently become. Down a crooked alleyway we found an antique shop, or junk shop. A bell tinkled as we pushed open the door. The proprietor, an old man in his seventies or eighties, gloomily returned our 'Bonjour, monsieur'. The place was crammed with the usual stuff, moth-eaten Persian rugs, brass kerosene lamps with etched glass chimneys, old tobacco tins, biscuit tins, rickety cane-backed chairs, kitchen implements, wooden printing blocks, scuffed leather-bound books. I lifted a rust-pocked enamel sign for Ricard pastis from a shelf and behind it I discovered the icon: a pocket-sized wooden panel some five inches by four, featuring the Holy Family and the Three Wise Men, done in dark ambers and blue-greens and blacks that seemed to glow in the dark shop interior, the Holy Infant at its centre swathed in a creamy white cocoon of supernatural light. The paint was wrinkled with age, its layers worn away in some areas to reveal the underlying smolt-grey and ochre ground, its three-dimensional quality palpable when I brushed it gently with my fingertips. It exuded mystery, reverence, antiquity. It's beautiful, I whispered to you. But I hesitated to buy it; I felt there was something immoral in buying icons, pieces which had very probably been looted or stolen from those who held them dear for reasons which had little to do with our modern conceptions of art. And, as if to confirm my unease, the proprietor suddenly said, Not for sale. It is a personal thing, you know? And we began to make some small talk with him.

When he discovered I was from Ireland, though, his attitude changed. Now his story was that he was waiting for the right person to buy it, he'd been waiting years. But most people, he said, were tourists, they did not appreciate these things, they did not esteem their proper value, which was not monetary, it was not even artistic, but spiritual. And he knew the Irish to be a spiritual race. You are Catholic? he asked. I nodded and shrugged uncertainly. Of course he's Catholic, you said. He brought me to Easter Sunday Mass in Saint-Eustache, and you waxed lyrical to the old man about the ceremony, the incense and the music, the shafts of sunlight falling through the gloom from the tall high windows. And you are not Catholic? he asked you. No, you said, but I'm thinking of becoming one, it's such a beautiful religion. Such a true religion, I mean, because it is true to our feeling that there is a world beyond this one, it has the beauty of truth, you said. Yes, said the old man, you will be a Catholic, and you will marry this fine man, and your first child will be a son, and may the Holy Family look kindly on his birth. Alas, I never married myself, he said, and I have been waiting for this moment, for such a fine couple to discover this icon. And by now I was so implicated that I had to buy it, and I was happy to find an excuse to do so. The old man named a price: it did not seem exorbitant for something that was priceless, and I didn't haggle. And when we examined it together in the light of day, its colours seemed to glow even more, with an undeniable authenticity, and we were proud of ourselves at having been the recipients of such a gift.

After Paris you had to go to London for a few days; I went on to Belfast, and the next morning I wrapped the icon in a silk handkerchief, put it in my pocket, and brought it to Beringer for him to see. I never told you this until now. Without saying anything, I took off the silk handkerchief, and handed him the precious object. Mm, he said, and looked at it carefully. Very nice, very nice indeed, he said, and he took out his loupe and went over to the light of the window, and looked at it again, examining it in detail. Then he looked at the back, and at the front again. Yes, he said, lovely, masterly, I might say. Beautiful work. I was smiling proudly. But of course, he said, and he paused before delivering the blow, it's a fake. The smile fell from my face. Oh, don't be too hard on yourself, Mr Gabriel, it's still a lovely piece of work. Whoever made this, he did everything right, proper techniques, done in the old style, well, except for a few little things. And he held the icon up. See the way the panel is convex? Yes, that's because it was cut from an oak barrel-stave, I said. It was one of the things which had convinced me about it. Oak barrel-stave, correct, said Beringer, that's what it is. But look at this, he said, and he showed me the back of the panel. What? I said. Well, said Beringer, if you look at the saw-cuts, they've been made with a modern power-saw, a circular saw, and they didn't have saws like this in when, oh, 1700 or so, whenever this might have been made, were it the genuine article. And here's another thing. He turned the panel over to show the image. See this strip of paint running around the edge? Yes, I said. I'd loved that little detail, a strip of dark rust red that framed the scene and somehow lifted it into another dimension.

Well, said Beringer, and he took a long, nicotine-stained thumbnail to it, and lifted off a tiny piece of the paint – Don't worry, he said, the whole thing'll come off by itself anyway in a matter of months, here, feel this, he said, and he passed me the tiny rust-red flake. Feel it, he said. Doesn't it feel like a plastic film? Yes, I said reluctantly. That's because it is, said Beringer, it's modern acrylic paint. But outside of those little details, why, it's a lovely piece of work, you have to admire the man that made this, oh, he knew what he was doing. And for all we know, maybe it was made for a genuine market, for a true believer. What does it matter if it's old or new, so long as it's done in the right way? I nodded ruefully. And might I ask, Mr Gabriel, how much you paid for it? I named the price. Oh, good price, good price. Though of course were it the real McCoy, you could maybe multiply that by ten. Or twenty. Still, you can consider it a bargain. You've got yourself something special. You've gone with your instincts, and that's what you should always do, you have to trust yourself, said Beringer, even if you're wrong. Because if you don't trust yourself, who will?

I have the icon before me as I write, Nina, the icon that we placed against the mirror of the vanity unit in Room 412 in

Hôtel Scribe, admiring it at intervals throughout our week in Paris. Lee Miller had stayed in Room 412, David Scherman was next door, 410 or 414, you didn't know which. Though I expect it must have changed since then, you said, and in any event, maybe this 412 is not what 412 was then, because when you asked the concierge if this was Lee Miller's room, the Lee Miller who was here during the liberation, he shrugged, and said, Who knows? The Liberation was a long time ago. But try and picture it as it was then, you said, pretend it is Lee Miller's room. There's her camera case hanging on the door knob, can't you see it? It's a Rolleiflex case, the camera itself is on the dressing table, over there, among the jars and bottles of perfume and chemicals, and there's a table in the middle of the floor with a Hermes Baby typewriter on it, and a half-empty bottle of cognac, and a full ashtray, and piles of paper, there's all sorts of junk overflowing from the drawers and wardrobes, cases of K rations piled up against the walls, cases of cognac and fine wines, the whole lot buried under cartons of flash bulbs, you said, and I began to join in the game. There's loot everywhere, I said, everything from lace to leather, the iron bed is strewn with books and German military crests and silver ashtrays with swastikas on them, and binoculars and pistols and bayonets, and there's a pair of jackboots in the corner, and a silver candelabra. And there's half-a-dozen jerrycans of petrol out on the balcony. Petrol? you said. Oh, I am sorry, Lee, I meant gasoline, I said. I'd been putting on an American accent. I guess I've been too long away from good old Uncle Sam, I said. And who might you be? you said. Why, if you're Lee Miller, then I must be David Scherman, I said. Don't be too sure of that, you said, Lee Miller had a lot of lovers. And for a moment I was piqued. Then I caught the mischief in your expression, and I said, Well, can I be Monsieur X, then? And you said, Who shall I be then? Madame Y? No, you can keep on being Lee Miller if you like, I said. Snap, you said, and you winked at me with your left eye. The *L'Heure Bleue* you'd put on earlier had faded, and we went to bed in an imagined aura of cognac, photographic fluids, cardboard boxes, gasoline and gunmetal. *Parfum Exotique.*

Barkston Gardens Hotel, Earls Court, London

ONLY AN
INFINITE PRESENT

Blackbird self-filling pen

L eonardo da Vinci observes that if you look at a damp-stained wall long enough, you will begin to see landscapes in it, adorned with mountains, rivers, rocks, trees, valleys, and so on. And you will also see fleeting figures, and strange expressions of faces, and people dressed in outlandish costumes. The effect, says Leonardo, is like listening to a carillon of bells, in whose clanging you may discover every name and every word you can imagine. So when last night a surveillance helicopter perched itself for some hours in the sky above Ophir Gardens, I could hear the syllables of your name, Nina, repeated in the washing-machine spin-cycle noise of its engines. Then I would hear my own name, Gabriel, then both our names together, Gabriel, Nina, Gabrellianina, till they would become scrambled and garbled back into the meaningless chaos from whence they had come.

Just after dawn the helicopter swooped away and dwindled into silence. I was left with the not unfamiliar feeling that I had somehow been drained of my identity by this infringement of my acoustic space. And I was reminded again of how, in the 1970s, young Catholic men like me would be routinely stopped by British army patrols, spread-eagled against a wall, and interrogated for some hours as to our identities. Our names. Where we lived. What we did for a living, if anything. Our parents' names. Those of our relatives, our friends, our colleagues, our associates. We soon learned that these details were already known anyway, as they were checked by a field-radio link to a central database; so these regular interrogations seemed a gratuitously thorough exercise. Some names, though, Irish names, proved difficult for the English soldiers: Fintan, for example, would be pronounced by them as Victor, Ciaran as Karen, and Manus as Menace. Fiach was Fake. Then there were the Irish-speaking zealots who would refuse to respond to questions put in English, though they spoke it better than they did Irish, and would demand an interpreter to be present at their interrogations: but this procedural difficulty was often easily circumvented, as an Irish-speaking companion would provide that service, the two acting as interpreters for each other. I was once forced to become one half of such a double act myself, having been latched on to by a drunk, Irish-speaking acquaintance of my father, on the way home from the pub one night.

Such episodes were clearer in my memory when I related them to you, back in 1982 and 1983. Isn't it extraordinary, I'd say, that the Powers That Be seem to know everything about everyone – or at least the Catholic population, I could not speak for the other side, though it did seem their identities were not so thoroughly examined – yet they can't identify who really is who, and who's doing what. Well, you'd say, so-called intelligence is one thing; knowing what it means is another, and the same information can be used to draw very different conclusions by different parties, with different vested interests. It depends how you look at it, you'd say. That's why they invented MO2, because we don't draw any conclusions, we just exist. The information is what we are. And again I would try to get to the bottom of what precisely you were, or what you and your colleagues did. Let me put it like this, you said. When I was brought up for my differentiation, as they called it, it was a kind of interview, Callaghan was there and he had this side-kick I'd never seen before. Callaghan introduces him as 'my esteemed colleague Mr Bentley'. Bentley's this chap in a lovely suit, really dark blue with a faint grey chalk stripe, must be Savile Row, he's wearing Crocket & Jones black Oxfords, but he's also got this unconventional touch, floppy-collared linen shirt, light blue with a pink needle-stripe, and quite a stunning tie, deep russet moiré silk, and Callaghan, he's wearing his usual baggy professorial tweeds.

Anyway, there's just the two of them, we're in Callaghan's office. Lovely room, he's got the original warehouse wide-planked flooring sanded and waxed – nothing so crude as that polyurethane varnish – and he's got a few Persian tribal rugs scattered on them, and there's some lovely Art Nouveau furniture, a burr walnut drinks cabinet with a sunburst motif on it, nice settee and chairs in cut moquette, that kind of thing. Good art on the walls, you'd like it, Gabriel, there's a Maurice Wilks landscape, and a Paul Henry, one of those Connemara ones which is mostly sky, clouds tumbling all over the place. There's a nice Colin Middleton from his Surrealist phase.

Callaghan pours us all a good glass of brandy to begin, and offers me a cigarette from a cedar box, though he knows I don't smoke, it's all very informal. Bentley lights up a pipe, and Callaghan gestures for me to sit on the settee. Bentley and himself sprawl out in these easy chairs. Well, says Callaghan, Miranda, if I might call you Miranda, we've looked at your differentiation outline, and it's very good, very well thought out, says Callaghan. Yes, very well thought out, says Bentley in a cut–glass Oxford accent, and the way he says it, it's not like he's repeating what Callaghan said, he's adding to it, he puts a different spin on it, and Bentley smiles meaningfully as he says this, and then Callaghan says, Yes, we'd just like to explore it a bit further, get a clearer picture of what you have in mind. Yes, says Bentley, a clearer picture. Of what you have in mind, says Bentley, and again this seems to mean something else to what Callaghan meant. But first, says Callaghan, purely procedural matter, don't you know, let's be sure we've got the right woman, and he laughs as if he's just made a joke, and Bentley says, between puffs of his pipe, Yes. The. Right. Woman.

So Callaghan's got this dossier on his lap, and he opens it and says, Miranda Bowyer. Born London, 11th June, 1951, parents Arie Bouwer, Dutch national, and Eleanor Bowyer, née Birtwhistle, and so on, the dossier's got where I went to school, my university career, what I subsequently did, they've got everything, they've got things about me that I'd forgotten, maybe things about me I didn't even know. And every so often he looks up at me and says, Correct? And I nod, and Bentley says, Yes. Correct. Well, that's good, says Callaghan, we like to know who we're dealing with, and he laughs again. And this time Bentley doesn't echo his words, but he says, Well, Miranda, if I might call you Miranda, we've looked very carefully at your outline, it's excellent, design consultancy, it's a good niche market thing, we'll go into all that later in more detail, but for now, it seems to me that the best way to advance this little session is for you perhaps to give us a broader understanding of your role in the organisation, well, not so much that, but we'd like you to be clear about what we do. I mean, what do you think we do? says Bentley, and Callaghan says, Yes, what do you think we do?

So I'm a bit put out by this. And oh, do take your time, they

both say together then, and they look at each other like
Tweedledum and Tweedledee, and I'm beginning to feel like
Alice in Wonderland, so I start talking off the top of my head,
and I says, Well, I'm looking at the art on the wall here, and
it seems to me it must be representative in some way of
what you do. You've been very careful in researching my
background, and I'm sure the organisation is equally meticulous
in its design choices. Take the Maurice Wilks, now. And
Callaghan and Bentley crane their necks to look at it, as if
they'd never seen it before, it's one of those *Bridge at Cushendun*
pieces, but a good cut above the normal, nice scumbling to
the clouds, Wilks, born when, 1911, 1912, year of the UVF
gun-running operation, Protestant background, son of a linen
designer, why, his father might have worked in these very
premises, I said, and Callaghan and Bentley nod sagely at this,
and Maurice goes to the local College of Art, he's a star pupil,
exhibits at the RHA when he's only nineteen. Starts to specialise
in landscapes, spends a lot of time in the Glens of Antrim,
Connemara, Donegal, those kinds of Irish landscapes, mountains and skies. It's ostensibly very conventional, the kind of
thing the art-conscious Ulster middle classes like to hang on
their walls, but there's a nice touch of French Impressionism
there too, and it's very well painted. Young artists these days,
they could learn a lot from Wilks. And Wilks sees himself more
as an Irishman than an Ulsterman, I'd say, though I've never
met him. Isn't he living in Dublin now? So the Wilks sends
out a message that art can transcend political allegiances, that
there are things that are important beyond this fiddle.

The Paul Henry, much the same kind of thing, but the
Middleton, it's a bit more challenging, and I go on about the
cultural traffic between Belfast and Paris, I throw in a mention
of Sir John Lavery, and they like that. Isn't that the Lavery that
painted the Royal Family? says Bentley. Yes, says Callaghan,

and those rather dashing paintings of the Orange parades, great colour sense, don't you think, those vibrant oranges and purples. Then I talk about the furniture a little. Drinks cabinet by Anderson & McAuley, when they were the big department store in Belfast, top of the range piece, made for linen merchants, shipbuilders. Same kind of design that went into the *Titanic.* Ditto the suite and the rugs, and I gabble on a bit more about the décor, you said, and I can see Callaghan and Bentley exchanging approving glances, so I see I'm on the right track, and I end up making a great speech about how communities can only be reconciled by pursuing common interests, that living with beautiful things must necessarily work against narrow sectarian interests, you know, kind of William Morris philosophy, and that MO2 is the kind of organisation that seeks harmoniously to integrate its objectives with the aspirations of the majority of the citizens of Ireland both North and South, it's all a bit of tautology really, or codology, but it seems to go down well with Callaghan and Bentley. So they say, Well, Miranda, consider yourself differentiated, and I say, Is that it? and they smile and nod. And the budget I gave them in advance, it's approved in a matter of days, and I begin setting myself up. And here I am, Fawcett & Jones, at your service, Angel.

I didn't know you knew so much about Irish art, Nina, I said. You gave me one of your looks. That's because I usually listen to you talk about it, Angel, you said, you do it very well. And anyway, when I started off, I didn't know that much, but then I made it my business to know. That's the challenge of the job, there's always something new to learn, you said, and I didn't know whether you spoke tongue in cheek, or not.

As I write, Nina, it is Thursday 28th July 2005, precisely three weeks after the bombing of London by radical Islamic terrorists, and the IRA has just made a statement calling upon all its units to 'dump arms' by four o'clock this afternoon, and instructing its volunteers to assist the development of purely political and democratic programmes through exclusively peaceful means. In other words, the IRA has said that its war is over, without using those precise words. And I wonder if the helicopter last night had anything to do with that announcement. For helicopters are about being seen and heard, as much as they are about seeing and hearing. They're a signal that something's happening, or about to happen. Part of the choreography, an audio-visual aid, if you like. The IRA statement was delivered on a DVD in a quiet Belfast accent by a former IRA prisoner, Seanna Walsh, a name which was pronounced variously by the political commentators, and to tell you the truth, I was not familiar with this supposedly Irish name myself. But that a real person should be assigned such a role was in itself significant, for previously all IRA statements had been issued by the pseudonymous P. O'Neill. Walsh was standing against a backdrop of green ivy in what I took to be his back garden, and I could hear a child crying and a blackbird singing behind him as he spoke the momentous words. So it seemed appropriate for me to write this letter with a Blackbird Self-Filling Pen, made by Mabie Todd & Co. Ltd of London in 1938, who also made Swan, Jackdaw and Swallow pens. It's a green Blackbird, done in various hues of marbled green, with black inclusions, the logo of a stylised blackbird in flight stamped on the body and the head of the clip. The gold nib glitters as I write. Any time I have a Blackbird in my hand I cannot help but think of the Early Irish poem my father taught me. You remember, Nina? I used to recite it to you:

> *int én bec*
> *ro léc feit*
> *do rinn guip*
> *glanbuidi*

*fo-ceird faíd
ós Loch Laíg,
lon do chraíb
charnbuidi.*

It was, I explained, a piece of marginalia, inscribed by a monk in the margin of his ecclesiastical text as he was distracted by the beauty of the moment. Or a piece of graffiti, you said, someone who wanted to say, I was here. Perhaps, I said, except that the someone is anonymous. And yet maybe we feel that we do know him, for all that he's nameless. It sounds beautiful, you said, what does it mean? Oh, it's untranslatable, of course, I said, and I've tried it different ways, all with their own failings. But it might go something like this:

> the little bird
> that whistled shrill
> from the nib of
>   its yellow bill:
>
> a note let go
> o'er Belfast Lough –
> a blackbird from
>   a yellow whin.

Whin, you said, we have that word in Yorkshire too. The whinny moors of Yorkshire. Somehow it's not the same as *gorse*, is it? No, I said, we speak a different language to the Southern English. And I went on to say that this was the first piece of writing – apart from practice runs – that I'd ever done on a typewriter. I wanted to see how it might look spaced out in regular type, for all that it had originally been done with a goose-quill and oak-gall ink.

I'd bought the typewriter, an Imperial Portable, in

Woolworth's in 1972, Saturday 4th March, to be precise. For some time it had been a custom for three or four of us to meet for coffee on Saturday afternoons in the Abercorn Restaurant, just across the street from Woolworth's. Paul Nolan would be there, we'd gone on Civil Rights marches together in the late sixties – 1968, the year of revolution, we saw ourselves as Belfast equivalents of the Paris students. And in 1968 we thought the thing would be over in a matter of months, things would change for the better, and everyone could get on with living their lives in a just society. Little did we know. Four years later we'd meet in the Abercorn and talk literature and art and politics, wondering where it was all going to end. It wasn't a regular date, but most Saturdays there'd be a casual gathering. Anyway, on this Saturday, as it happened, I was so engrossed by my Imperial Portable, excited by the prospect of trying it out, that I gave the Abercorn a miss. And so, for one reason or another, did my friends. Most Saturdays we'd be there; this particular Saturday we were not. At about four o'clock I was just about to board the bus home, the blackbird poem was in my mind, and I was visualising myself pecking out the words on the unfamiliar keyboard, when I heard an almighty explosion. The IRA never claimed responsibility for the Abercorn bomb that killed two young women – they happened to be Catholics – and injured more than seventy; but it was widely accepted that it was indeed the IRA, and it was one of the atrocities cited today as commentators cast their minds back over the years of the Northern Ireland conflict.

So the typewriter saved you, you said. The Imperial Portable. Who knows? I said. Maybe my father and mother saved me, when they taught me Irish. Maybe the Irish monk who wrote the poem saved me. Maybe the blackbird saved me, as it sang in a whin bush eleven hundred years ago. Maybe the worm it had just fed on saved me. When something terrible happens, everyone has their story about how they were saved – they'd forgotten their passport, and had to turn back for it, and so missed the plane that crashed a matter of hours later, how their bicycle had a puncture, if that splinter of glass had not been lying on the road at that precise spot, had the drunk not smashed his empty bottle on the pavement the night before, had the landlord not served him that last bottle to take out, why, they'd have been cycling past the scene of the explosion at about that time, they'd very likely be blown to bits, how they had a premonition, and decided to take the bus instead of the tube, how in hindsight they now knew what that dream they'd had two weeks ago meant, how in a vision they'd seen blood run down the glass of an aeroplane window, how they'd got drunk last night and called in sick that day, this or that random or purposeful interference with the normal pattern of their lives, tiny blips that become meaningful under the pressure of the extraordinary event, and so a series of coincidences, or what now seem to be co-incidences, is made into a narrative that makes some sense of what is beyond normal sense. But the stories only skim the surface. Who can say what circumstantial chain lies behind our actions, and our thoughts? Yes, you said, I often think of that, when I think of how my mother died. Because in many ways it seemed so unnecessary, so gratuitous. But then it is always difficult for us to imagine why someone should take their own life, you said.

As the noise of the helicopter dwindled away into the distance I heard a blackbird singing in the garden of Ophir Gardens, and I wondered what went on in the blackbird's mind, as it broadcast its lovely aria of loops and spirals, whether it merely delivered a territorial claim, or if it too revelled in the beauty of its song. I was still in that heightened state which sometimes accompanies lack of sleep when your postcard arrived, and it took me only a matter of minutes to recognise the source of your message. *Only an infinite present.* It was, again, a reference to Yves Klein. On 9th April 1951, he was in Madrid when he witnessed a display of American supersonic aircraft. They appeared like silver knives in the blue sky, he wrote in his diary that day, and traversed the hemisphere in a split second. Soon time will be conquered, and then we will no longer have past nor future, only an infinite present. I am determined to put all that I write, as well as all that I say, in the present – a perpetual present, said Klein. Later, when he presented his monochrome blue paintings to the public, he responded to accusations of charlatanism by saying, In the atomic era, where all material things can suddenly disappear – blasted out of existence – leaving room for only the most abstract things imaginable, one might be permitted to recount the following story, from ancient Persia:

One day, a flute-player began to play only a single continuous note. After he had repeated this performance for some twenty years, his wife suggested he might profitably listen to some other flute-players, who produced a range of sounds – high notes, low notes, notes in sequences, and so on – that might perhaps be more interesting and melodious. To this, the flute-player replied that he should not be blamed for finding the one note that others still sought.

And it sometimes occurs to me that all these letters of mine are but an attempt to discover one note, the one blue note that might explain why you did what you did, why you left me the way you did, because the more I think of it, the more inexplicable does it become to me. More inexplicable than it was then, for you were wholly guilty to me then, and so I burned your letters, because I wanted you to be dead to me.

But little by little your postcards have begun to change all that.
For you are very much alive, and I wonder what made you
choose this card, of Barkston Gardens Hotel, Earls Court,
London, a photograph taken at noon on a summer's day – the
trees are in full leaf, the sun almost directly overhead, as I can
see by the shadow of one of the parked cars – a scene of almost
spellbinding banality. Yet there is something eerie, almost
sinister about it. It is noon, yet the street is deserted. Out of
curiosity I looked up the hotel on the Internet, and I see it is
still a going concern, though it is now described as being in
South Kensington, which I daresay is more fashionable than
Earls Court. But this place looks like a location for a noir spy
thriller, photographed at a time which must long predate our
relationship. As you know, I am not expert in cars – I didn't
drive when I knew you, though I did learn, after my father's
death – but, apart from the venerable convertible parked in
the right foreground, the cars have a mid-1960s look about
them. Let's say 1965. And then I remembered your telling me
that your mother ended her life in 1965 in an Earls Court
hotel, that she had been saving her medication for months,
that she had booked herself into the hotel for a weekend, that
she had said goodbye to you that Friday morning as you left for
school – no, she had kissed you, something she kept only for
special occasions, you thought it strange at the time – and had
taken an overdose later that night. She was found the next
morning when the maid came to do up the room.

I cast my mind back to that night in New York when I
thought you bore the aura of your mother's perfume,
hawthorn blossom after rain, and you told me of your father's
time in the Erinoid factory at Lightpill, how he would lie
awake at night listening to the groans and clanks of the goods
trains, their whistles sounding in the dark like cries of happiness
or sadness, and then he would hear the triumphant shriek of

the Great Western express as it rushed past on its way to London, the long plume of its smoke borne like hawthorn blossom against the night sky. And he would think of you then, and of your mother. He didn't really speak about it until a couple of weeks afterwards, you said, and even then I wonder if he was speaking about her at all. You know, Nina, he said, one has to follow one's instincts. And he told you a story, how during the War he was faced with a choice, like that presented to a bomb-disposal expert, whether to cut this wire or that, except in this instance he had to decide quickly whether a telephone message received from a known double agent was a bluff or a double-bluff, whether the information was true or false. The decision he made resulted in the death of four men. I trusted my instinct, he said, and I cut the wrong wire, in a manner of speaking. But I had to trust myself, because if you don't trust yourself, who will? And there will be times when you are wrong, but at least you can say that you are true to yourself, Nina, said your father. I took it that he referred to some other wrong choice in his personal life, or to my mother's suicide, you said. Or that perhaps the two were connected.

Years later, when I suspected that he had been unfaithful to my mother during those two years in Stroud, I thought it unlikely that she would have condemned him for it; she was not given to those sort of moral judgements. But she did pride herself on her judgement of character, her judgement of situations, and the parameters that people set themselves. She'd made a career out of it. That's what her colleagues used to say about her, that she had great judgement, a great instinct for doing the right thing. I used to wonder what that meant, maybe it's some kind of epitome of what you are, that every choice is a summary of all the decisions you make in the past, you said, and I was struck by your use of the present tense, as if the past were somehow revisited, perhaps continually revised, by present thoughts, words, or deeds. Let's assume she finds out about my father's infidelity, if that indeed were the case, you said. I think she would have judged herself more harshly than him, because she had misjudged his character, someone she thought she knew as well as herself. That was what disturbed her most. And who am I to question that? How can we question our parents' instincts? you said. For it was those instincts that brought us into being.

Prompted by the memory of your father, I've taken up another Dutch-made pen, one from the same batch of 'new old stock' that included the Merlin. Like the Merlin, it languished in the time capsule of a Delft stockroom for some fifty-seven years, never inked until it came into my hands, and, apart from some gibberish written as a test run, these words concerning itself are the first it has written in its life, its purpose unfulfilled until now, as I inscribe its name, CIBA, on this page. It's an elegant little pen, given an almost funereal dignity by its black and pearl-grey livery, and I am reminded of standing at the grave of my own father, as I did two months ago on the anniversary of his death, gazing at the silver-grey lettering engraved on the black marble tombstone: Seoirse Mac Connmhaigh, as he styled himself, not the George Conway of his birth certificate. Through Irish he had become another person.

At the funeral it was remarked, by family friends and relatives I had not seen for years, how much I looked like Seoirse, or George, depending on what side they came from; it had never struck me, for I always thought I took after my mother. But when I looked in the mirror that night I could see a resemblance I had never seen before, and saw in my own face his bone structure, the grey eyes that were like his eyes looking back at me. I'd been given the privilege of casting the first spadeful of earth into the grave, and, as it pattered on the lid of the coffin, I thought of an expression that sometimes occurred in the old Irish stories he told me as a child. *Fód a bháis*, the sod of his death: the place where the hero is destined to die, explained my father. I imagined a patch of ground the size of a boot-sole which when trod upon opens a portal to the next life. Later on, I thought of a landmine. There is no avoiding one's sod of death, no matter what road we take in this, the journey of our lives, whatever purposeful meanderings or deviations, whatever U-turns or whatever sidetracks we make, the sod of death awaits us all, as surely as the CIBA pen, by whatever chain of tiny accidents, has reached my hand. Nor would I have looked for the CIBA, had I not been moved to become a collector of pens that day I saw my father's Conway Stewart, or one which resembled his, in the dusty annexe of an auction room.

CIBA is an acronym of the Swiss company Chemische Industrie Basel, whose Dutch subsidiary in Maastricht no longer makes pens, but it does still produce a wide range of electronic materials, inks, graphics, paper, plastics and rubber. It began its life in Basel in the 1850s producing fuchsine, a new chemical dye derived from coal-tar, so called because of its resemblance to the deep purple red of the fuchsia flower. In 1859, after the Battle of Magenta in Italy, in which the Franco-Sardinian alliance defeated Austria, the new colour was named magenta. The victorious general, Marie Edmé Patrice de Mac Mahon, was created Duke of Magenta by Napoleon III, and later became President of France. His ancestor Mac Mahon from Clare was one of the 'Wild Geese', the army of Patrick Sarsfield which, after its defeat at the Battle of Aughrim, and under the terms of the Treaty of Limerick of 1691, left Ireland for France.

There is an avenue Mac Mahon in Paris, one of those which

leads to the Arc de Triomphe. We did not walk it when we were there, but we did stroll along boulevard Magenta, and, scanning the blue signs of the intersecting streets, we could not resist taking rue de la Fidelité, which led us into rue de Paradis, where we found the Musée du Cristal. You remember, Nina, the displays of crystal urns and wine-glasses and baroque candlesticks and glass flutes and punchbowls multiplied a hundredfold in the mirrored rooms, the fantastic tinkling chandeliers composed of a thousand multifaceted pieces, chandeliers reflected by my later memory of those that glittered overhead that evening in New York at the Ambassador's reception. And I thought of Tommy Geoghegan, whom we met a few days later, quite by accident it seemed, in one of those dark lobby bars off Washington Square, all polished oak and brass and discreet waiter service. The violently blue suit he'd worn at the reception had been replaced by a light tweed jacket and a polo shirt, his red face had toned down to a healthy pink, and the mild boorishness he'd displayed that night now seemed like brash charm. I could see why people, as you'd said, would take him into their confidence. And he was intelligent. He'd begun by enquiring after my father. I didn't know you knew my father, I said. Yes, he said, I met him at one of those Esperanto conferences, in Dublin. Marvellous man, almost convinced me that Esperanto, by replacing English as an international language, would provide a shield for minority languages such as Irish. Quoted James Connolly the Irish rebel to me, did you know Connolly spoke Esperanto? said Tommy Geoghegan, and I confessed I didn't. Well, it fitted very well with Connolly's socialism, or communism, call it what you will, said Geoghegan, and of course it fitted very well with your father's ideas. What was it? for smaller nations to consent to the extinction of their language, would not hasten the day of a universal language, but would rather lead to the intensification of the struggle for mastery between the languages of the greater powers, I think Connolly said something like that. And of course Zamenhof thought the same, he had a vision of a world united by a mutual respect in which the smaller nations could participate as readily as the great powers. And, if you look at it, it's not unlike what we in MO2 are trying to achieve, even out the differences, said Geoghegan. I must say, Gabriel, I'm glad to see you with Miranda, a very special woman – you'd gone to the powder room by this stage – but then you don't need me to tell you that, he said, leaning forward confidentially, and I caught a whiff of his Old Spice aftershave.

Afterwards, I remarked on it disparagingly to you. Oh, I don't know, you said, it's a very underrated scent, very clean and smooth, nice lemon and lavender notes above the sandalwood, you shouldn't be put off by the name. Or the bottle. You remember the ad, *Girls like it – is there any better reason to wear Old Spice*? I've worn it myself, you said. Have you? I said, I hadn't noticed. Then it must have been when I wasn't with you, Angel, you said.

LOOK FOR A LONG TIME
AT WHAT PLEASES YOU

Croxley

Nothing is ever truly lost, my father used to say, for every thing in the universe is in the place where it finds itself, and is observed by God, who sees everything. By the same token, though I have so far failed to come across an equivalent of the red and black Dinkie pen that first attracted you to me, I know that my quest is not fruitless. I don't know how many thousands Conway Stewart made of this particular model, but, scattered as they might be across the world, some of them broken and cast aside, buried in landfills or in the backs of sofas, perhaps ground underfoot in a purposeful or careless moment, I trust that enough remain for one of them, one day, to find its way to me. Not that it will be identical to yours, for the parameters of each design allow for random variations that make each pen subtly individual.

The taxonomy of Conway Stewart pens is complex: serial numbers run from No. 1 to No. 1216, but the system is not chronological, for many of the higher numbers are early models, and vice versa; and each model comes in a range of colours and designs and sizes, with different caps, clips, bands, levers and nibs, so that the permutations run into the many thousands. Your Dinkie, for example, is a 540, but that number comprises over a hundred variations, of which your ring-top Red and Black Mottled Vulcanite is only one. I'm writing this with a Dinkie 540, as it happens, not a ring-top like yours, but one with a pocket-clip. I bought it from an eBay seller in Hong Kong, who told me it came from the last effects of a lady widowed by a colonial administrator, and its Peacock Plumage livery – a spilled petrol swirl of violets, emeralds, mauves, purples, sapphires, tortoiseshells and black, also known as Butterfly Wing – has an Oriental shot silk iridescence. It's too small for me to hold altogether comfortably, so it's difficult to control, but that makes me form my words all the more deliberately, watching the letters as they appear on the page to form these sentences. As a tribute to one of its many colours, I loaded the Dinkie with violet ink, and its unfamiliar smell reminds me that there are little perfume atomisers made to look like fountain pens: unscrew the cap, and instead of a nib you find a button that releases a glazed rainbow of scent when pushed – 'Parfum Exotique', aromas standing in for words. You remember, Nina, reciting Baudelaire's poem as we stood by his grave in Montparnasse. It was Easter Monday, Cemetery Monday, as I dubbed it, for we had then gone on to the necropolis of Cimetière Père Lachaise, wandering the long avenues and intersecting alleyways between the graves and vaults and sepulchres of bankers and statesmen and princesses and movie stars and artists, mausoleums shaped like pyramids and beehives and gazebos, adorned with baroque marble angels and imposing statues of those interred beneath them.

We visited the grave of Oscar Wilde, which was fronted by a massive block bearing a winged Egyptian deity, its plinth covered with lipstick kisses. Marcel Proust's grave was an unexpectedly plain, flat, black marble slab. It seemed unvisited, but the equally simple grave of Colette – Colette who, like Lee

Miller, was one of your heroines – was covered with fresh cut flowers, and, as we approached, a young woman, whose frizzy hennaed hair shone like a beacon above her plum-coloured velvet dress, added a single tuberose lily. You know what the French say about the tuberose, you whispered. No, I said, what do they say? They say a young girl should not breathe its fragrance after dark, in case it might prove dangerous to her chastity. Colette was very fond of the tuberose. What is it she wrote? a cloud of dreams bursts forth and grows from a single, blossoming stem, you said. And it seemed that of all the flowers there the tuberose gave out its scent the most, a heady, almost luminous aroma. Though I don't know what it does to the cats, you said. The cats? I said. Yes, they say that cats visit her grave in droves every night, because she was very fond of cats, time spent with cats is never wasted, she used to say. I would have expected Lee Miller to have mentioned the cats when she visited Colette, but she didn't, you said, and you went on to recall Lee Miller's Colette piece, which appeared in the March 1945 issue of *Vogue*.

You'd imagined yourself there in Lee Miller's shoes, you'd memorised whole sentences of her *Vogue* piece, as if you had stepped back in time up the dark staircase into Colette's third-storey apartment in the Palais Royal gardens. Colette's sitting up in a bed covered with tawny furs, her frizzy hair like a halo against the cold light from the tall windows, you said. She talks about the black market, the end of the war, the erratic electricity supply, and then she enters her past, darting here and there to choose an object, or a book, but never leaving the bed, for I'm an extension of her body, her hand guiding my arm to reach an envelope of pictures from a high shelf, none of them in order, and they slither out all over the bed and off the bed as she skims through them, each summoning up an anecdote, which in turn attracts another object, a souvenir, a keepsake, a letter from Proust or a portrait of her by Man Ray, towards the bed. She's what, seventy-one, seventy-two, and her many lives run through my mind's eye like sepia flashbacks, you said, Colette the siren, the gamine, the lady of fashion, the diplomat's wife, the mother, Grand Officer of the Légion d'Honneur, Colette the author of the Claudine books which inspired a stage play and a whole range of products, Claudine cigars, Claudine uniform, Claudine soap and perfume, though Colette's own cosmetics shop went bust, and there's a many-layered aura in the tall-windowed room that's lined with bookshelves and alcoves, there's butterflies in picture-frames, and glass-domed jars with votive offerings in them, little floating hands and ships and acrobats, sealed in holy water. There's glass paperweights with flamboyant marble swirls in them, and snowstorms, and crystal balls.

Then she shows me the manuscripts, you said, the early ones neatly written in school exercise books, pink and blue printed covers labelled in purple ink. The later ones are a labyrinth of scrawls and crossings-out and arrows, from which she makes fair copies with big spaces between the lines, which in turn fill up with more alternatives and second or third thoughts, you said, more cancellations, and so the whole process of spinning the yarn begins again. Until I read Lee Miller on Colette I had no idea that Colette, the natural writer, as I'd thought of her, the mistress of the spontaneous phrase, worked in so laborious a manner. She shows me her pens, seven of them standing in a big blue jug. There's ones with broad soft nibs for first drafts, and ones with fine hard points for writing between the lines, and a special one bought by a special someone for her in the Twenties, that she uses when she's stuck. She keeps trying the switch by her bedside but the electricity's been off all day, and when I leave it's almost dark. I remember the last glimmers of light imprisoned in the crystals, and the iridescent blue of the framed butterflies, and the whites of Colette's eyes, you said, as if repeating a long-rehearsed quotation.

I take it you spoke French to her, I said. Well, Lee Miller did, her French was nearly perfect, you said. As is yours, I said, and you gave a self-deprecating shrug, but it was true, your French was much better than mine. I could read French with only occasional recourse to a dictionary, and I had felt a glow of self-congratulation when I discovered I could follow most of the Easter Sunday sermon in Saint-Eustache, but then the priest's enunciation had been exquisite, and I knew the theme – of darkness, light and resurrection – well enough from similar childhood sermons. It was familiar territory, and I knew the signposts. And I thought I could speak French reasonably well, but when I did, my collocutor, assuming I knew French well, would unleash a torrent of words in which my comprehension would immediately flounder. But you, Nina, were never out of your depth: French was a second element to you. Your whole body language would change as you spoke, adopting a vocabulary of Gallic shrugs, pouts, frowns and gesticulations, as if you were clothed by French, and became someone other than the one I thought I knew. I loved and admired you for it, and wondered sometimes if I envied you, if envy ever entered into love, for both are emotions, whereas admiration is dispassionate. And, half-jokingly, I'd propose that the whole world should indeed have learned Esperanto, for then we would not need to learn the languages of different nations in order to communicate with them. But that's precisely the point, you'd say, the point is the difference. *Vive la différence*, as they say. When I speak French, when I listen to French, I think differently, and I say things other than what I'd say, were I speaking English, you said. And of course I knew this myself, for Irish, after all, was my first language, and I not only thought differently in it, but felt differently. Or at least I did once, for now my Irish is like a ghost of itself behind my more accustomed English. As it was then.

We'd gone to Montmartre one day. From the steps of Sacré-Coeur, we gazed down at Paris, radiantly clear in the meticulous April light. I always think that Paris is like the French language, you said, the way it's departmentalised, as you pointed out the various districts, Saint-Germain-des-Prés, the Tuileries, the Latin Quarter, Montparnasse, the Invalides, the Marais. Of course the boundaries, the definitions, have been eroded over the years, but then so has the language, if you're to believe the academicians. But the old fabric is still there under all the changes. Look, over there, and you pointed to a green space in the distance, that's the Jardin des Plantes, rue Mouffetard's not far off, you can't see it, but we'll have to go there, they have a brilliant market, it's been on the go for centuries. It's this steep narrow street, it's packed with shoppers, stalls along the pavements, open shop fronts with their awnings out, butchers, trays of calves' liver and tripe and the lovely pot roasts they do, all parcelled up with butcher's string, it's a work of art, and those yellow chickens with the heads and feet still on them, then there's the greengrocers, big fat knobbly tomatoes, all kinds of fresh salad stuff, and the fishmongers, marble slabs awash with cod and halibut and seabream and ray and conger eel and lobsters and sea urchins, and God knows what other kinds of creatures, I know what they are in French, but I couldn't tell you the English for them. And the cheese counters are really unspeakable, I don't know how many hundreds of kinds they have, and you have all these smells wafting around, between the cheese and the fish and the fruit and vegetables and flowers, the smell of anchovies and olives and Gitanes. Then you come to the end of the street, you turn a corner, go down an alleyway, and you're in an empty Roman amphitheatre, it's been there since Paris was, if not before.

That's what I love about Paris, you never know what's round the next corner, you said; and from my small experience of the city, it seemed true. I remember especially the evening we dined early in one of the streets off rue Montorgueil. Chez Bibi, that was the place, we were the first customers, and Madame Bibi herself, as we supposed her to be, engaged us, or rather you, in a long colloquy regarding the merits of the food we were about to eat. And the food was good, if a little heavy, solid Bordelaise cooking with wine-reduced sauces, and the wine was good too. By the time we stumbled out, satisfied and half-dazed, rue Montorgueil was thronged with people out for the night, the restaurants and cafés overflowing on to the pavements, and the cool evening air was resonant with conversation and clinking glasses.

We walked north, we crossed a boulevard; suddenly, as if a curtain had descended, the buzz of rue Montorgueil died behind us and we entered a silent zone, a maze of grey deserted streets and alleyways, which turned out to be the garment district. You remember, Nina, how entranced we were by the window displays, the cards of loom elastic, buttons, needles, pins and hair-clips, reels of cotton thread displayed like colour charts, long fat bolts of pink and blue and green cloth, the dresses that seemed thirty years out of date, the tailor's dummies posed in attitudes of faint surprise? I never knew this place existed, you said, and I was somehow pleased that we were both foreigners now, explorers of a strange new world.

We turned a corner and for the first time we saw people: two women in their forties, maybe, each followed by a string of youngsters. Each carried a pillowslip. The bins outside the shops were overflowing with scrap material and oddments, and these families, we realised, were rag-pickers. Each would stop at a bin and rummage it quickly and professionally, choosing some pieces, discarding others, stuffing them into the bulging pillowslips. There was obviously a hierarchy of stuff, whether chiffon, organdie, tulle, lace, gauze, poplin, whether plain or patterned, whether this pattern or that, and we wondered why some pieces were deemed more valuable than others, for they all appeared equal to our eyes. And where did they all end up, what patchwork did they make? It's like something out of Victor Hugo, you whispered. We walked on, and in about two minutes we entered the red light district of Porte Saint-Denis to a swirl of competing perfumes.

Paris did indeed seem intricately classified, and had I known then what I now know about the history of artificial languages, I might have expanded your analogy of the city as language. For the earliest attempts at a universal language arose from the medieval idea that man, by reconciling himself to the City of God, in which everything had its proper place and purpose, might attain to a perfect knowledge of the universe. The whole sum of things might, it was thought, be brought by division and subdivision within an orderly scheme of classification. To any conceivable thing or idea capable of being expressed by human speech might therefore be attached a corresponding word, like a label, on a perfectly regular and logical system. Words would therefore be self-explanatory to any person who had grasped the system, and would serve as an index or key to the things they represented. Say you want to find a book in a library. You look it up in a catalogue, where you find its reference number – say, PZ0477.f.26D. If you have learned the system of classification of that library, the reference number would tell you where to find that particular book out of millions; moreover, it would indicate what kind of book it was. The initial P would at once place the book in a certain main division, and so on with the other numbers, till those at the end of the series would lead you to a particular bookcase, a particular shelf, and finally to the book itself.

Just so, a word in a philosophical language. I was not altogether surprised to learn that one of the most interesting of such languages was invented by a Frenchman, Jean François Sudre, a musician educated at the Paris Conservatory. Walking the city as a student, he had been struck by its many sounds, from the tolling of the church bells to the screech of a knife-grinder's stone. It struck him that all these had a musical value, which could be expressed by the seven notes of the scale, do, re, mi, fa, sol, la, si. As the city broadcast itself, so everything in the city, everything in the world, everything in the known universe, could be expressed as a series of musical notes, whether played or written. So he proceeded to make up his vocabulary from the seven syllables of the scale, according to principles of philosophical classification. Initial *do* indicated a class of key, that of Man, moral and physical; *dodo* gave a sub-class, religion; *dododo* a third sub-division, and so on. The other major classifications were *re*, clothing, household, family; *mi*, human actions, bad qualities; *fa*, country, agriculture, war, sea, travel (*fafa* stood for sickness and medicine); *sol*, arts, sciences; *la*, industry, commerce; and *si*, society, government, finance, police. By shifting the accent from one syllable to another, he formed within a single stem the verb, the noun of the thing, the noun of the person, and the adverb corresponding to a given idea.

Sudre published the principles of his language in 1817, calling it Solrésol, which meant 'language' in Solrésol, and he thought its resources practically unlimited, not least because such a system lends itself to all possible forms of graphic, phonetic, and optical expression. If the seven notes of the musical scale are pronounced in the ordinary way, you can speak the language like any other; but you can also sing it, or play it on an instrument; with bells and horns, you can communicate to a ship in distress; substitute the seven colours of the rainbow for the seven notes of the scale, and you have an optical language, to be spoken by means of flags, lanterns or rockets.

Enthusiasts of Sudre's language – they included Jules Verne and Victor Hugo – thought that elaborate works of oratory might be produced by means of son et lumière, or poems in the form of banquets, for the system could as easily appeal to the sense of taste. And it did not stop there, for perfumes might as easily be employed. The coloured knots of a textile rug could be a literal text, the pattern in a dress a commentary on its own style. To a speaker of Solrésol, birdsong might contain unintended meanings. I do not know, Nina, whether Baudelaire knew Solrésol, but it seems to lie behind that poem you used to quote to me, 'Correspondances', in which Baudelaire speaks of the trees of the forest giving forth confused words, of perfumes that are like the skin of babies, or green meadows, or oboe music; a world in which perfumes, colours, sounds, all correspond. Thus everything in the universe is meaningful. There are messages to be read in the stars, in the stones of the road, in the coloured lichens on a stone wall, if you look long enough.

Which brings me to your postcard, and what it says: *Look for a long time at what pleases you.* It's like something you might find in a fortune cookie. A bon mot in the bonbon. And I've looked at your postcard for a long time, because it pleases me to try to unravel its meaning. *Dolls, 1690–1700, Lord and Lady Clapham in formal dress, Photo © Victoria and Albert Museum*, according to the caption. I know these dolls, for I too saw them in the V & A Museum, where you must have bought this card, but then I did not look at them as messages from you. It was my last birthday, you remember, just last October, I was there, perhaps you too were there, when you bought this card and the other of *Two Dutchmen and Two Courtesans*, did you share the same gallery space as me, and breathe the air I breathed, did you brush against me unwittingly, unseeingly, or with full knowledge and complete consent? Would you have known me, whatever I'd become since last we met, or not? Whatever the case, the two cards must be connected. Because they both come from the same source, and they both come from you. Even when we buy postcards as souvenirs or decorative objects, we have a possible recipient in mind. And you must have been thinking of me then, you must have been thinking of us. Perhaps the *Two Dutchmen and Two Courtesans*, poised in their tentative minuet, could stand for the first stages of our relationship, our getting to know each other, wavering between ourselves as singletons, ourselves as couple; and Lord and Lady Clapham might be what we were towards the end, or rather – the thought has only now occurred to me – what we might have become, these two ensconced in their elaborate high-backed chairs, impassive and self-satisfied, their attitudes and dress unaltered through the centuries, had you not left me as you did. And as we become them, their dress becomes us well: I picture myself in the red coat with the over-big, redundant buttons, the nonchalantly tied silk cravat, the brocaded waistcoat, the wig of human hair; your outfit is slightly more modest, but the expression given to your face, it seems to me, is more circumspect, more calculating, that of a lady who is one step ahead of her consort, though convention demands her to be placed slightly behind. She takes the longer view of their mutual history. Is this how it ended up between us? Or is this what time might have done to us?

The Dinkie, being a Dinkie, doesn't hold a lot of ink, and it ran out on me two sentences ago, if questions are sentences. If you are reading this now (and I hope one day you shall) you'll have noticed the broken flow in the writing, where the last few words petered out and I had to go over them again, like picking up a dropped stitch in a piece of knitting, except of course with knitting you'd be using the same needles, whereas I welcomed the break as an opportunity to change pens, for my hand was getting cramp from the small Dinkie.

I pondered my choice for some time. Should it be the American Wahl Eversharp Doric in Silver Grey Web, an important, legal-looking instrument, whose twelve-sided columnar design recalls the Doric porticos of American courthouses, and which one can picture in the hand of a judge, signing procedural documents, or sentences? Or another Onoto made in the year of my birth, this one with a transparent amber barrel that shows what ink remains? Or the 1939 Conway Stewart 175, which, because of its dull and unprepossessing photograph on eBay, I was able to pick up for a song, hoping that a better pen lay behind its poor image, and so it proved, as a thorough cleaning brought out the glowing splendour of its Toffee Swirl with Rose and Mauve Inclusions body, while the gold trim shone up like new? Eventually I settled on this much plainer pen, one which could not be further from the gemlike iridescence of the Dinkie I laid down for it. It's a big black Croxley, made just after the War by the stationery manufacturers John Dickinson Ltd, and named after Croxley Mills in Watford. Here, in 1830, the original John Dickinson had set up his new 'continuous web' mechanised paper manufacturing process, which replaced the handmade techniques of the day. Dickinson had first made his name in the Napoleonic Wars, when he came up with a paper for cannon cartridges that did not smoulder after firing, thus preventing the many fatal premature explosions which occurred when a new charge was rammed down the barrel. Today John Dickinson plc is among the largest stationery manufacturers in the world. I wrote my notes for the Esperanto book in their Black n' Red notebooks. And, as it happens, I'm writing this on Dickinson Croxley Script A4 paper; you can see the watermark if you hold it up to the light. But this is all by the bye, for I only discovered this information a few minutes ago, after a Google search on John Dickinson, before I began writing this with the Dickinson Croxley pen. The reason why I chose it is because engraved on its barrel are the words

MANCHESTER UNITY OF ODDFELLOWS
The best Friendly Society

and, intrigued by this inscription when I first saw it on eBay, I could not resist buying it. I got it for a few pounds: Croxleys, though they are very solidly made, with great nibs, are not deemed to be as collectable as some other English pens, and the black colour, together with the inscription, lowers the value of this one even further. The Oddfellows, as I discovered, are an organisation akin to the Freemasons, claiming like them a leading role in the French Revolution, and an ancestry stretching back to biblical times, in this instance the expulsion of the Israelites from Babylon in 587 BC. And it struck me, in the course of remembering our relationship, that perhaps the organisation you worked for was a kind of Oddfellows, once a clandestine organisation with code-names and passwords, which had evolved into one which, ostensibly at least, worked for the greater good of society.

I remember your quoting to me a saying of Talleyrand's, *La parole a été donnée à l'homme pour déguiser sa pensée*, words were given to man to disguise his thoughts, and perhaps that is true, for though my writing here, as you can see, is as calm and measured as my choice of words, it would not have been so had I written to you first thing yesterday morning after seeing the Irish stamp on your card, and the Dublin postmark. Then, my hand would have trembled had I put pen to paper, for Dublin, as you know, was a turning point in our relationship, like a door that closes off one prospect and opens up another; and I did not know whether to feel pleasure or pain that you were on the same island as me. It was some hours before I could calm myself sufficiently to write. But at other times I have not so deferred the moment, I have responded immediately and honestly, you can see how my writing is wavered by excitement or emotion, the hurried scrawl of my words as they struggle to keep pace with my thought. And then again, because I sometimes do not know what to feel or think, I write slowly to discover what those thoughts or feelings might be, finding them sometimes to turn out quite differently to what I had expected, for whatever happened in the past, even the immediate past, is changed when viewed in retrospect.

We had gone to Dublin for the weekend to celebrate my promotion to Head Keeper of Irish Art at the Belfast Municipal Gallery. We'd known each other for a year. Six months before, the Assistant Keeper, Sam Catherwood, had dropped dead of a stroke; and some months after that Freddy Burrows, the Head Keeper, took early retirement. Although I was next in line, I didn't really expect to get the job; posts like this usually went to outsiders, so I was pleasantly surprised when I was told hours after the interview that I had been successful.

We stayed at the Shelbourne Hotel. I toyed with the idea of booking Room 217, where JFK and Jacqueline had stayed in 1958 during his presidential campaign, but it proved a little beyond even the means of my new salary. As it was, I managed to get 412, the number of Lee Miller's room in Hôtel Scribe, telling the desk not to let you know that I had asked for it in advance. So when the key was handed over, you were delighted. Great number, you said to the concierge, and you turned to me and laughed, and he smiled discreetly and said, Yes, madam, it's a very good room, overlooks the Green, I'm sure you'll be very comfortable there. Imagine, Angel, of all the rooms they could have given us, they give us Lee Miller's number in Hôtel Scribe, isn't that amazing? you said. Yes, I said, and did you know that James Joyce used to drink both in the Hôtel Scribe, and in the Shelbourne? Really? you said, and I said, Yes, really, though I didn't know it for a fact, it was more of a likely possibility, a way of letting you know that this was my territory now.

My job often brought me to Dublin, and I knew it well, whereas you'd only been there fleetingly. We ended up that night in Mulligans pub in Poolbeg Street, where Joyce set a scene from one of his *Dubliners* stories, 'Counterparts', it's one of those dark pubs where the light seems filtered through nicotine and settling Guinness, and the Guinness there is really very good, you remember? That paradoxical edge of bitterness behind the creamy-buttermilk-thick black. Do you know 'Counterparts'? I said, and you said, No. Well, it's rather a depressing story, really, there's this clerk in a law firm, Crosbie & Alleyne, Farrington, he's called, and he's supposed to be copying out this contract between these two parties, Bodley and Kirway, they're called, you know how it was in those days, dip pens and inkwells, no photocopying, and he's not really on the job, he's the kind of man who slips out for the odd jar every now and again, and his boss, that's Alleyne, he's got this broad Belfast accent, comes in and says, Where's the Bodley and Kirway contract? and Farrington makes some poor kind of excuse, he says, But Mr Shelley said, sir, he says, and Alleyne mimics him, he says, Mr Shelley said, sir, well, kindly attend to what I say and not to what Mr Shelley says, sir, says Alleyne, and when Farrington tries another excuse, Alleyne says, Do you take me for a fool? Do you think me an utter fool? and Farrington looks round him at all the other clerks, and pauses for effect, and says, I don't think, sir, he says, that that's a fair question to put to me, and all the clerks titter nervously at this impertinence, so of course the boss really flies off the handle then, and it ends up that Farrington has to make an abject apology to him, and he knows that from here on out his life is going to be hell in the office.

He badly needs a drink after all this, but he's just spent his last penny on the glass of Guinness he'd slipped out for when he was supposed to be copying the Bodley and Kirway contract, so he pawns his watch, he gets six shillings for it, and he goes on a pub-crawl, he meets these various cronies on the way, and he tells them the story of how he faced down the boss, he acts Alleyne shaking his fist in his face, then he acts himself delivering the smart remark, and who should come in but another crony, so he has to tell the story again, only better this time. And all this time he's standing the rounds, no one else seems to have any money.

Anyway, they end up in Mulligans, the small parlour at the back, we were in one off the snugs just off the front bar, and I gestured with the hand that wasn't holding my pint, down there, I said, they made it into an Art Deco bar in the thirties, it's really rather special in its own way, but this, and I gestured again, to the dark surroundings of the front bar, this hasn't changed since Joyce's time, and anyway, I said, two young women with big hats and a young man in a check suit come in, Joyce is very good on dress, one of the women's wearing an immense scarf of peacock-blue muslin wound round her hat, it's knotted in a great bow under her chin, and she's wearing primrose-yellow gloves up to the elbow, and Farrington starts to make eyes at her, he thinks she's making eyes back at him, but then when the party gets up to go she brushes against his chair and says, O, pardon! in a London accent, and he realises she's way beyond his class anyway, and he starts to think of all the money he's spent on his so-called friends, there's nothing he hates more than a sponge, and then someone proposes an arm-wrestling match, and Farrington gets beat twice by the one of the cronies he was standing drinks for, a mere stripling, and he ends up getting the tram home by himself, past the barracks, it's dark and cold and wet, he doesn't know what time it is, his watch is in the pawn, he's spent all his money that wasn't even his in the first place, and he doesn't even feel drunk, and when he gets home his dinner's cold and the fire's out, one of his boys tells him his wife's out at the chapel, and he starts to mimic him, Out at the chapel, at the chapel if you please! And he takes a walking-stick and starts to beat him, and the boy cries out, O, pa! Don't beat me, pa! I'll say a Hail Mary for you if you don't beat me, pa, if you don't beat me, I'll say a Hail Mary, and that's the end of the story.

You grimaced. Poor boy, you said, I don't suppose the Hail Mary did him any good. What a funny religion. Yes, I said, Joyce thought so too, but then who would he have been without the Catholic Church? You know, *Introibo ad altare Dei*. Speaking of which, I think we need another pint, and I went up to the bar for another two, and I was standing with a five-pound note in my hand trying to catch the barman's eye when someone brushed against me, and said, Sorry, and then took a little step back and said, Gabriel, Gabriel Conway! Despite the summer heat he was wearing a donkey jacket, and one of those Bob Dylan caps, he'd a beard, you remember him, and it took me a few seconds to place him, it was Hughie Falls, I hadn't seen him from university days, he'd been in the PD then, the People's Democracy, we'd gone on Civil Rights marches together, or at least he'd been on the same marches as me, so I ended up including him in the round, I was feeling expansive, and to tell you the truth, maybe I wanted to show you off to him, you were looking really well that night, sky-blue linen jacket, white linen knee-length skirt, red slingback open-toed shoes.

Anyway, we joined you in the snug, I introduced you to him, and in retrospect I think his eyes narrowed a little when he heard the name, Miranda Bowyer. Pleased to meet you, he said, and, leaning confidentially across the snug table, he started to engage me in a reminiscence of the old days, of the great victories we had won and the tragic setbacks we had suffered, and when the pints were finished he insisted on buying a round of half-uns, and these were going down nicely when he got round to asking me how I was doing. So I told him about the promotion, and his eyes definitely did narrow this time. So, he says, part of the establishment, is it? The cultural wing of the British war machine? And I took it for a typical Belfast heavy slagging, no real malice intended. Yes, I said, fully-fledged capitalist running-dog lackey, and went up for another round of whiskeys, or rather, just the two, you put your hand over your glass when I asked if you wanted another, and when I came back, Hughie Falls and you were engaged in some kind of animated discussion, and when I put the drinks down he began talking to me in Irish, bad West Belfast Irish, mangled grammar, terrible pronunciation, and I realised that he was quite drunk, not that we were entirely sober. And I also began to realise that his remarks before had been serious, or that the drink had made him serious, that and the bad Irish, for it wasn't the kind of Irish that could handle any subtlety of expression.

So I played along with it a bit, answering him in Irish, realising as I did that much of it was lost on him, I might as well have been talking Swahili, and then I got fed up with it and started to answer him in English, and this really set him off, he began to rant about how I'd betrayed my birthright, me above all people, who had the good fortune to have Irish as a first language, people would give their eyeteeth to have had that opportunity, or at least he said what he thought the equivalent might be in Irish, it came out something like the teeth of their eyes, and then he said, *Is fearr Gaeilge bhriste ná Béarla cliste*, better broken Irish than clever English, it was one of those tired old saws that Irish fanatics always ended up coming out with, and I said to him in English, Oh, piss off, Hughie, you know that's nonsense, and by the way, your broken English isn't much easier to follow than your broken Irish, and with that he slammed his glass down, the whiskey jumped out on to the table, Well, fuck you, Conway, he said in English, when the day comes you'll be one of the ones they string up from the lamp-posts, and he left.

What was all that about? you said. Oh, the usual, I said, that I'm a Castle Catholic, a collaborator with the occupying forces, you know, what he was saying when he first sat down, we thought it was a bit of a joke. Yes, you said, when you were up at the bar he asked me what I did, and when I told him, he more or less accused me of being a spy for the Brits, he brought up the imperialist war machine again. But of course if you see it from his point of view, well, maybe you are a bit of a Castle Catholic, don't you think so? Bought and sold for English gold? And I saw a glint in your eye I found difficult to fathom. Oh, come on, Nina, I'm just doing a job, and I do it well, I'm good at what I do, I said. Oh, no one doubts your ability, Angel, you said, but you know as well as I do that ability wasn't enough to get intelligent Catholics like you a job in the old days. Before you went out on those Civil Rights marches, back in the Sixties. When did you start in the Gallery? Oh, what year was it, 1975, I said. And what were you doing before that? you said. Well, nothing much, Nina, I left university in 1971, went on the dole for a year, did a clerking job for a year, saved up enough to go round Europe for a few months, came back, went on the dole again, read a lot of books. Quite typical for people of my generation, I said.

And then you got this nice job, you said, how did that happen? Well, I said, a bit exasperated, the way it usually happens, I saw the ad, I applied, I went for the interview, I got the job. Oh, come on, Angel, surely there was more to it than that, you said. No one encouraged you to go in for it? No, I said. You wouldn't by any chance have met a man in a bar? you said, you know, just a week or so before? Someone connected to the Gallery? Like John Bradbury? John Bradbury? I said, the collector, sits on the Board of Trustees, that John Bradbury? Yes, you said, I don't know any other John Bradbury. Well, now that you mention it, yes, I happened to meet him in the Wellington Park, you know, in the back bar, some of us used to gather there, I forget who introduced me to him, might have been John Hewitt, you know, the poet. Yes, you said, and you had a long and interesting conversation with him, did you not? Oh, come on, Nina, I said, what are you getting at? As it happens, I found him very charming, and he knew his art, unlike a lot of the others on the Board. He knew Gerard Dillon, we had a great conversation about him, and Bradbury was very interested to know my father knew him. As a matter of fact, he even knew my father, spoke highly of him, was knowledgeable about Esperanto. Knew a bit of Irish, for that matter, and what little he knew was better than Hughie Falls's Irish. So what? I said.

Well, you said, you wouldn't be where you are now had John Bradbury not happened to bump into you that night, you said. Oh, don't be ridiculous, Nina, we didn't even discuss the Gallery, it was just talk about art. Just talk about art, you said. He didn't mention the job at all? Well, I said, and I was struggling to remember that evening, we'd both ended up well jarred, and as I thought about it, I knew you were right, just before he left he said to me, I really enjoyed our chat, Gabriel, and oh, by the way, we're looking for someone in the Gallery, there'll be an ad in the *Irish News* next week, look out for it, won't you? He said something like that, I said. Yes, you said. That's because John Bradbury is MO2, you said. And so are you. So maybe Hughie Falls isn't that far off the mark. Don't be ridiculous, Nina, how can I be MO2 when I don't even know it? I said. You mean without your full knowledge and complete consent? you said. Well, Angel, you said, it's like this. Some of us know from the beginning what we're getting into, and we consent to it, and others don't, because it takes them a while to arrive at full knowledge, and when they do, either they give complete consent, or they don't. Some of them quit, the ones who take a long time take early retirement, whatever. Everyone of us has to make that decision, it just takes longer for some to arrive at it.

So now you know, what are you going to do about it? you said, and I didn't know how seriously to take you, I realised that you too were a more than a little drunk. I hesitated, and before I could reply, you said, You see, Gabriel, you really are rather naïve. You really do think that art exists in some superior realm, untouched by politics, without the intervention of the Powers That Be. But I'm different, I know what I've got into, and I go along with it, I've made that compromise, but you think of yourself as being uncompromising, and uncompromised. I've made my decision, but you think there's no decision to be made. You're undecided, even though you don't know it. But if it takes me to make a decision, then I make it, just as I could walk out the door of this pub now if I wanted to, you said. But you don't want to, I said weakly. No? you said, and you got up and walked out.

I sat there for a few long seconds, stunned, thinking this was only play-acting, that you'd be back immediately. Then I got up and went after you.

It was pouring rain outside, one of those July thunderstorms. I thought I glimpsed the heel of your red shoe disappearing down a side street, and I ran after you, but when I turned the corner, the street was dark and wet and empty. I ran on anyway, thinking maybe there'd be an alleyway you might have taken, and there was, I ran down that alleyway, and down another, but you were nowhere to be found. Then I went back to the pub, thinking you might have relented and returned, I went up to the barman and asked him if you had come back, you know, the good-looking girl with the dark hair I was sitting with, she was wearing a light blue jacket, white skirt, and he looked at me pityingly and said, no, she hadn't been back, but you never know, would I like another drink in the meantime. And I said, yes, I'll have a large Powers, for I could think of nothing else to do, and I still held out hopes that you might return, and I sat there drinking until closing time.

I stumbled along the corridor of the fourth floor of the Shelbourne and jiggled the key in the keyhole of Room 412, trying it this way and that until eventually it swung to. A bedside lamp was on and you were lying in bed with your eyes open. It took you a long time to come back, Angel, you said. And I lay down with you, and after a while we entered that realm which is so familiar yet so strange, where we lose each other in ourselves, and wonder if we are who we are, or someone else, and then we fall asleep still not knowing. Now I remember the perfume you put on that night before we went out, and the square-shouldered black bottle that it came in, *Fracas* by Germaine Cellier, 1948, a needle-sharp tang of bergamot above a shadowy musky stink of tuberose. And now

I remember the corollary of that phrase of yours I read two days ago, *Look for a long time at what pleases you.* You'd quoted it to me in Paris when you talked about Colette, apropos of what I can't recall. You know what Colette says? you said, and I said, No, what does Colette say? and you said, Look for a long time at what pleases you, and a longer time at what pains you.

IN DREAMS BEGIN
RESPONSIBILITIES

Conway Stewart Scribe Camouflage

I realise that my last letter was somewhat longer than those I had previously written. So many connections are beginning to occur to me, and that letter could have been even longer. I failed to mention, for example, that your postcard bore not just one Irish stamp, but two, one of them a 4c, the other a 48c, whose combined value, I thought, must exceed that required for a postcard to Northern Ireland, so your choice of them must have been deliberate. As you know, I was a stamp-collector in my teens, specialising in the stamps of Ireland, which appealed to me not only out of nationalistic sentiment, but because Irish stamps have always had a tradition of good design. These are no exception: they belong to the Irish Wild Flowers series of 2004, designed by the artist Susan Sex, and feature elegantly simple representations of the Violet (4c), the Dandelion (5c), the Primrose (48c), the Hawthorn (60c), the Bluebell (65c), Lords and Ladies (€2) and the Dog Rose (€5). That your card should bear a violet was especially significant, for you knew that it would remind me of John Donne's poem 'The Ecstasy', which we used to quote to each other:

Where, like a pillow on a bed
A pregnant bank swell'd up to rest
The violet's reclining head,
Sat we two, one another's best.

I would begin, and you would reply with

Our hands were firmly cemented
With a fast balm, which thence did spring;
Our eye-beams twisted and did thread
Our eyes upon one double string ...

and so on, till, holding hands and staring into one another's eyes, we would recite the last verse in unison. As for the primrose, it symbolises resurrection, among other things, but 'the primrose path of dalliance' also springs to mind. So you flit between alternatives, following the butterfly nature of your star sign. But you knew I would pick up on the stamps, for you were slightly bemused when I told you of my teenage passion for stamps; and perhaps you remembered Walter Benjamin's essay, 'Stamp Shop', which I'd quoted to you as evidence that stamp-collecting could be an intellectually respectable pursuit. To someone looking through old piles of letters, says Benjamin, a stamp that has been long out of circulation on a torn envelope often says more than a reading of dozens of pages. And, further on: Stamp albums are magical reference books; the numbers of monarchs and palaces, of animals and allegories and states, are recorded in them. Postal traffic depends on their harmony as the motions of the planets depend on the harmony of the celestial numbers, said Benjamin.

Perhaps it was not entirely unexpected that the son of a postman should have become a stamp-collector: my very first collection was of the foreign stamps my father would bring home, having begged them from the addressee, and I still remember the pleasure given to me by those glimpses of exotic lands, the black swan and the lyrebird of Australia, the springboks of South Africa, the tigers of Malaya. You remember, I told you how one day he arrived home with a rare item, a postcard he had discovered at the back of the dead-letter box, bearing an Edwardian stamp with a 1903 postmark, and the phrase, in what looked like a woman's handwriting, *See you tomorrow, usual place and time, Yours, ever, N.* Those were the days, said my father, when you could post a card in the morning and be sure that it would arrive by that afternoon. He was an occasional reader of science fiction, and suggested playfully that the box had a slit in its back which was a portal to another universe, parallel to ours, but sixty years behind, through which the card had slipped. And I wondered who N might have been, whether in this universe or that, and what the consequences of her correspondent's likely failure to attend the assignation. At any rate, the card, with its implications of alternative existences, led my father to remember Edmund Edward Fournier d'Albe, who had been elected as Chairman of the Irish Esperanto Association when it first met in 1907, and whom my father met towards the end of his life. He was very old, said my father, but he still radiated a powerful intelligence, an extraordinary man, both his Irish and his Esperanto were perfect, and poetic.

Fournier d'Albe was indeed an extraordinary figure, a Fellow of the Institute of Physics, Vice-President of the Radio Association, and the author and translator of numerous scientific books. He shared the year of his birth, 1868, with James Connolly. He was a fluent speaker of German, French, Italian, Irish, Manx and Esperanto, and had published an Irish–English dictionary and phrase-book. In 1912, the year of the sinking of the *Titanic*, he invented the type-reading optophone, which, by converting the light refracted from a page of printed matter into musical notes, enabled a blind person to read. He was responsible for the transmission of the first wireless picture – of King George V – on 24th May 1923; and in 1926, at the 18th World Congress of Esperanto, held in Edinburgh, he delivered a paper on 'Wireless Telegraphy and Television'. In 1907 he published *Two New Worlds*, 'an attempt to penetrate the mystery of time and space with the help of the most modern resources of scientific research': in it, he proposed a hierarchical clustering model for the structure of the universe which anticipated modern fractal theory. Fournier's fractal can be visualised if we take one of a pair of dice and look at the side representing the number 5, known as 'Phoebe Snow' in gambler's slang. Four of the dots are located at the corners of a square and the fifth is located at the centre. Let us imagine that each dot is really a miniature Phoebe Snow, and further, that each dot of the miniature Phoebe Snow is a microscopic Phoebe Snow. This constitutes three scales of the self-similar structure; but Fournier d'Albe went much further and imagined the pattern repeating ad infinitum, in a dizzying blizzard of self-replication. Worlds lay within worlds in nested frequencies. Atoms and stars, electrons and planets, cells and galaxies all moved to the same measure. Clouds, coastlines, earthquakes, the fluctuations of the stock market, all corresponded. A flag snaps back and forth in the wind, and a column of cigar smoke breaks into an anxious swirl. A pirouette of litter on a street corner heralds a tornado. A pin drops in an auditorium, a bomb goes off. Like patterns were apparent everywhere. The All was immutable, but the detail was ever new. The event, the incident, the individual was unique, unprecedented, irrecoverable; but the equilibrium was eternal.

In addition to his other achievements, Fournier d'Albe was a noted investigator of paranormal phenomena. While he recognised that the vast majority of these were spurious, a matter of imposture and the desire of many people to believe in an afterlife, or to believe in anything, there nevertheless remained some instances that were inexplicable to science; and he thought that these might be accounted for by some kind of slippage between the infinite worlds proposed by his theory. He was familiar with the work of W.J. Crawford and had corresponded with him briefly before his suicide in 1920. In May 1921 he travelled to Belfast, where he took up lodgings for four months, during which time he conducted an intensive study of the phenomena produced by the Goligher circle. After observing a séance at the Morrison home, and another at the late Crawford's, Fournier d'Albe rented an unfurnished attic at 40 Fountain Street, in the city centre, to which he transferred the equipment used by Crawford; and here he conducted investigations into a further eighteen sittings, summarising his findings in a monograph, *The Goligher Circle*, published by John Watkins of London in 1922.

He had gone to Belfast hoping to find a medium who was somehow in touch with an alternative reality, a correspondent with another universe. But as he subjected Kathleen Goligher to more and more rigorous controls it became apparent that trickery was being used, and he came to 'a definitely unfavourable conclusion regarding the whole of the phenomena'. A final sitting on 29th August produced no results. Kathleen Goligher indicated that due to indisposition she would not be giving any sittings to Fournier d'Albe, or to anyone else, for at least twelve months; and she never again submitted herself to scientific scrutiny. Fournier d'Albe had found the Goligher Circle to be 'an alert, secretive, troublesome group of well-organised performers'. He seemed to have proved conclusively that the 'operators', far from being agents of a world beyond the grave, were none other than the members of the Goligher Circle themselves. Yet Fournier d'Albe's findings were disputed by those who wished to believe, and to this day there were still those who believe in Kathleen Goligher's ability to produce ectoplasmic rods and cantilevers, just as there are those who believe in Uri Geller, or the reality of alien visitations.

D'Albe kept a meticulous record of his dealings with the Goligher Circle, going so far as to note the weather at the time. I learned that the summer of 1921 was a typical Irish one: 1st June, for example, was showery and cool, while 6 June was hot and sunny. I was much taken by the coincidence that 40 Fountain Street, where the sittings took place, is the current location of the XL Café, and, as I read these brief reports of the weather, I imagined myself walking along the street one of those June days, feeling the breeze or the rain or the sun on my face, before going in for a cup of tea, where I might meet your counterpart. Then it occurred to me that the circumstances might not have been so idyllic.

D'Albe's stay in Belfast coincided with a period of civil unrest that came to a head shortly after the opening of the first parliament of Northern Ireland on 22nd June, when Catholics were driven en masse from their homes and jobs by the UVF. There must have been gunshots to be heard as well as the rappings produced by the Goligher Circle, for the UVF had attacked Catholic homes in the New Lodge Road, not far from the city centre. My own father's father had been expelled from his job as a fitter in Harland and Wolff's, the shipyard that built the *Titanic*. In an attempt to discipline the loyalists, the government in Westminster recruited a Special Constabulary, but when a number of them joined Protestant mobs in Belfast on 10 July, they came to be regarded as enemies of the Catholic community. *Plus ça change.* The Specials were part of the loyalist mob which infamously attacked the Civil Rights march at Burntollet Bridge on 4th January 1969. Hughie Falls was there, among the injured, and his photograph appeared in the *Irish News*. Long-haired, bearded, eyes staring wildly, blood pouring from a head wound, he cut a heroic, Christ-like figure, and for many months afterwards did not lack female companionship.

Is that the Hughie Falls you knock about with? my father asked me when he saw the picture. Yes, I said, not being inclined to deny him. Well, said my father, he might be a hero, but his father, Tommy Falls, was a rogue. How's that? I said. He was a scab, said my father, he broke a postal workers' strike back in the Thirties. And how did the strike end up? I said. My father sighed. Oh, we had to go back, without a penny more than what we started with. So it was pointless anyway, I said, whether Tommy Falls was a scab or not. Not pointless, said my father, it was a matter of principle. Of comradeship. And that was the end of that conversation.

You knew my father a bit, Nina, you knew he was a man of principle. And yet. You remember that time he bumped into us in the XL Café? He had taken quite a shine to you, you know, I think sometimes he even flirted with you a little. There'd been a little item in the paper about him that morning, about his work with Irish and Esperanto, how he'd kept them going when it was neither profitable nor popular, that kind of thing, and you complimented him on it, wondering how he'd found the time for it when he was working – he'd been retired a year by then – that his job as Inspector in the Post Office must have quite demanding. Oh, not at all, he said, I was a bit of a straw boss, you know, I just put in an appearance every now and again, and I could nip out whenever I wanted to, like now. The postmen did the real work, the way I used to.

It's like this, he said, I was given an offer I couldn't refuse. Gabriel's mother put me up to it, it was all her fault, he said, and he winked ruefully at me, for I knew the story well. Yes, he said, it was just after the War, the top brass approached me, said if I went for Inspector, I'd have no problem, only I'd have to go on a training course to London. And the last thing I wanted to do was to go to London, you see, conscription was still in force then, on the mainland as they call it, and I didn't want to risk that, being a member of His Majesty's Armed Forces, it would go against everything I believed in, said my father. But you went anyway, you said. Yes, said my father, it was either that or a lifetime of misery from Gabriel's mother. But you escaped, you said. By the grace of God, said my father. But you work for Her Majesty's Royal Mail, you said boldly, raising your eyes to the Crown insignia on his peaked cap. But I don't carry a gun for her, said my father, the pen is mightier than the sword, and anyone can hold a pen freely, be he Irish or English or Catholic or Protestant. It was the Irish who brought the pen all over Europe, the monks who held the flame of learning aloft throughout the Dark Ages. In this sign shall you conquer. That's what I've tried to teach Gabriel. Do you think I've succeeded, Miranda? Oh yes, Mr Conway, I'm sure you have, you said, and you fondled the little Dinkie that dangled at your breast. Nice pen, said my father.

When he left, I told you the other side of the coin, that my father had been interned for six weeks in 1941, suspected of being a member of the IRA, which in Belfast at that time consisted of a few dozen militarily incompetent idealists. I think the Powers That Be thought they might be in league with the Nazis, which maybe wasn't too far from the truth in the case of the more fanatical elements, I said. Maybe your father's promotion was a quid pro quo for his imprisonment, you said. First they give him the bad news, then they give him the good news, you know, bad cop, good cop routine. That's a bit far-fetched, Nina, I said. There was what, a seven-year gap between his internment and his promotion, do you think they work that far ahead? Or that far in retrospect? Well, you never know, you murmured. No, I said, the interesting thing was, it was a case of mistaken identity, my father had nothing to do with the IRA, the person they wanted was his twin brother, Gerry, they lifted George instead of Gerry. Anyway, they got Gerry too. He was in for the duration, they let him out in 1945, I said. And what happened to him? you said. Oh, he died in 1964. Heart attack. It was the first time I saw my father cry. When the news came – this uncle of mine, Joe Marley, they called him the Angel of Death, because he always got the job of breaking the bad news when there was a death in the family, or in a neighbour's family, for that matter – he came to the door, my father answered it, and he knew by the expression on the Angel's face, he didn't have to be told, that Gerry was dead. And he burst into tears, he sobbed for a good half hour.

He died young, you said. Yes, I said, after Gerry got out of prison, it was difficult for him to get work, as you might guess, just the odd casual job working in the bakery or the docks. He'd give most of his wages to my Auntie Maureen, and save a little for himself, enough to go on a monthly binge. He wasn't a heavy drinker, you understand. It was a very controlled thing, once a month for years, he'd go out on a tear, all the pubs of the Falls Road, or quite a few of them, for there were a great deal of pubs in the Falls then, each with their own wee quirks and characters. Joyce would have had a field day there. And my Uncle Gerry would come home speechless with drink, and fall into bed and sleep all the way through the next day. Then he'd get up as if it never happened, the monthly oblivion. But I like to think he had some crack along the way. He was a great storyteller, like my father, and like him he read a lot of books, taught me to play chess. And oh, yes, he collected stamps. He gave me his stamp album before he died. A more innocuous man you couldn't imagine.

They put the Tricolour on his coffin when they buried him, I helped to carry the coffin, I still remember the weight of it and the way it cut into my shoulder, I was only sixteen. And perhaps I never fully understood then why my father had been so deeply affected, but now I think he must have felt guilty, because Gerry had done real time for Ireland, and he hadn't. And my father was the Irish speaker, Gerry wasn't. Gerry was a foot soldier, but my father must have admired him for the stupid courage of his convictions, Gerry who was just as intelligent as him, if not more so. My father had done well in life, George had done well, and Gerry hadn't. George had compromised with the Powers That Be, and Gerry hadn't. George took the King's shilling; Gerry remained penniless, I said. But your father was right, to take the opportunity to advance himself, you said. But he didn't particularly want to advance himself, it was my mother who wanted him to advance himself, I said. And you, Angel, what about you? you said. What about me? I said. Well, isn't there some kind of parallel of compromise here, like father, like son? you said. And we began to rehearse an argument which by now had become familiar.

When I began this letter yesterday I had a suspicion I would get round to my uncle's story sooner or later, so I've been writing this using two pens alternately, a paragraph in one, a paragraph in the other. One is a Kingswood in Pearlised Blue Onyx, which demanded to be chosen not for its attractive colouring, but because engraved on its cap is the inscription

WALDRON WELCOME HOME
1939–45

from which I presume that it was one of a batch given to the homecoming soldiers of Waldron, a village in East Sussex which lay in Bomb Alley, where German aircraft would drop their bombs on their way to and from London. Most of its young men went to the war, and twenty-two of them died in action. Those that survived were given a pen, mightier now than the sword, as they entered civvy street. I wonder how many of those pens found employment; this one, at any rate, has seen some action, for there is a ghost of a personalised scratch to its nib as I write, and it sends a shiver up my spine to think that I touch what he once touched, that I hold in my hand an instrument held by the hand of a soldier. The other pen is a Conway Stewart Scribe made in 1941 or so, in green and brown patchy swirls veined with black, a pattern known as Camouflage. If you lost this pen in a field, it would be difficult to find. But the pen led me to discover that the Surrealist artist Roland Penrose had been one of the Chief Advisors to the Camouflage Development and Training Centre set up in 1940 by the War Office, and was the author of *The Home Guard Manual of Camouflage*. He was also, at that time, conducting an affair with Lee Miller, whom he married in 1947. He had painted his own car in a disruptive pattern, and on one occasion had experimented with a matt green camouflage cream, which he smeared on the naked body of his lover as she lay on the grass of a friend's garden, covered with netting taken from the raspberry patch. Penrose was delighted with the results, declaring that if you could hide such eye-catching attractions as hers from the invading Hun, smaller and less seductive areas of skin would stand an even better chance of becoming invisible.

Penrose was not the only artist involved with camouflage; in fact, its principles had first been outlined in 1897 by the American painter Abbott H. Thayer, in an article called 'The Law which Underlines Protective Coloration'. The spectator, he said, seems to see right through the space really occupied by an opaque animal. Nature, he believed, acts like an artist, and the study of these optical effects belongs to the realm of pictorial art and can only be interpreted by painters. For art and camouflage are two sides of the same coin: art makes something unreal recognisable, the other makes something real unrecognisable. Thayer also thought that the concept might have military applications, but these were not followed through until the First World War, when Lucien Victor Girand de Scévola, an artist serving in the French infantry, established the first *Section de Camouflage*. He was influenced in his approach by the Cubist work of Picasso, in which familiar things – bottles, pitchers, glasses, newspapers, the paraphernalia of café life and conversation – were taken apart and put together again in a series of flat, intersecting planes, sometimes showing different aspects of the same thing simultaneously. I well remember at the beginning of the war, wrote Gertrude Stein, being with Picasso on the boulevard Raspail, when the first camouflaged truck passed by. It was night, we had heard of camouflage but we had not seen it, and Picasso, amazed, looked at it, saw it, and then cried out, Yes, it is we who made it, that is Cubism. And a playful remark made by Picasso to Jean Cocteau, that the army would better dazzle the enemy if they were dressed in harlequin costumes, might have led indirectly to the concept known as 'dazzle painting'.

Developed by the marine painter Lieutenant Commander Norman Wilkinson in 1917, dazzle painting, rather than trying to blend in with the sea and sky, which are visually inconstant, used a system of stripes, blocks, zigzags and disruptive lines to confuse enemy observers. The intention was not to hide the object, but to make it unfamiliar. For much of our ability to identify what we see is based on our experience of seeing similar things in the past. Vision depends on memory. In our memory is stored a vast thesaurus of images, to which we constantly refer when looking at the world, so that we can identify a thing quickly without spending time working out what it is. And the art of illusion depends on this visual process: Roland Penrose, for instance, had collaborated with the stage magician Jasper Maskelyne, who was practised in making his audience see things that were not there, and not to see things that were there. W.J. Crawford, examining the phenomena produced by the Goligher Circle, jumped to the wrong conclusions because he already knew what he wanted to see; he was led astray by his expectations, and possibly his desire, for his attraction to Kathleen Goligher is evident in his writings. He was beguiled by love and memory, just as we retain the image of the loved one long after she has gone from our sight. And Nina, I never lost sight of you through all these years of your absence from me, much as I tried to. Oh, after three or four years I thought I had forgotten you, but then you would appear to me in dreams, unbidden, and I would consent to the reality of your presence, even when I knew I was dreaming.

We can easily suspend our disbelief in dreams because they are so wonderful. When I was younger I would fly in my dreams, soaring and swooping like an angel above the city, seeing it spread below me like a map, and when sometimes it occurred to me that it was impossible, that I must be dreaming, I used that lucidity to revel in the experience, and I would fly with even more spectacular agility.

So it was when I dreamed of you. Most of the dreams took place in cities that resembled Belfast, or cities I had visited with you, like New York, Paris, Dublin and Berlin, or cities I had visited alone, like Lisbon, Rome, and Prague, or cities I had never visited, like Tokyo and Madrid. I would be walking along a crushed cinder path by a dark canal in the shadow of a semi-derelict factory when I would catch a glimpse of the heel of your red shoe vanishing under the arch of a bridge, and I would hurry to catch up with you, half-walking, half-running, till I came to a flight of stone steps, I could hear the click of your heels as you ascended and the steps became an alleyway between high blank walls that led to a street of closed shops, which led in turn to a row of mean houses with incurious pale children loitering by the doorways, who barely took you under their notice as you passed by, for I can see you clearer now as the gap between us closes, you are wearing an apple green 1920s jacket with a pink floral print pleated dress that sways a little against the sway of your hips as you turn off into an entry that takes you into a close, and I follow you through a doorway into a gloomy room, it looks like a workshop, for it smells of oil and metal and a massive lathe gleams in the corner, and now you pause at the foot of the stairs, and turn towards me, and I see your face for the first time, and you smile wordlessly, beckoning with your eyes as you lead me up the stairs to a bare attic with a mattress on the floor, where you take off the jacket and the dress and the 1920s flesh-tinted bra and pants and garter-belt and stockings, we both lie down, and we are about to embrace each other when I wake.

It now occurs to me that the attic resembles the attic where the Golighers held their séances. Here, W.J. Crawford had conducted experiments that proved to his satisfaction that Kathleen Goligher could extrude psychic matter, or 'plasm' from her body – from the join of the legs, as Crawford delicately put it – to form semi-flexible rods and cantilevers which could lift a small table, manipulate hand-bells and trumpets, and create various sound effects which gave coded answers to questions asked of the unseen 'operators' of the structures. The operators, according to Crawford, were independent spirits who, having passed through the portal of physical death, wished to communicate to us that death was not the end of being, but the beginning of a new life. The world in which they lived was contiguous to ours, and very like it in many respects, for it had mountains, lakes and rivers, as real to them as ours were to us, so much so that many of the operators referred to our world as the shadow world, and theirs as the real one. The psychic structures were a link between the two worlds. Crawford, after numerous experiments, succeeded in obtaining impressions caused by these structures in a dish of clay. He discovered that when Kathleen Goligher wore stockings, the impressions were lined with stocking marks.

The common-sense explanation for this phenomenon, that the marks had indeed been made by a stockinged foot under cover of the darkness of the séance room, was contemptuously dismissed by Crawford. He had taken every conceivable precaution against any such imposture. The medium's hands were held firmly by other members of the Circle, while Crawford tied her legs to her chair with a variety of ligatures, including whipcord and black silk bands. He theorised that the psychic structures were covered by a film of matter which oozed round about the interstices of the stocking fabric. Being of a glutinous, fibrous nature, it assumed almost the exact form of the stocking fabric. It was then pulled off the stocking by the operators, built around the end of the psychic structure, which, when placed in the dish of clay, naturally left an imprint similar to a stocking. But the thing that left the mark was not a foot in a stocking, said Crawford.

Convinced that he was on the brink of something extraordinary, nothing less than a scientific proof of immortality, Crawford went over his findings again and again. He began to experiment with different types of stockings, and more elaborate restraints. He purchased brown stockings, blue stockings, white stockings, and grey stockings for the medium, made out of different fabrics – wool, cotton, silk. Sometimes he had her wear stockings of a different design on each leg. He encased her legs in high boots. He made a special box with a bar which was locked over her feet; a piece of wood was then tightly fitted around the tops of her ankle and screwed into the top of the box. Nevertheless the plasm was able to force its way up the foot and leg of the medium, between her stocking and the tightly laced long-legged boot.

When he asked the operators to levitate the table they did so with ease. He filled a tin dish with a very watery white clay, and asked them to dip the end of a structure in the clay and leave marks on the floor. Soon afterwards, he heard them do just that. The dipping sounded exactly like a cat lapping up milk. Crawford had a fine ear for acoustic textures. Sometimes 'peculiar fussling noises' were heard in the region of the feet just prior to phenomena. He noticed that when the medium wore thin silk stockings the noises were accentuated. They occurred in spasms, and were caused, thought Crawford, by the friction of the psychic particles on the stocking fabric. Many people interested in psychic matters, said Crawford, assumed the evolution of the plasma to be a quiet and tranquil affair; but of course nothing could be wider of the mark. Considerable labour attended the production of the phenomena, and the medium was sometimes heard to groan as if undergoing birth-pangs. Crawling under the table in the dark, he had felt her feet at such moments, and had noted a whirlpool of internal muscular movement round foot and ankle and the lower part of the calf. He also felt a flow of material particles from the medium's ankles and legs, cold and disagreeable to the touch. Further, when he placed his hands on the outside of her haunches, he could feel little round packets of psychic stuff filling in on the backs of the thighs; and when he felt her breasts during the occurrence of psychic action, they became very hard and full.

Crawford's posthumous publication, *The Psychic Structures at the Goligher Circle*, is comprehensively illustrated. There are many photographs of stockings, the fabric of some showing signs of being ruffled and distended, as though severely mauled by the transit of the psychic matter through the extremely narrow passageway between boot and stocking, thought Crawford. It was well known that photography would show up faint processes invisible to the naked eye, and enable minute comparisons to be made, he said. Photographs of imprints made by real stockings in clay were compared to those made by psychic simulacra of stockings, and found to be remarkably similar. Enlarged, these impressions took on curiously abstract forms, as the white clay, like the surface of a moon, was dented, hollowed, dimpled, ribbed, and pitted by the fabric. Strangest of all is the series of twenty-six photographs which conclude the book. These purport to show the psychic structures extruded from the body of Kathleen Goligher. To a disinterested observer, however, the structures look like strips of white fabric – linen, perhaps, for the Golighers worked in the Belfast linen mills. Crawford has labelled the photographs, from A to Z, and provided explanatory captions, for example, 'A plasmic column under the table, used when very powerful levitations are required'. For all the world it looks as if someone has tied a bandage to Kathleen Goligher's ankle, and pinned the other end to the underside of the table. The other photographs, 'Plasma collected near the feet of the medium forms into a lump and advances along the floor', 'Plasma inside the medium's shoe', and so on, are no more convincing. If anything, they are proof that Crawford was deceived by a cheap conjuring trick, the whole business quite literally fabricated.

And there is something deeply disconcerting about the photographs. As I tried in vain to see how they might be amenable to Crawford's interpretations, it struck me that their atmosphere of pathological derangement lies in how they contravene the rules of portraiture. They show a female figure seated in a Windsor chair against a black backdrop, the upper half of her body draped with a black cloth. They are, presumably, photographs of Kathleen Goligher. But all except one have been taken in such a way as to exclude the sitter's head. And that one has been cropped. A neat square has been cut out of the top left-hand corner, where Kathleen Goligher's face should be, and I wondered if this was a form of vengeance. Elsewhere – in Crawford's first book, *The Reality of Psychic Phenomena* – there are photographs which do show Kathleen's Goligher's face, notably the studio portrait used for the frontispiece. She is an attractive young girl of about seventeen. Her long hair, parted on the right, is tied at the back with a ribbon and draped in three ringlets to the left of the open neck of her sailor blouse. With her long nose, her full lips and the rather mysterious myopic gaze behind the rimless glasses, she bears more than a passing resemblance to the young W.B. Yeats, and I now recall that your phrase, *In dreams begin responsibilities*, is a quotation from Yeats. And I wonder how much that phrase says about the peculiar relationship between Crawford and Kathleen Goligher, five whole years during which she permitted herself, with the collusion of her family, to be examined forensically by him, or, to put it bluntly, to be groped by him. What on earth was going on?

The relationships of others are often unfathomable to us, Nina. I wonder if Crawford did love Kathleen Goligher, whether consciously or not, and if she somehow returned his love by keeping up the charade for those long years, wanting his dream to be a reality for him. Perhaps, attracted by Crawford's picture of her as a gifted medium, she came to believe that she had indeed extraordinary powers, or was persuaded to think so by the other members of the Circle. If a reputable scientist, far above her in social status – for the Golighers were poorly paid textile workers – could believe in her, why could she not believe in herself? Or perhaps the whole thing was done for money, though there is no mention of money ever changing hands. And what happened at the end, what caused Crawford to kill himself? Who was responsible, in what dream did that responsibility begin? Did Kathleen Goligher, exhausted by the pretence, reveal her pretence to him, whether consciously or not? Did she tell him the truth out of love, or pity, or contempt? We shall never know.

I can still see the attic room of my dream that resembles the Goligher séance room, the bare boards with nail-heads glinting in them, and the faded blue striped wallpaper with faded pink roses on it, as photographed by Crawford, except Crawford's photographs are black and white, and in any case I had this dream several times before I ever set eyes on Crawford's books. I think the wallpaper was a throwback to that of my childhood bedroom. The chronology of such dreams is always confusing, for they repeat themselves with terrible familiarity, and the same motifs recur again and again as the long past resembles the immediate past. At other times, I would meet you in Warsaw. I would be walking in the Old Town, re-membering how it had been razed by the Germans in the war, and was now a copy of the Old Town, painstakingly recon-structed from the rubble, from old photographs, architectural plans, and memories. I am in one of those streets that specialise in amber jewellery, and you are peering into a shop window, when you turn, and we see each other face to face. It's been a long time, Nina, I would say, and you would say, No matter, Angel, the past is past, we're living in this moment, now, come here and look, how beautiful these things are. And you would take my arm and, like children at a sweetshop window, we would feast our eyes on necklaces and earrings and pendants, and we would remark on the fantastic centrepiece, a great chunk of raw amber that had a millions-of-years-old butterfly imprisoned in its glowing candy-coloured depths. And we would be so engaged when suddenly there would be an almighty explosion, a shop at the end of the street would collapse under a column of smoke, and then the next shop would explode, and the next, and I would realise how implicated Belfast was with Warsaw, the whole row collapsing like dominoes, the series of explosions getting nearer, nearer, until, as we stood rooted to the ground, we were swept into oblivion, and I woke.

I look again at your postcard captioned, *Sunlit interior of Grand Central Terminal, c. 1940*, and your message, *In dreams begin responsibilities*. When it arrived the day before yesterday it struck me that it was similar in style to your first postcard, that of the Empire State Building being struck by lightning. When I compared them, I now saw that both indeed had come from the same source. Both had the heading, *New York Flashbacks*, and both were copyright of the Underwood Photo Archives Ltd, San Francisco. Moreover, I now realised that they must have come from a booklet of postcards, for, when I looked at them more carefully, I could see that both had a serrated edge where they had parted company with their spine, leaving behind residual little blips of paper hardly perceptible to a recipient more concerned with the message than with such forensic details: both were leaves from the same book. And I pictured you flicking through the series, thinking of me, appropriating these two from a number unknown to me, but not entirely unimaginable, for I vaguely recalled seeing booklets like this in metropolitan bookshops, of some two dozen or thirty postcards, and black-and-white photographs titled *The Statue of Liberty*, *Times Square*, and *Ice-skating in Central Park* flashed through my mind.

I wondered if you had chosen both at the same time, premeditatedly, having already decided that your one-sided correspondence with me would be a long one, that each card would be a significant link in a chain, that the whole sequence was pre-planned and orchestrated, or if the second New York postcard had only occurred to you at some later stage, or if, indeed, it had been chosen on impulse that very day, the day before the day before yesterday, when you sat down to write my name and address, and the message, *In dreams begin responsibilities*.

No, hardly an impulse, I then thought, for the card bore an Irish stamp, and it seemed unlikely that you would have taken the whole booklet with you from London, but then maybe again you did, intending perhaps to select one of the images contained in it, not necessarily this one, for a purpose not entirely decided when you embarked for Ireland. For all I knew, you had a whole stack of cards to choose from. Whatever the case, the photograph is a beautiful and myst-erious one, the interior of the station like a vast antechamber to another realm. Shafts of light striated by the glazing bars of the great half-moon windows stream down onto the con-course, where little knots of people have gathered accidentally or purposefully caught between arrival and departure, and one figure stands bathed in a pool of light as if waiting to be beamed up into another dimension. And I know that you would have intended this image as a reference to a dream I once had when I was going with you.

I told you about it the next morning. I was about to board a train bound for New York from Great Victoria Street station in Belfast – a journey entirely feasible in dreams – when you came running up to me and I said, Nina, what a lovely surprise, I thought you were in London. I was, you said, but I was speaking to your father on the phone, and he told me that you had just left for New York, so I thought I'd join you, we'd a lovely time when we were there before. So we boarded the train and went straight to the dining car, where we had a lovely candlelit dinner, caviar and oysters and lobster and champagne, and then we met a nice American couple, we played whist with them for a while before retiring to berth in the sleeping car for the night. We climbed into bed and let ourselves be rocked a while by the rhythm of the train, imagining its plume of smoke trailed like a line of foam as it sped across the dark Atlantic, and then I realised I was dreaming, and said, Nina, this is a dream. And you said, Yes, I know, but let's stay in it for a while, it's such a nice dream, and then I woke to find you lying beside me in my bed in Ophir Gardens. This is just as good as the dream, you said, and I said, Yes, but we'll have to be very quiet, my father's sleeping next door. Then the door opened, my father walked in, and I woke.

What a convoluted dream, you said, and how very Catholic. Well, it's got a lot of perspectives in it, I said, maybe that's what Catholic means, it reminds me of a Gerard Dillon painting, it's called *Self Contained Flat*, he painted it in London in the early Fifties, I think he got the idea from one of those medieval paintings in the National Gallery, you know, where they show the same saint doing different things in the same panel, as if the different bits of a narrative all happen in the same space, in the same time, a kind of God's-eye view. Well, Dillon shows his little bedsit in London, crammed with different perspectives, there's a bit of Cubism in it too, here's Dillon walking in the door, and here's the same door opening on to a little garden where Dillon's digging potatoes, here's the poky kitchen with the gas stove and a little table with a blue milk jug, and a daffodil in a water-glass, and so forth, and the cat perched on the windowsill above the door, and Dillon in the foreground at a table with a blow-torch and a bottle of meths and pair of pliers and a screwdriver, he liked to show himself as a worker artist, though he's wearing a very raffish blue check shirt and a nice waistcoat, and there's a naked figure lying prone on the bed in the top right corner, you know the Gauguin painting, *Spirit of the Dead Watching*? it's a reference to that, the woman lying on the bed with her head turned to one side, looking at us with her eyes closed, as if Dillon's whole painting was maybe dreamed by her. It's a very happy painting, I said, someone who's pleased with himself and his little self-contained world, but it's got that touch of melancholy in it.

There was more than a touch of melancholy in some of my other dreams about you, Nina. Sometimes I would find myself wandering a Belfast with bits of London embedded in it, such as Leadenhall and Threadneedle Street, an area of monumental banks and churches. You would step out from behind a column of a gloomy portico, looking as beautiful as ever, if a little older than when we were going together, you're wearing a navy wool suit with a knee-length skirt, and an electric blue Art Deco scarf tied round your throat, and little sapphire stud earrings, and dark blue stockings and black ankle boots with a Cuban heel, and I would say, Nina, you've come back, I knew you would come back, and a panic-stricken look would come across your face, and you would say, No, no, Angel, I don't know what I'm doing here, in these clothes, you must be dreaming, you must have summoned me to appear in your dream, you must stop it, Angel, I can't be here.

And then I knew I was dreaming, but I wanted the dream to continue, so overpowered was I by your beauty, so over-whelmed by your palpable presence, for I reached out and touched your cheek, I could feel the warmth of your flesh, and I said, No, Nina, please, stay with me in the dream for a while. What can it matter to you, if it's only a dream? We can be happy for while in the dream, it can be just as it was in the old days, and then you can go back to your own life, I won't bother you again, just give me this one night, I said. And tears would well in your eyes, and you would shake your head dumbly, and I would go on, Please, Nina, just one night, I'll take you to this lovely restaurant I've just found, for just then I remembered the restaurant from another dream of Belfast-London, where there were better restaurants than in the real Belfast, and I could picture it in my mind's eye, it was in one of those alleyways off Corporation Square, Bologna, it was called. You'd really like it, Nina, it's a real find, just very good simple Italian food, they do this tricolore salad with mozzarella and tomatoes and basil and olive oil, just that, with a grind of black pepper and a pinch of salt, and the tomatoes burst with flavour against the milky mozzarella, little pillows of mozzarella, perfumed with basil, and then the grassy peppery tang of the oil, and then there's the lamb chops, they've been marinaded in olive oil and lemon juice and rosemary, all they do is char them on both sides on an iron griddle, they're oozing with pink juices inside, or maybe you could have the roast pork, shoulder of pork that they do on a spit over a fire of juniper branches, and then their divine zabaglione, some espresso and a grappa, I said, the grappa's really special, and then we could go to the 77 Club, they've got this brilliant singer, she does Billie Holiday num-bers, well, yes, I know what you're going to say, no one can do Billie Holiday like Billie Holiday, but this woman, she's something special, she does it with respect, no false histrionics, and she gives the songs her own edge, she puts her own experience into them, as well as what she understands of Billie's experience, it'll be just like you told me, Nina, how you imagined it, I can see her with that white gardenia in her hair, you said, isn't it strange how the song makes you see the singer, she's standing in a spotlight in a bar in New York, you said, and it's dark but there's those little tea-lights in faceted glass holders on the tables and you can see hands holding cigarettes and cocktail glasses, a face or two maybe, the smoke curling up and drifting into the spotlight, and we'll be there, Nina, it'll be like that, Nina, I said.

And you shook your head sadly, and said, No, Gabriel, it won't be like that, I've changed since then. Is that what I said to you? I can't remember, it's such a long time ago, I've forgotten so much, you said. Please, Nina, I said, you can't have changed that much, just be what you were to me then, just a little, just for this one night. And you said, Perhaps I never was that person, Gabriel, perhaps even then you made me up, perhaps you were in love with a dream of me, and not the real me. And then I would remember how you had said that to me in real life. Goodbye, Gabriel, you said, and you stepped back into the shadows, and I would wake with my eyes full of tears.

Last night, inspired by your postcard, I dreamed of you again. The happy dream this time, where we take the Belfast train for New York. Just as you settled in your seat you sprayed a little perfume on your wrists. What's that? I said. *Chamade*, you said, by Jean Paul Guerlain, 1969. I always liked the word, it's after Françoise Sagan's novel, *La Chamade*, a double-edged word. *Son coeur battait la chamade*, her heart was beating wildly. But *la chamade* is also a drumbeat signalling retreat. And so the dream proceeded as it had before, except when I found you in my bed in Ophir Gardens, my father did not come in, for he has been dead these seven years. And you were about to surrender to me when I really did wake. You were not there, but it seemed to me your perfume lingered on the pillow for a good half-hour: Spanish lilac, hyacinth and tuberose, calmed by murmurs of amber, jasmine, lily of the valley. Then a lingering, coffiny base of cedarwood.

THE LANGUAGE OF STAMPS

TOP RIGHT-HAND CORNER.
HAVE YOU FORGOTTEN ME.
LOVE POST
WILL YOU BE MINE?
ONE PENNY
RIGHT-HAND SIDE OF SURNAME.
I AM LONGING TO SEE YOU.
ONE PENNY
I AM ALWAYS THINKING OF YOU.
LOVE POST
I LOVE YOU TRULY.
ONE PENNY
I SEND YOU A KISS.
LOVE POST
DO YOU LOVE ME.
ONE PENNY
I CANNOT BE YOURS.
ONE PENNY

TOP LEFT-HAND CORNER.
LEFT-HAND SIDE OF SURNAME.

BOTTOM RIGHT HAND CORNER.
WHEN ARE YOU COMING TO SEE ME.
LOVE POST
ONE PENNY
FORGET ME NOT.
ONE PENNY
DO WRITE SOON.
ONE PENNY

BOTTOM LEFT-HAND CORNER.
NO.
YES.
ONE PENNY
LOVE POST
I AM ALWAYS TRUE TO YOU.
LOVE POST
THIS AND MY LOVE.
ONE PENNY
I WILL NEVER FORGET YOU.
LOVE POST

N

Wasp Clipper

Again I find I'm playing catch-up with myself, for I had intended to dwell a little on the fact that your last card, that of Grand Central Terminal, had also been posted in Dublin, and bore a 60c Hawthorn stamp. Again, the face value of the stamp seemed high. It, too, must have been deliberately chosen. In Irish folklore, the hawthorn is the fairy tree, especially a lone hawthorn, for under it you may find a portal to the fairy world which lies contiguous to ours. And I am reminded of your description of your mother's perfume, *Après l'Ondée*, hawthorn and violets doused in rain, how perfume can so magically evoke the presence of someone no longer in this world. As for your latest postcard, it's been posted in Drogheda, with a 65c Bluebell stamp, and I had written a good few sentences in response to that when my pen malfunctioned.

I had only myself to blame. I had recently acquired a Wasp Clipper made in the US in the thirties by Sheaffer, quite a beautiful pen in a layered olive green and silver-grey web pattern shot through with sparkling gold threads that create an illusion of extraordinary depth. But the nib had lost most of its iridium, and was an unsatisfactory, scratchy writer. And I wanted this lovely pen to be a working pen, so I thought I would take the good nib from a Parker pen that had lost its cap, and substitute it for the poor Clipper nib. As it turned out, when I disassembled the two pens and tried out the marriage, it wouldn't work: the Parker nib was just that much bigger than the Clipper, and I couldn't get both nib and feed to fit the section. So I rummaged around in my spares box and eventually found an old Conway Stewart feed that was a little narrower than the Parker feed, and tried that, and lo! the combination worked perfectly. I filled up the Wasp Clipper Parker Conway Stewart, and began to write. The line was nice and smooth, if a trifle wet, and I was writing quite pleasurably with my Frankenstein's monster of a pen when it dried up on me. I shook it, and tried it again; nothing happened, so I shook it little more violently, whereupon it spat out a series of blots across my words.

That marriage wasn't quite right either: the feed was just that little bit too narrow. I crumpled the ruined page into a ball and binned it, and took up a 1940s Wyvern Perfect Pen in Rose Pearl and Black instead, which I knew to be more reliable. The whole experience made me reflect on my gradual and somewhat reluctant discovery that many vintage pens, considered purely as writing instruments, are far from perfect. Oh, they look beautiful, but they leak, they blot, they flood, they skip, they scratch, or the filler mechanisms don't work – worst of all is the plunger filler invented by Sweetser, the roller-skating transvestite, which gives all sorts of trouble because it depends on a very precise vacuum seal, and even if you replace a worn seal, you can never trust them to fill satisfactorily again. Whereas a cheap modern cartridge pen by Parker or Sheaffer will last you for years, and write unhesitatingly with a consistent line every time you pick it up.

When I was last in London I bought a Japanese Muji

cartridge pen in their Tottenham Court Road shop – it cost just ten pounds – for purposes of comparison with my vintage collection. Any time I'm in London I usually end up buying something there, and I've just looked up Muji on the net to remind myself of their products. At the heart of Muji design, says their website, is the Japanese concept of *kanketsu*, the concept of simplicity … *Muji's simple, anonymous, unostentatious products subtly blend in with their background and bring a quiet sense of calm into strenuous everyday lives.* My life is not that strenuous, but I especially like Muji's stationery range – steel rulers, mini tape-measures, acrylic hole punches, brightly coloured paper clips and bulldog clips, aluminium business-card holders, credit-card cases, and various other little receptacles and boxes which are good to look at and feel good in the hand. I like their inexpensive notebooks, which take fountain pen ink very well despite their low price, and I like their clothes: I'm wearing a white linen Muji shirt today, very simple classic design, very cool. And I've just picked up the Muji pen, I'm writing with it right now. It really is very well designed, a simple brushed aluminium tube with a nice circumferential groove in the end of the barrel into which you can securely post the cap, cap and barrel appearing seamlessly joined, as they do when the pen is closed. Granted, the stainless steel nib has a little fancy scrollwork on it, possibly imitating a Mont Blanc nib, but the Muji bears no other markings beyond the words 'iridium point'.

I like the fact that it bears no name, that it is confident enough to let the design speak for itself, but it's ever so slightly boring. The nib has been made to write like a ballpoint to suit modern hands, with an unvaryingly inflexible line: admirable in its own way, efficient, but characterless. And I love the quirks and idiosyncrasies of my vintage pens, none of which write the same, even when made by the same maker, with the same nib. I love their differences, their implications of alternative ways of writing.

So I return the Muji to its drawer and look at my pen collection again. There are spaces vacated by three pens I sent away for the kinds of repair I couldn't manage with my novice skills, one of them a black Celluloid Mabie Todd Blackbird Topfiller with a translucent amber upper barrel which enables you to check the ink level. It was a lovely writer when it worked, but then it developed a tendency to flood, and leak on my finger and thumb, due to a faulty seal between section and barrel. It's been gone for over a month; pen repair shops often have this kind of waiting list. But its absence reminds me that I was wakened again this morning by the song of my neighbourhood blackbird; and then I remembered the dream I'd been wakened from, which concerned my father, and which causes me to now write with a Silver Grey and Black Marble Blackbird.

I was walking down a white road that led to a blue sea. I could smell turf-smoke, and knew I was in Donegal. It had just rained. Water gurgled in the ditch, and tinkled down the limestone ruts of the road, its music echoing the song of an unseen blackbird. Then I saw my father, standing by the yellow bungalow, and I thought, he must have retired to live here, he was always very fond of *The Yellow Bungalow*. But then I saw the broken windows, and the weeds sprouting from the thatch. My father was holding a packet of letters in his left hand, and writing something on them. Return to sender, I thought. He began to walk away from me down the limestone road between the grey stone walls past the ruined houses and the rusted farm machinery lying in the fields, walking with that slightly swaggering postman's gait, he stopped, looked over his shoulder at me, and smiled, and entered the graveyard through the creaking gate, and I ran to follow him, and I'd almost caught up with him when he lay down on a flat grave-stone, took off his peaked cap and laid it on this chest, and crossed his arms, and, as I watched, his body in the blue-black uniform began to shimmer, merging with the gravestone, and by the time I reached him he was gone, and I could not even make out the name on the stone, for it was covered with moss and lichen. Then I heard the blackbird singing again, and I woke to hear the real blackbird singing.

You knew my father, Nina, you remember that swaggering walk of his. And you remember how he used to run a Saturday afternoon Esperanto class in an upstairs room of The Compass Bar in Ireland's Entry, near the Law Courts. He'd tried to persuade you to sign up for the course, you know he'd taken quite a shine to you. And one day in the XL Café you seemed to go along with it for a while, but then, very diplomatically it seemed to me, you wriggled out of it. When he had gone, I said I thought you'd handled the situation very well. Can you see me as an Esperantista? you said. Why not? I said. Well, I just don't think it's the kind of movement that attracts women, for one thing, seems more like an old boys' club to me, you said. And I conceded that I didn't know many women who were involved in the movement, but I knew that some marriages had been made through Esperanto, and that there were several hundred Esperanto speakers in the world whose first language it was. What a bunch of oddballs they must be, you said. But don't you think it admirable that two people should fall in love through an ideal, and that they're prepared to follow that ideal though, by teaching it to their children? I said.

You laughed. Like you, Angel, the way you were brought up in Irish? Don't you think you're just a little bit of an oddball yourself? Not that I don't love you for it. But you don't seriously believe that these minority pacts are going to change the course of history, these people going around with green stars in their eyes. And speaking of stars, you're a typical Libra, Angel, you'll do anything for a quiet time, go with whatever the flow is, you weigh things up and make sure you're always on the right side of the scales. And maybe it's not only the stars made you that way, it's the way you were brought up, between Irish and English. Maybe you don't really believe in anything, because you know the world is different in Irish than it is in English, you can never decide on what the world really is, or what it should be, you said.

But you know that too, I said, your French is nearly as good as your English, you think in French sometimes. But it's not native to me, you said, I chose to learn French. Whereas you had no choice, your parents made that choice for you. Then again, maybe it was in their stars, you said. But by the same token, Nina, maybe it was in your stars that you should learn French. Oh, don't be silly, Angel, you know I really don't believe in all that stuff, it's only a metaphor, but if I did, I could say that the stars only give a general picture, it's up to the individual to fill in the detail, the devil is in the detail, or God, for that matter, wasn't it Flaubert who said, *Le bon Dieu est dans le détail?* Not that he ascribed his own writing to God, he meant that whatever one does, one should do it thoroughly, as best as one can, that's why he spent days looking for *le mot juste*, you said.

Well, Nina, Flaubert said a lot of things, didn't he say that of all lies, art is the least untrue? I could go along with that, I said. Yes, you said, but you think that what you see in art should be true for everybody. And Flaubert said, there is no truth, there is only perception, you said. Oh, for God's sake, let's stop this, Nina, we're starting to sound like Mutt and Jeff, I said. More like Abbott and Costello, you said. Abercrombie and Fitch, I said. Marks and Spencer, you said. Jeeves and Wooster, you said. Gilbert and Sullivan, I said. Lennon and McCartney, you said. Chang and Eng, I said. Who? you said. You know, the Siamese Twins, I said, Yin and Yang. Oh, all right then, Thompson and Thompson, you said. Who? I said. You know, the twins in Tintin, you said. Tintin and Snowy, I said. Dorothy and Toto, you said. Tom and Jerry, I said. The Owl and the Pussycat, you said. Leda and the Swan, I said. Lady and the Tramp, you said. Bubble and Squeak, I said. I don't see the connection, you said. Well, you can imagine a pair of dogs called Bubble and Squeak, can't you? I said. Oh, all right then, if you're going to allow that kind of thing, Fish and Chips, you said. Rhubarb and Custard, I said. Crosse and Blackwell, you said. Smith and Jones, I said. You gave me a querying look. As in Alias, I said. Bonnie and Clyde, you said. Barrow *and* Furness, I said. What do you mean, Barrow and Furness? you said. You know, the shipbuilding place, like the Clyde, I said. That's a bit thin, you said, but all right, Samson and Delilah. Samson and Delilah? I said. Yes, Harland and Wolff's, the two big cranes, they're called Samson and Goliath, isn't that right? All right then, Antony and Cleopatra, I said. Abelard and Héloïse, you said. Hero and Leander, I said. Scylla and Charybdis, you said. A rock and a hard place, I said. Gin and tonic, you said, on the rocks. Jekyll and Hyde, it's a cocktail, I said. First I ever heard of it, you said, I think you're making it up. But it would be a good name for a cocktail, I said. So would Punch and Judy, for that matter, you said. Or Tom and Jerry, I said. We already had that one, Angel, and besides, I'm tired of this game, Rosencrantz and Guildenstern are dead.

You remember, Nina, we used toy around with pub names, too, though we tried to avoid those silly English names, like The Rat and Parrot, or The Slug and Lettuce, though the disease had crept into Belfast too, there was The Whip and

Saddle bar in the Europa Hotel, the most bombed hotel in Europe, where all the foreign correspondents would hang out. No, we tried to make our names plausible, along the model of real Belfast bars like The Elephant, or The Fly, or The White Fort, or The Compass itself, for that matter, whose navigational connotations derived from its being built on the site of a former open dock that was filled in back in the 1870s. Joy's Basin, they called the dock, it was built by one of the Joy family of Belfast. Joy's Basin? you said, that would make a good name for a pub. Yes, I said, but maybe a bit in bad taste, the United Irishman Henry Joy came from the same family, they hanged him in Cornmarket in 1798, not too far away. About fifty paces from where the Abercorn Restaurant used to be, I said, remembering that there was still a dock called the Abercorn Basin. At any rate, we came up with The Meridian, and The Plimsoll Line, and The Foremast (there was already a Crow's Nest), and The Tug, and The Clipper, and Long Haul, and would have considered The Starry Plough, but for its political implications. From there it was an easy step to The Green Star.

My father, in his introductory session, would have delivered to The Compass class a brief biography of Ludwig Zamenhof, mentioning the Irish origins of the green star that was the Esperantist emblem. And he would have outlined to them how Zamenhof arrived at the fundamental principle which was to guide his new language, how one day, when he was seventeen or eighteen, in about 1876 or so, he had been walking to school in Warsaw when suddenly he noticed a sign which read *ŠVEJCARSKAYA*, meaning place of the porter; in other words, a porter's lodge; and then he saw another sign which read *KONDITORSKAYA*, place of sweets, in other words a sweetshop, or confectioner's. And then, envisioning all the various places of trade and business in Warsaw, the hundreds of grocers and butchers and bakers and candlestick-makers and hairdressers and restaurants and public houses, he saw how by means of a suffix, *-skaya*, the many could be made one, that one word could be made into other words that need not be separately learned, and hence one did not require a multiplicity of words for the multiplicity of things in the world. A ray of light fell upon those huge, terrifying dictionaries, said Zamenhof, my father would say, and they began to dwindle rapidly before my eyes. So Zamenhof began constructing his language with a basic stock of root words to which a series of prefixes and suffixes could be attached to generate a wealth of different meanings. My father would add that Zamenhof's Jewishness and his knowledge of Hebrew might also have led him to this illumination, for a logical economy of root consonants is common to both languages. And, my father would proceed, when you come to The Compass class, when we assemble in this upper room, I don't care whether you are Jew or Catholic or Protestant or Mohammedan, for as Esperantists we are all brothers – and there were indeed no sisters, you were quite right, Nina, in your stylish dress you would have looked out of place among these drab-suited old men and young men who looked older than their age – and though we are few in number, my father would continue, we may, by the grace of the one God that made us all, and by our own efforts, spread the gospel of Esperanto throughout the world.

He would finish by giving an account of the first Esperanto Congress, held in Boulogne on Saturday 5th August 1905, when the new Esperanto flag, a green rectangle with the green star in a white quarter in the upper left-hand corner, flew together with the French tricolour from the flagstaffs and windows of the Municipal Theatre. It was the first time Zamenhof had spoken in public; he did not even know if his words would be understood by the seven hundred or so delegates who came from many different countries, each perhaps with their own notions of how the language should be pronounced. He began nervously, but his confidence grew as he saw his audience respond with nods of comprehension and appreciation. This present day is sacred, he said. Our meeting is humble; the outside world knows little about it and the words spoken here will not be telegraphed to all the towns and villages of the world; Heads of State and Cabinet Ministers are not meeting here to change the political map of the world; this hall is not resplendent with luxurious clothes and impressive decorations; no cannons are firing salutes outside the modest building in which we are assembled; but through the air of our hall mysterious sounds are travelling, very low sounds, not perceptible by the ear, but audible to every sensitive soul; the sound of something great that is now being born. Mysterious phantoms are floating in the air; the eye does not see them, but the soul sees them; they are the images of a time to come, a new era. The phantoms will fly into the world, will be made flesh, and assume power, and our sons and grandchildren will see them, will feel them, and take great joy in them.

Zamenhof spoke on, realising that his audience, so willing to understand, was hanging on his every word; and when he ended by reciting a prayer he had composed for the occasion, a prayer not directed to the God of any national or sectarian religion, but to some mysterious Higher Power, a thunderstorm of acclamation broke out in the hall, and complete strangers embraced, and shed tears of joy. And my father would then conclude his introduction to Esperanto by telling how Ludwig Zamenhof, heartbroken by the events of the First World War, died on 14th April 1917. It was my father's first birthday, and Zamenhof was fifty-seven, the age, Nina, that I am now.

It's taken me some time to respond directly to your latest card, but I seem to have spent years in my mind since it arrived just yesterday. I note the stamp, the 65c Bluebell, a flower also known as wild hyacinth, behind which lies one of those Ancient Greek stories concerning the jealous cruelties of the gods, which so much resemble our own. It concerns the beautiful youth Hyacinthus, who was loved by both Apollo, the Sun-God, and Zephyrus, the God of the West Wind. But Hyacinthus preferred Apollo, and Zephyrus looked for revenge. So one day, when Apollo and Hyancinthus were throwing the discus, Zephyrus blew it out of its proper course, striking Apollo's lover on the head and killing him instantly. Apollo, stricken with grief, raised from his blood a purple flower, on which the letters, *Ai, Ai*, were traced, so that his cry of woe might live forever on the earth. But since the bluebell that is native to these islands bears no such message, it was called *Hyancinthus nonscriptus*, not written on.

And your postcard is barely written on, just my name and address, and the initial of your name, that I last saw twenty years ago, the slanted ascender of your *N* beginning on a curlicue and rising to an apex with the downward sweep of the diagonal, then rising again to end as it began in a matching curlicue. It is an elegant *N* that makes me think of the *N* we saw emblazoned on the bridges, monuments and state buildings of Paris, *N* that stands for Napoleon, whose remains are enclosed, like the last of a series of Russian dolls, within six coffins locked within a massive tomb of porphyry. You remember, Nina, how we thought *N* might more happily stand for Jules Verne's Nemo, the captain of the *Nautilus*, Nemo meaning Nobody, whose underwater realm knew no boundaries of nation, or language for that matter, for Nemo and his crew communicated among themselves in a kind of Esperanto.

Language takes many forms, as witnessed by your postcard, THE LANGUAGE OF STAMPS, a vintage curiosity, perhaps some eighty or ninety years old, which purports to show how the position of a stamp on an envelope or card can bear a coded message: upside down in the bottom left, DO WRITE SOON; right way up in the top left, DO YOU LOVE ME; slanted in the same corner, I SEND YOU A KISS; right-hand side of the surname, FORGET ME NOT; and so on. You've placed your Irish Bluebell in the top right-hand corner, which could mean either HAVE YOU FORGOTTEN ME, or nothing at all, since this nowadays is the conventional position for stamps, and we are not used to seeing any other. More meaningful to me is the fact that you were in Drogheda when you posted it the day before yesterday, some thirty miles nearer to me than you were. I know that you would have been thinking of my father, for you could not have forgotten my telling you that, when I was ten, he had taken me on a pilgrimage to Drogheda to see the head of the Blessed Oliver Plunkett. The Blessed Oliver Plunkett, my father had often told me, was the Archbishop of Armagh at a time of relentless persecution of Catholics. He had set up a college in Drogheda in 1670, which was razed to the ground a year later. In 1679 he was arrested on a trumped-up charge of fomenting rebellion; and in 1681 he was executed at Tyburn in London by hanging, disembowelling, quartering and beheading, the head and forearms being salvaged soon afterwards, hidden in two tin boxes, and thence transported to Ireland, while the rest of the body remained in England.

It was December, the anniversary of Plunkett's beatification, and bitterly cold. It was early afternoon when we arrived, and already it was getting dark. It was a long way from the railway station; as we walked the grey streets I knew that we were in a foreign town. The clothes in the shop windows looked different, and the butchers displayed unfamiliar cuts of meat. A fine rain was beginning to fall when we got to the church, which was strangely empty. There was an odour of wax and decaying incense. My father and I were the only ones who knelt by the shrine in a side-chapel, where the head of the Blessed Oliver was displayed, blackened and unrecognisable as having belonged to a human being, seeming to float in the gloom that was lit only by a few guttering candles; and for weeks afterward the head occupied my dreams, hanging bodilessly in a dark space that was at once remote and claustrophobic, like that inside a confessional box.

You'd asked me about Confession, you were intrigued by the concept. You have to make what's known as an examination of conscience, where you review the past week, and see what sins you might have committed, we used to go to weekly Confession back then, I said. What sort of sins? you said. Well, that I was disobedient to my parents, or that I stole something, or, when I was old enough to have them, that I had impure thoughts, thoughts about girls that is. And how old were you then? you said. Oh, you'd be surprised, Nina, you can have impure thoughts when you're ten or eleven, maybe younger. And did you steal, Angel? Well, not much, I said, maybe I shoplifted a few sweets, that kind of thing, or I'd take a few coppers from my father's pockets when he lay sleeping on the sofa after doing a night shift. What they call venial sins, that you don't get sent to hell for, you only have to do time in purgatory, I said. But what if you didn't commit any sins, what then? Oh, sometimes you made them up, I said, because if you said you hadn't committed any sins since your last Confession, the priest would be reluctant to believe you, and he would say, Are you sure, my son? For instance, you wouldn't have picked a fight with your brother or sister, or you wouldn't have been tempted to steal an orange or an apple from a greengrocer's display, when no one was looking, or maybe you'd be reading one of your mother's magazines, and you'd see a picture of a woman, and you'd have impure thoughts about that woman, the priest would say, and you'd think about it? And you would say, Maybe I did, Father, because it was entirely possible that you would do such a thing, or think such a thing, and the priest would give a little sigh of satisfaction, and say, Ah, I thought so, my son, we're none of us perfect, and then he'd absolve you from this imagined sin, I said. But that's bizarre, Angel, you said, it's like something out of Kafka. Oh, don't knock it, Nina, I said, it was a good exercise in contemplation, good exercise for the memory, trying to remember what you might or might not have done in the course of that week, reliving those dubious encounters with oranges and apples and women's magazines. And it did teach you to examine your conscience, to realise that everything you do, every decision you make, every thought, or every thought you imagined you'd had, or might be tempted to have in the future, is important, that it is judged by some absolute standard of morality. That anyone can be guilty of something, if one looks hard enough at oneself. It taught you to know yourself, I said.

I say this now, Nina, knowing how I judged you, you whom I once thought wholly guilty, and yet I still don't know who you are, Nina, and that is why I still love you. I know I might have pictured you wrongly in the past, and you must forgive me for trying to picture what you might have become, imagining what experiences have lined your face, and where, whether the creases in the forehead, the wrinkles at the corners of the eyes and mouth, what weight you might have put on, and how it might suit you. I need to hold on to some picture of you, even as I know I might be wrong. And when sometimes, leafing through a history of costume or a vintage fashion magazine, I picture you in this outfit or that, dressing you like a doll in eighteenth-century petticoats and flounces, or in an elaborate Japanese kimono, or a 1920s coat and dress ensemble of Art Deco printed silk, you must forgive me for that too, as you must forgive me for sometimes picturing you naked, for you must have known in advance that such thoughts would occur to me, and you must have allowed for that, when you entered into correspondence with me again, with your full knowledge and complete consent, just three months ago, though it seems a lifetime. I think we should spend some time away from each other, you said, the second-last time we met face to face. It was June 1984. We'd just come back from a weekend in London where we'd quarrelled endlessly, you remember, it began when we went to the National Gallery, I expressly wanted to look again at Titian's *The Death of Actaeon*, a painting I'd always loved. The narrative that lies behind the picture, as I recounted it to you, is Ovid's *Metamorphoses*.

Ovid begins by telling the outcome of the story first, as if assuming it to be already familiar to his audience – this is the story of Actaeon, he says, upon whose brow strange horns appeared, and whose dogs greedily lapped their master's blood. And if you look for the truth of the matter, you will find it in the fault of fortune, and not in any crime of his, says Ovid. Anyway, Actaeon and his comrades have been hunting since dawn. It's high noon, and their nets are dripping with their quarry's blood, says Ovid, so they call it a day.

Then he cuts to another scene, to a beautiful grotto with a stream, and a waterfall, where Diana, the goddess of the woods, is wont to bathe after hunting. On this particular day she's just come back from the chase, and she lets herself be divested by her nymphs of her robe, her spear, her quiver, and her unstrung bow. And while the nymphs are pouring water over her naked body from big Grecian urns, Actaeon has lost his way, wandering through the unfamiliar woods with unsure footsteps, as Ovid has it. And he enters the grotto, covered in spray from the waterfall, whereupon the nymphs begin to beat their breasts and scream at the sight of him, and they crowd around Diana, trying to hide her body with their own, but Diana stands head and shoulders above them, and her cheeks are as red as the rosy dawn as she stands in full view without her robes. And not having her bow and arrow to hand, she dips her hand into the stream, and throws water into Actaeon's face, and says to him, Now you can tell everybody that you saw Diana naked – if you can tell.

And, though he doesn't know it yet, horns begin to sprout on Actaeon's head, his arms become legs, and his hands feet, his clothes and his skin turn into a spotted hide. Then she puts fear into his heart, and he begins to run, wondering why he has become so swift of foot. And then he sees himself reflected in a pool, he sees the stag's head, and the horns, and he tries to speak, but all that comes out is a groan. What can he do now? For though he's got the body of a stag, he's still got the mind of a man, and he's thinking, I can't very well go back to my palace now, I'd be too ashamed, but then again, I'd be very afraid if I stayed out here in the woods. So he's standing there dithering when his sees his dogs running towards him – Ovid's got these great names for the dogs, Nina, I said, like Hunter, Fury, Barker, Growler, Gazelle, Catcher, Gnasher, Spot, Runner, Soot, Whirlwind, Wolf, and so on – and he starts to run, the whole pack chasing him, and he wants to cry out, I'm Actaeon, I'm your master! but no words will come, and then the lead dog sinks his teeth into his shoulder, and the rest of the pack pours onto him, tearing at him till his whole body is one great wound, and the worst thing is, his comrades have got wind of what's going on, they catch up with the dogs and urge them on, all the time shouting for Actaeon, and complaining that he's missing all the action, and Actaeon lets a groan out of him, not quite a human cry, not quite the cry of a deer, and then he dies.

There was a lot of debate after the event, says Ovid, some saying that Diana was more cruel than she was just, others saying that when it comes to defending one's virginity, strong measures are needed; and both sides had their arguments well marshalled. But as for Ovid himself, he says the whole thing was just an unfortunate accident, that Actaeon was just in the wrong place at the wrong time, I said.

And what do you think, Angel? you said. Oh, I don't know, I said, but it would seem that the gods, or the goddesses, have as little control over circumstances as human beings, and as little control over their passions. I prefer to look at the painting, I said. By now we were standing before Titian's *Death of Actaeon*. It's a big painting, almost six feet by six and a half, and I had stood before it alone many times, imagining myself to enter the dark wood of its landscape, never fully able to resolve its blurs and ambiguities. In a significant departure from the Ovid story, Titian shows Diana present at Actaeon's metamorphosis, standing in the left foreground, almost life-size, holding a bow which lacks a string. It's as if she's part of the action, and yet not, I said, maybe she's a projection of herself, or maybe Actaeon's fate is her dream. At any rate, Titian made a lot of changes to the painting, and some people think it's unfinished. It's an autumnal painting, all those sepias and russets, the leaves of the trees beginning to turn. Maybe the unfinished look is the point. The dogs especially, the way they emerge out of a flurry of brushstrokes, made up of contradictory layers of paint. They're a series of afterthoughts, a kind of ongoing process. You know, Nina, *The Death Of Actaeon* is always at the back of my mind, I carry it around in my mind, but I can never see it clearly enough, it shimmers and changes as I try to imagine it. And when I go to see it for real, like now, I realise that even then I can't see it clearly enough, it's as if the painting has changed since I last saw it. And every time I look at it, I see things I never saw before. Or maybe I did see them, but never noticed them. Maybe I've forgotten seeing them, I said.

So the painting's really about your own thought processes, you said. Well, I hadn't thought of it that way, Nina, but maybe it is, I said. But then it would seem to exclude whatever I might think of it, you said. I mean, it doesn't seem to have occurred to you that it might mean something different to me. Well, you didn't venture to tell me, Nina, I said. And you didn't venture to ask, you said. You were too busy with your own analysis, your self-analysis. But you might as well know that in 1965, just after my mother died, they brought us to the National Gallery on a school trip, I was fifteen, remember? And Titian wasn't really on the agenda, we were going to look at the Rembrandts, the self-portraits, and we were just passing the *Actaeon* en route, when it caught my eye, and I stopped and looked at it. Maybe I only stopped for a few minutes, they had to send someone back for me, I don't know how long I looked at it. But I could see my mother in the Diana figure, the way she held herself with such disinterested aplomb, such gravity. And afterwards, when I read up on the background, the painting seemed more than ever to be about what can happen between men and women, when they stumble on some terrible revelation about the other. I could see the story of my mother and father in Titian's painting, you said. But it was your mother who suffered most, not your father, I said. How do you know? you said. Who are you to say who suffered most? I prefer to think of her as being empowered by her death. Like Diana, unleashing the invisible arrow. *The Death of Actaeon* means something to me, Angel, but all it is to you is a talking-point, a conversation piece. And you carry a picture of it around in your head for years, you weigh its pros and cons, never arriving at any conclusions. You're very good at pictures, Angel, you picture this, you picture that, but it really hasn't much to do with the real world, has it? Art, for you, is a little safe haven. Like your father's beloved Esperanto, a cosy little back room where a dozen or so oddballs talk about changing the world, when they all know the whole thing was doomed to failure about fifty years ago, it's all cloud-cuckoo-land. Don't you think you're like that, Angel, like your holier-than-thou father, ever so slightly pompous, with your useless pictures of the world? you said, and I was taken aback that you should speak of my father in this way.

And you, I suppose you're going to change the world? I said. Nobody changes the world, you said, history isn't a matter of personalities, of kings and statesmen making the big decisions, history's the manufacture of consent. That's what MO2 does, we're in the Chinese whispers game. But at least I've no illusions about it. I consent to it. And I take pleasure in what I do, because I like to create beautiful things, you said. Isn't that what I do? I said. No, you said, you think your pleasure is morality, you think you're better than the next person because you can appreciate something they can't. And you've made a picture of me, Angel, you carry it around in your mind like an icon, and for all I know you might adore it, but it's the wrong picture, Gabriel, it's not me. It's a kind of fake, you said, and I'm tired of tramping around galleries looking at pictures with you, be they real or fake, and with that you turned on your heel and left.

We made it up a little afterwards, when I came back to the hotel room and found you were wearing *L'Heure Bleue*, as if to remind me of our time in Paris, or to remind yourself of our time in Paris. But it began again in Belfast, or rather it ended in Belfast. We'd gone out for dinner, to Restaurant 77, the best restaurant in town, it was your idea. The condemned man's last meal. Afterwards, we were, as I thought, about to get a taxi to your place when you said, I think we should stop seeing each other for a while. What do you mean, stop seeing each other? I said. It was a circumstance I had never envisaged. Oh, I knew we had had our difficulties, but they consisted of mere ideological differences, easily resolved, and this struck me like a bolt from the blue. You were silent for a moment. What do you mean, stop seeing each other? I said again, less confidently this time. Yes, Angel, maybe if we stop seeing each other we'll learn to see each other better. We both need a little time and space away from each other, you said.

I felt as if my world had turned upside down. You can't mean it, Nina, I said. You mean everything to me, I said. I can't live without you, I said. How can you say that, I said, after all we've done together, after all we've said to each other, you said you loved me, I said. We say a lot of things, Angel, and they're true for when we say them, but things change, you said. But it's not over, is it, Nina? It can't be over, you'll come back to me, won't you? Give me some hope that you'll come back, Nina, I said. Oh, Angel, I don't know my own mind at the moment, I live in hope as much as you, don't press me too hard, you said. And I said more, and you said more, and I could not change your mind. I have to leave now, you said. You'll be in touch? I said. I'll write, you said. You kissed me gently on the cheek, and left me.

When I woke the next morning I thought it had all been a bad dream, and when I realised you had indeed said what you said, I felt bereaved. I had not felt like this since the death of my mother, nor would I feel like that again until the death of my father. And, remembering that time, I am writing now with a funereal black Waverley pen made in the 1920s, whose unusual spear-shaped nib has a teardrop vent-hole. Like the Dutch pens, the Merlin and the CIBA that I used to describe our happier times, the Waverley had never been inked until it came to my hands. It is like new, this pen that is almost as old as my father was when he died.

You remember my father, Nina. He must have been in your mind when I saw you for the last time. It was Saturday 30th June 1984, a week after our last meal together; I had arranged to meet him for a drink after his Esperanto class in The Compass, and I had just stepped from the sunlight of High Street into that maze of alleyways that lies between it and the Law Courts, when you stepped out from a dark colonnade, and said, Angel, Gabriel. My heart leapt. Nina, I said. And we stood awkwardly for some long seconds. Well, fancy meeting you like this, you said. Yes, fancy that, I said. How are you, Gabriel? you said. How do you think I am, Nina? I said. Oh, don't be hard on me, Gabriel, I've thought about little else since that night, I've thought about my whole life, what I'm doing, or what I'm supposed to be doing, you must give me some time, you said, and you proceeded to tell me an elaborate story of how your boss, Callaghan, had taken you to lunch at Restaurant 77 one day – isn't that an irony? you said ruefully – and had suggested to you that perhaps it was time for a change of scene, that Eastern Europe was the coming thing now, that you had done very well in Belfast, but that maybe Warsaw would suit your talents better at this particular time, and my heart gave a lurch as I heard this. You mean you might be leaving altogether? I said. Oh, I don't know any more, Gabriel, I don't know what I'm doing, you said. And then I saw you look at your watch, and you said, Gabriel, I really must be going. I'll be in touch, I promise, I will write, and you left.

I looked at my watch; I had arranged to meet my father at

five o'clock, and it was now five past. And then I heard an almighty explosion. You know the rest, Nina. You must have pictured me running towards The Compass Bar, standing aghast before the smoking rubble, being restrained by the police and army, waiting for what seemed like an eternity before I saw my father being carried out, weeping tears of relief when I saw that he was still alive, though I could see that one of his legs was shattered. As it turned out, they had to amputate.

My father managed well enough; even when he suffered phantom limb syndrome, he used to joke about it, or perhaps it wasn't a joke. After Nelson lost his arm at the Battle of Santa Cruz de Tenerife, said my father, he could feel fingers digging into the missing limb, and Nelson thought this was direct evidence for the existence of the soul. And I never thought I'd find myself agreeing with an English admiral, said my father. What hurt him more was the thought that the cause of Esperanto had been directly attacked by the bomb. It was just like the persecution of Esperantists in Nazi Germany and Soviet Russia, he said. There were dark forces abroad, said my father, who would do anything to keep the Irish people apart from one another, and he would quote from his beloved Zamenhof. When I was still a child in the town of Bialystok, said Zamenhof, I gazed with sorrow on the mutual hostility which divided the people of the same land and the same town. And I dreamed then that after some years everything would be changed for the better. And the years have passed; and instead of my beautiful dream I have seen a terrible reality. In the streets of my unhappy town savages armed with hatchets and pickaxe handles have flung themselves at those who practise another religion, or speak a different language to themselves. For there will always be those whose interests are to foster such hatred, said my father.

No one ever claimed responsibility for The Compass Bar bombing that killed five people, three Catholics and two Protestants. Some said it was a rogue Republican element. Some said it was a rogue Loyalist element. And quite a lot of people said that whoever was responsible, it could not have happened without the collusion of rogue elements within the security forces, whether actively or by omission, that it had been sanctioned at some level in the maze of clandestine operations that lay behind official government policy.

It took me some days to put two and two together. Until then, I'd thought of MO2 as just another of those well-meaning and ultimately pointless local business development agencies. But the more I thought of it, the more it seemed to me that you must have known, that MO2 had prior knowledge. You knew I met my father most Saturdays after his class, you knew my movements, you knew how to intercept and delay me. And if that were so, you saved me, but you did not save the others, and I could not forgive you for that.

Your brief letter, sent from Paris ten days later, only served to confirm my suspicions. You had left MO2, you said, you could not bear to live with it any longer, you had taken up a new life in Paris, you hoped that I was well, and that I would forgive you for what you had done, but it was all over between you and me, you could not bear the pain of looking me in the eye again. Words to that effect. Later that day, 9th July 1984, I learned that York Minster had been struck by lightning, and its South Transept razed by the subsequent fire. And in the days that followed, I heard how the four-hundred-year-old stained glass of the great Rose Window, made to commemorate the defeat of the House of York in the Wars of the Roses, had been riven into some forty thousand fragments, though the panels had miraculously stayed intact within their embrasures, having been releaded some years previously; and in the months that followed, I heard how restoration began, as adhesive plastic film was applied to the crazed mosaic of the glass panels, which were then removed one by one, disassembled, and reassembled, tessera by tessera, using a specially developed fixative which had the same refractive index as the old glass, whereupon the completed work was sandwiched between two layers of clear glass for added security, and mounted back in place: which intervention means we will never again see what was seen before the fire, the dims and glows of stained glass unmitigated by an added medium, however clear. And I remembered how we two had once seen the glass as it was, as it had been.

As I cast my mind back now, Nina, I no longer know the truth of what we were together, or what you were to me. I look at your last postcard again. *HAVE YOU FORGOTTEN ME*, the stamp says, or it might say nothing. I trace the *N* of your name with my finger, and, as I put my hand to my face, I seem to catch a whisper of some perfume. What is it, Nina, *Je Reviens*, or *Vol de Nuit*? But it escapes me, I can find no name for it, and I do not know what message your next card will bring.

THIS TESTAMENT SAVED THE LIFE OF Pte. W. HACKET 1st WOR Regt
AT ARMENTIERES. AUG·20·1915·NOW IN 2ND GEN EASTERN HOSPITAL
DYKE Rd BRIGHTON · BULLET PASSING THROUGH OUTER COVER
AND ALL THE LEAVES AND STOPPED AT THE LAST PAGE.

G. L. WILES   BRIGHTON

NINA

Conway Stewart Dinkie

*D*ear Gabriel, you wrote. I had looked at your letter for some time before I opened it. The stamp bore a Belfast postmark, and I was filled with hope and trepidation because we now breathed the air of the same city, or had done yesterday at least. My name and address was in blue ink, the colour of eternity, but also of death, and I thought of the blue vein in your wrist, how you would often raise it to my face for me to smell whatever perfume you were wearing. Eventually, with trembling hands, I took a knife and slit open the thick cartridge-paper envelope. A postcard fell out; I would look at it later. For now, I was more concerned with your many words.

It's been a long time, you wrote, *and I hardly know where to begin. But when I wrote those words on the first postcard I sent you, I remembered how you used to sing that Rolling Stones song, 'Long Long While'. You remember?*

> *Baby, baby, been a long, long time*
> *Been a long, long time, been a long, long time*
> *I was wrong girl and you were right.*

It was the B side of 'Paint It Black', 1966, you said, you liked it better than the A side because it had less pretensions about it. Very simple lyrics, but Jagger sings them with real emotion, you loved that little off-key catch in his voice, you said. I hadn't realised then that you were such a Rolling Stones freak, and you would say you weren't, it was just if you had a choice between the Beatles and the Stones, you'd go for the Stones any day. More edge. But I knew you liked Mick's style in general, and, despite your protestations, I think you were fascinated by that English middle-class bad boy thing, you liked the fact that he read books as well as listening to the blues, and you liked the clothes. Not that you dressed like Mick Jagger, but you had just a little touch of flamboyance. That first time I saw you in the XL Café, the first thing I noticed, beyond your face, was the tie you were wearing, looked like a Forties tie, pale grey with a washed-out pink diamond pattern, went nicely with the Donegal tweed jacket. I think maybe I fell in love with you a little just then, because it seemed that you wore the clothes almost at a distance from yourself, you didn't seem to be a natural dresser, it was something more considered, as if you had a picture in your head of how you should look, or how you might look to others. And, as I got to know you, I thought it was a little bit like how you looked at paintings, admiring but not fully entering them, and I liked that hesitancy in you, the way you adjusted your tie as I looked at you from the corner of my eye.

Anyway, it's been a long, long time, and you'll want to know why I started this whole thing, this correspondence. And I hardly know myself. But it must have started with the cards, I'd buy postcards in whatever place I'd be, not to send to anyone, but as mementoes, or just because I liked the pictures. I stored them in a shoebox, a men's shoebox, Church's brogues, you could still smell the leather off the cardboard. Years of postcards. And I was flicking through them one day when I saw that one I began with, the Empire State Building struck by lightning, I couldn't even remember where I bought it, but it reminded me of us in New York, you remember, how excited we were, lightning flickering above the skyline of the city, us laughing in the downpour. We'd taken shelter in one of those dives off Bleecker Street, you remember, it was like something from the 1940s, there was a black girl doing Billie Holiday numbers, standing on a little raised platform under a spotlight, and those little tea-lights in faceted glass holders on the tables, you could see hands and cigarettes and cocktail glasses, a face or two, and the smoke drifting up into the spotlight. And she was really good, she sang the songs with respect, but she put her own heart and soul into them too, and when I glanced at you over the tea-lights I could see that there were tears in your eyes, and then tears came to my eyes too.

So when I saw the lightning in New York postcard, I thought of you, and of our time there, and thought it might have been possible that you'd been in my mind when I bought it, however subliminally. And then I started going through the shoebox again and I began to find a pattern, this card or that would remind me of this or that time we'd spent together. So many memories began to well up. Like Colette when Lee Miller met her, you know, going through her photographs. And I could have chosen others, too, besides the ones I ended up with. There's a lovely 1950s 3-D one of the Chrysler Building, all metallic greens and silvery blues, and I remembered how you'd talked about its automotive architecture, it had never occurred to me that the Chrysler Building had anything to do with cars, and you said, Well, that's one for your little red book, Nina, you're always looking for these little style details, maybe you could do something with that, and I said, Yes, it's like the way those big American cars with the big bench seats were made for the dresses, the big flared skirts and petticoats, and I wrote down 'Chrysler Building haute couture' with my Dinkie pen that first brought us together, you remember …

Dear Nina, how could I forget? I'd been looking for a match for that pen ever since it occurred to me to begin collecting. And I found it just last week, or perhaps it found me. I'd had a couple of long-standing requests in with Beringer, you remember Beringer, his shop in Winetavern Street? One of them was for the Dinkie, the other for a Parker Royal Challenger, 1939, I'd just missed one on eBay, and the more I'd looked at its photograph, the more I wanted one, I loved the Art Deco stepped clip, very Chrysler. So I called in with Beringer on the off-chance. Ah, Mr Gabriel, he said, the Royal Challenger, he said, and he took the pen from his breast pocket and handed it to me, barrel first. It was indeed lovely, brown pearl bodywork with a black chevron pattern that matched the clip, it's another take on the Parker arrow emblem. How much do I owe you? I said, and he named a price, I named a lower price, he came down a little, I came up a little, and so on, till we met halfway, as we knew we would. Ah, you drive a hard bargain, Mr Gabriel, he said, but I'll tell you what, just to show there's no hard feelings, here's a little luckpenny, and he shot his cuffs, held open his two hands before me, made fists of them, and said, Pick a hand. I looked at him somewhat sceptically, and touched his left hand, and when he opened it, lying on his palm was the twin of your Dinkie. Of course it wouldn't be an identical twin, Conway Stewart never made two of these black and red mottled rubber models alike, but as it looked as near to yours as I could remember, I was delighted.

I didn't know you did magic, Beringer, I said. Oh, only for special customers, Mr Gabriel, it wouldn't do to let the general public know that an antiques dealer has stuff like this up his sleeve. As a matter of fact, I learned that one from your late father, God rest his soul, he said, and I suddenly remembered that when I was a child my father had a whole repertoire of these tricks, making things appear from nowhere. So here I am now, writing with the Dinkie that came from nowhere – though Beringer, true to form, did give me an elaborate account of its provenance. When I saw it I realised it wasn't quite as spectacular-looking as some of the pens I'd acquired before it – the Oriental Peacock Dinkie, for example – but nevertheless its colours glow with the intensity of my memory of them, and it gives me pleasure to write with a pen that resembles yours so closely, as I here transcribe the words of your letter, knowing that by writing them again in my own hand, following the loops and curves of your thought, I will gain a better understanding of them.

... *you remember, red and black,* you wrote, *le rouge et le noir, I wrote all those letters to you then with my Conway Stewart Dinkie. I don't know who started that business, writing to each other practically daily sometimes, whether it was you or me. You used to joke about it, said it would be good training for MO2, all those memoranda I had to write, or was supposed to write. But when I began sending the postcards, I knew I couldn't write at any length, I had to work up to it, for I didn't entirely understand myself what had happened. You must know that after I left you I was very confused. 'Paint It Black' kept going through my head*

> *I see a red door and I want it painted black*
> *No colours any more I want them to turn black ...*

So I got out, I'd saved up quite a bit from my business, enough to last me a good few months, and I went to Paris, where I knew I could get a job with my French, the French like Englishwomen with a bit of style who can speak good French, though I had to tone down my French accent a bit, make it more English, for that's the whole point, that you're an Englishwoman speaking French.

And for six months I did nothing, I got a little apartment near Les Halles, in rue Montmartre, I'd just go for long walks, trying to forget how we'd been in Paris together. Then I got a job in a fashion photography agency. And I fell for one of the photographers, and it took me a while to realise that it was because he reminded me of you, he looked at things in that admiring way, without quite engaging with them, he saw the world in terms of photographs, though he wasn't half as good as he thought he was. So I dropped him. And I hesitated about telling you this, but you might as well know, because everything I've done since I left you has led to this moment where I write to you again, now, after twenty years.

After the photographer, I took up with a married man, one of those minor French politician-intellectuals, oh, nothing physical, in fact I think he was a closet gay, it was a business arrangement if you like, I was his escort, the kind of woman his kind of man likes to be seen with in discreet restaurants. He was very charming, and very well read, we'd have this French Symbolist thing going, matching quotations from Baudelaire and Mallarmé, and eating with him was a real pleasure, if a trifle analytical, you know that way the French have to talk their food as well as eat it. He admired me, and I him. And I enjoyed the mutual flattery for a while, not to mention the discreet restaurants, but then it seemed to me he was flaunting me a little too much, I was becoming too much of an ornament, so I got out of that relationship too. And there were others, but nothing to write home about.

And you, you were like a ghost that would sometimes appear in my dreams, and I would dream of you being with other women, other ghosts perhaps. So very slowly I began to think of getting in touch again, but I deferred it for years, until I went through that shoebox full of postcards. And the more I thought of you, the more I thought of how we'd been together in different places, and how you saw the world, sometimes as I saw it, but sometimes quite differently. You used to joke, dear Angel, how I was always one step ahead of you, but if I was, you had a more considered view of the landscape. I always wanted to see what was round the next corner, while you took time to look at what was present. So I thought I'd send the postcards from different places, somewhere we had been together, others not. For I wanted to imagine what you would have made of those places, like Stroud, where I'd never even been myself, but I knew you would remember how I told you of my father's stint in the Erinoid factory at Lightpill, how I would dream of him driving the night train home to London, to me, his face lit by the glow from the open fire-box door, steam hissing from the brass pipes, the smokestack bearing its long plume of smoke through the darkness.

Of course Stroud had changed a lot from my father's time, the Erinoid factory had long since closed down, but that was the point, I was seeing it anew, through your eyes, as I imagined. They had set up a little Erinoid museum, you would have loved it, they had displays of Erinoid buttons, mock ivory and tortoiseshell, all the colours of the rainbow, door handles, umbrella handles, radio cabinets, the plastic rods that they used to drill out pen casings from, in fantastic marble effects. What they didn't have was the smell, though they told you about it, milk curd and formaldehyde, what a stink that must have been. And I remembered how my father's clothes would smell funny when he got home, I thought it was the smell of coal-smoke and steam from the engine. I think that's why I sent you the Berlin postcard, the one of the steam engine on the viaduct over Friedrichstrasse, but also because we got lost on the S-Bahn, you remember, we got off at the wrong stop and ended up in Kreuzberg, and we came across that little antique shop where you bought the Russian icon, I hadn't the courage to tell you I thought it was a fake, and what did it matter anyway, you were so delighted by it. And the subject was so fitting, an Annunciation, the Angel Gabriel appearing to the Virgin, you especially liked the blue of her cloak, it was like an Yves Klein Blue, you said, it was remarkable how it had kept its colour over all that time. You mean the blue he used to paint naked women with, and have them roll them around on a canvas? I said, and you looked at me suspiciously, thinking I was winding you up ...

I'd quite forgotten about that icon, Nina, I probably still have it lying at the back of a drawer somewhere. Maybe the blue's faded by now. But your mention of blue leads me to take up another pen, for the small Dinkie, as I knew it would, is beginning to tire my hand, so I've gone for a Cobalt Blue

Esterbrook with a 9556 Fine Writing nib, it's got a much
firmer feel to it than the flexible Conway. It's a very trust-
worthy pen. That's the thing about vintage pens, or at least
vintage pens of this low-to-medium price range, you don't
often get fakes. There's no point in faking something like a
Conway Stewart or an Esterbrook, the bother and expense
you'd have to go to would be counter-productive. Oh, of
course I've bought things on eBay that turn out not to be what
I thought they were, but that's because I read too much into
the poor description, or was inveigled by the eloquent description, or the photograph presented it in a flattering light, or I
imagined it might be better than the unflattering photograph.
I was the victim of my own wishful thinking. Most sellers are
not dishonest, it's just that sometimes they don't know what
they're selling, and describe it wrongly, or don't know how to
describe it. I still get annoyed when I see someone call a dip
pen a fountain pen. In any case, the buyer should always
beware. As it turned out, I got the Cobalt Blue Esterbrook for
what seemed to me a bargain price of some twenty dollars
from a seller in Canton, Ohio, and, as I loaded it with blue
Quink, I remembered the postcard you'd enclosed with your
letter. It had fallen to the floor face down; there was nothing
written on it, but the image on the other side had words
enough. It was a photograph of a New Testament with a bullet
embedded in its back, and a caption below, handwritten in
block letters:

THIS TESTAMENT SAVED THE LIFE OF PTE. W.
HACKET 1ST WOR. REGT. AT ARMENTIERS. AUG. 20
– 1915 – NOW IN 2ND GEN. EASTERN HOSPITAL
DYKE RD. BRIGHTON – BULLET PASSING THROUGH
OUTER COVER AND ALL THE LEAVES AND STOPPED
AT THE LAST PAGE.

And I knew that you must have been thinking of a story my father told you once, how he knew someone whose life had been saved in the same manner, a Belfast man who had been in the Battle of the Somme. He had seen the hole in the Testament with his own eyes, though the bullet was missing. And you replied that you'd heard of a similar incident concerning a soldier in the American Civil War, except that the bullet destined for his heart was stopped by a steel plate engraved with a portrait of his sweetheart. I looked at the photograph more closely. The bullet in fact entered the Testament back to front, from Revelation to Matthew, and the Testament is lying open at Revelation 22, the last chapter of the Bible, you can see THE END at the foot of the page, and my eye is caught by Verse 13, which reads, 'I am Alpha and Omega, the beginning and the end, the first and the last'. Then I read Verse 12, which says, 'And behold, I come quickly; and my reward is with me, to give every man according as his work shall be'.

And I take it that you meant these words for me.

In fact, you continued, *I'd thought of sending you a postcard of the Yves Klein Blue painting in the Tate, it would have done as well as any other, because I knew how fond you were of this blue, I knew what associations it held for you, the blue of the sea when we had that magical weekend in Donegal, and we stayed in the Yellow Bungalow, the blue of the Paris street signs, and of the Côte d'Azur, where you had never been, but knew from Yves Klein's writings. That's why I sent you a card from Nice, you had always wanted to go there, but we never managed, so I went proxy, I wanted to imagine it through your eyes. Yes, the one of the Turbine Room in the Bankside Power Station, before they turned it into the Tate. Sometimes I'd go to look at Klein's painting, I'd stand there for long minutes, getting lost in that deep blue, and sometimes I'd have the uncanny feeling you were looking over my shoulder at it, and I'd turn around, but the someone* standing there would not be you. It was like that when I chose the postcards.

You remember you told me about the Library Angel, how if you were doing a piece of research for a paper on some artist or other, you'd go to the stack in the library, and lift a book at random, and open it at a page, and it would contain precisely the information you'd been looking for, except you didn't know it until then? You'd say you'd been guided by the Library Angel. It was like that, Angel, you were my Library Angel when I flicked through the shoebox full of postcards, I felt your hand guiding mine. And as I did so, I'd think of what you must have thought of me when we last saw each other, the day of The Compass Bar bomb. Let's say I did go deliberately to intercept you, but without full knowledge as to why I was doing it. And before that day, I'd been thinking long and hard about the whole MO2 thing for a couple of months, things were beginning to change.

And two weeks or so before that Saturday, Callaghan, my boss, had taken me out for lunch, a rare event, he'd pretty much kept his distance up till then, let us all get along with whatever we were doing, he was very much into benign non-intervention. All that stuff I'd told you about MO2, well, it was basically true, but you knew I was ever so slightly winding you up when I gave it that conspiratorial spin. For really, I thought it was basically just a glorified local enterprise development agency, until that lunch with Callaghan. So, anyway, we talked of this and that, and then we've just ordered coffee when Callaghan says, Oh yes, Miranda, and how are getting along with that young man of yours, Conway, Gabriel Conway is it? And I said, Oh, fine, fine, though of course it wasn't so fine between us then, wondering why this had come up, he'd never expressed any interest in my personal life until then, in fact I didn't even think he knew I had one. Well, well, marvellous, says Callaghan, that's good to hear. Father runs an Esperanto class, George Conway, isn't that right? says Callaghan, Compass Bar? Yes, I said. Well, says Callaghan, we're thinking of putting one of our chaps in there, very bright, he'd pick up the lingo in no time at all, good community relations project, don't you think? Paul Eastwood, so happens he went to school with that Gabriel of yours, you might know him. Anyway, it's like this, I hope you don't go wanting to learn Esperanto yourself, it would look a bit cluttered, don't you think, two of our people there at the same time? He's starting, oh, Saturday week, says Callaghan.

And of course I told him I'd no intention of going to your father's class, which was true, but I thought it all a bit strange that Callaghan should be telling me this, and then Callaghan says, Oh yes, Miranda, and talking about new projects, you might be interested to know there's a very good British Council job in Warsaw coming up, we think it might suit you very well, Cultural Affairs Officer. Not that we're not pleased with your work here, far from it, but sometimes we get the feeling that you could be doing with broader horizons. Job satisfaction, and all that. Anyway, you'll think about it, won't you? says Callaghan. And that was the end of that interview. I'd a very uneasy feeling about the whole thing, call it instinct if you want. So I wanted to talk to you about it, but didn't quite know how, I wasn't even sure myself what I knew or didn't know, I couldn't very well have rushed into The Compass Bar and told everyone to get out, I think something funny is going on here. And I when was talking to you I realised how nebulous the whole thing was, though it didn't seem so nebulous after the bomb, and I was consumed with guilt afterwards. But I'm none the wiser now, after twenty years, whether MO2 was involved or not, and whether or not I was involved by implication.

So there you have it. It's taken me twenty years to try to pick up the pieces, and I don't even know what the pieces were. The only thing I knew was you. You remember our first time away from Belfast together, that weekend we spent in York? We'd gone to the Minster, you remember how dazzled we were by the stained glass? Oh, I'd been there once or twice as a child, but my memory of it was dim, and now I saw it through your eyes as well as through my own, the way the light broke and shimmered on the edges where the glass was framed *by stone, little rainbows playing on the stone tracery, so that it seemed the stone was glass. And we stood for an age before the great East Window, which depicts the beginning and the end of the world, from Genesis to Revelation and the Last Judgment. And God said, Let there be light; and there was light, you said. So God must have spoken in the dark, I said. I told you that my mother had told me that during the War, the blackout, they'd taken all the glass from the windows bit by bit and stored it away for safekeeping, and when the War was over, they'd pieced it all together again. And I thought you hadn't heard what I said, so rapt were you in looking, but afterwards you mentioned that during the War they'd also taken all the paintings from the National Gallery in London and stored them deep underground in a Welsh slate mine. They had to enlarge the entrance to the mine for the Gallery's biggest painting, you said, it was a Raising of Lazarus, you couldn't remember the artist's name. Stored in a dark tomb for so many years. And so many more years have gone by since we two set eyes on each other.*

I'd kept all your letters from the time we'd been together, and after I went through the postcards, I went through the letters, not in any chronological order, for they were all mixed up, though I knew the early ones from the yellowed envelopes that once were plain white, and the later ones that were mauve and pale green and lilac, I'd bought them for you in a little papeterie in the Île Saint-Louis, remember, and I saw myself as I was when I first read those letters back then, as if I were looking over my own shoulder at myself, and I thought I caught a whiff or perfume from each one, whatever scent I had been wearing when I read them first, and though I knew I must be imagining it, it nevertheless summoned up those times for me again. It's as if we're beginning all over again. I'll be in the XL Café next Saturday at noon. After all that has happened, I can't be sure that you'll be there too. If you are, you'll know me. I'll be wearing the Dinkie pen that first brought us together.

And I will be there, Nina, as surely as I now take up your Dinkie pen again to write the last words of your letter.

Ever, Nina.
Ever, Angel.

ACKNOWLEDGEMENTS

I am grateful to the artist and filmmaker Susan MacWilliam, who generously shared with me her researches into spiritualism, especially the work of W.J. Crawford and Fournier d'Albe. For some ten years she has been developing a body of work that explores the paranormal with reference to ideas of vision and perception, reality and illusion.

The editor and publisher gratefully acknowledge permission to include the following copyright material

AUDEN, W.H., 'Night Mail' from *Collected Poems* (Faber and Faber, 2007), reproduced by kind permission of Faber and Faber Ltd.

Bahnhof Friedrichstraße, copyright holder not traced

Barkston Gardens Hotel, copyright holder not traced

Belfast 1954 by John Chillingworth, © Getty Images

Bible, England, 1915, reproduced by kind permission of Chris Boot Limited

Book of Hours – Gemini © The Pierpont Morgan Library, New York. 2009. Gift of the Trustees of the William S. Glazier Collection, 1984 MS G.14, fol.7v

Dolls, 1690–1700 – Lord and Lady Clapham, reproduced by kind permission of V&A Images/ Victoria and Albert Museum, London

Lightning striking the tip of the Empire State Building, July 9, 1945, reproduced by kind permission of Underwood Photo Archive, Inc.

Against the cream blouse I
notice a little pendant cylindrical
jewel, some kind of etui or
lipstick-holder, I think. It's
done in a beautiful red and
black marble swirls that show
off the red highlights in your
Cleopatra-cut black hair and
it hangs from a lanyard that
is itself beautiful, interwoven
greens and reds and mauves
that have the sheen of silk.
You toy with it from time to
time, with one hand as the
other manages the business of
the tea and biscuits. Then you
reach for it with both hands
and you unclip it from the
lanyard, you rummage about
in your handbag and take out
a notebook, you unscrew the
little etui, and when I see the
gleam of a gold nib I realise
it is a distinctive fountain pen